Published by Kensington Publishing Corp.

IRISH COFFEE MURDER

Leslie Meier
Lee Hollis
Barbara Ross

Kensington Publishing Corp.
www.kensingtonbooks.com

KENSINGTON BOOKS are published by

Kensington Publishing Corp.
119 West 40th Street
New York, NY 10018

All Kensington titles, imprints, and distributed lines are available at special quantity discounts for bulk purchases for sales promotion, premiums, fund-raising, educational, or institutional use.

Special book excerpts or customized printings can also be created to fit specific needs. For details, write or phone the office of the Kensington Sales Manager: Attn.: Sales Department. Kensington Publishing Corp., 119 West 40th Street, New York, NY 10018. Phone: 1-800-221-2647.

KENSINGTON and the KENSINGTON COZIES teapot logo Reg US Pat. & TM Off.

First Printing: January 2024
ISBN: 978-1-4967-4030-4

ISBN: 978-1-4967-4031-1 (ebook)

10 9 8 7 6 5 4 3 2 1

Printed in the United States of America

Contents

IRISH COFFEE
MURDER

Leslie Meier

Chapter One

"Spring in Tinker's Cove," grumbled Lucy Stone. "It's an oxymoron. There is no such thing. The calendar says it's March, which meteorologists say is officially the first month of spring, so why is it snowing?"

Lucy, who had just entered the office of *The Courier* newspaper in Tinker's Cove, Maine, was complaining to Phyllis, the receptionist, and Ted, her boss. She paused to stamp the snow off her duck boots, pulled off her gloves, and unwrapped the muffler she'd wrapped around her neck; then, sniffing the air and noticing how her breath hung in the chilly air inside, she hesitated before pulling off her hat and unzipping her barn coat. "What's going on? How come it's so cold in here?"

"There's no heat," growled Phyllis, whom Lucy now noticed was sitting at her desk behind the reception counter wearing her purple plaid wool coat.

"Little problem with the boiler," said Ted, who was on his feet, pulling his black watch cap down over his graying hair and heading for the door. "Uh, I've got a staff meeting over at the Gilead office," he mumbled, somewhat shamefaced as he headed for the door. "I've called Frost and Winkle. They've promised to send someone over . . . well, as soon as they can. Seems a lot of folks woke up to cold houses this morning."

"Maybe Phyllis and I could work over in Gilead, too," suggested Lucy, thinking of the modern building that housed *The Courier* office there, which was a stark contrast to the aged office in Tinker's Cove. Sure, Tinker's Cove boasted the antique rolltop desk that Ted inherited from his grandfather, a noted regional journalist, and a genuine Willard clock that hung on the wall and had been keeping the time correctly for over a hundred years, but it also had drafty windows that rattled the wooden Venetian blinds, cockeyed floors that tilted and creaked, and a very old furnace that grudgingly supplied minimal heat to the newly fashionable original steam radiators. And today, no heat at all.

"No can do," said Ted, shaking his head. "They're putting new carpet in and everybody's jammed together in the conference room."

"New carpet!" exclaimed Lucy. "They're getting new carpet and we can't even get weather stripping for the windows?" Lucy and Phyllis had both nurtured a suspicion that they were treated as second-class citizens by Ted, compared to the lucky folks over in the Gilead office.

"And my chair," began Phyllis, chiming in. "This chair is busted and it's breaking my back!"

"I know, I know, ladies," admitted Ted, sidling toward the door. "It's all on the list. We can't do everything at once," he said, repeating a familiar line as he opened the door, letting in a vicious blast of cold wind. "I haven't forgotten you," he said, stepping out and closing the door behind him. The little bell that announced visitors merely offered a sad little ping, apparently too chilly to produce its usual jangle.

"We're on the list," snarled Lucy, pulling her chair out and sitting down at her desk.

"We're very low on the list," said Phyllis, rubbing her arms to warm herself.

"Why don't you go home?" suggested Lucy, powering up her PC. "I'll stay and wait for Frost and Winkle."

"No way. I'm not abandoning you."

"No. You should go. There's no reason for us both to freeze to death."

"Ah. I see the truck outside. I think we're saved."

This time the little bell on the door jangled heartily as Seth Winkle himself entered, rosy-cheeked and dressed in his insulated work clothes with his name and the company's logo embroidered in white on the jacket. "Bit cool in here," he observed, with classic understatement. "I'll see what's the matter and have you warm and toasty in no time."

"Oops!" exclaimed Lucy, noticing that the cellar door was blocked with boxes and bags of donated nonperishable foods that *The Courier* was collecting for a town-wide food drive. "Let me move some of that stuff out of your way."

Seth pitched right in, helping Lucy move the foodstuffs into the morgue, then disappeared down the stairs to the cellar. Lucy and Phyllis waited anxiously, listening to an atonal symphony of bangs and clangs. Moments later he reappeared, shaking his head and tut-tutting. "Wow, I haven't seen that model in a dog's age. You've got a gen-you-wine an-tea-cue."

"Can it be fixed?" asked Lucy, as if questioning the doctor about a sick child.

"Doubt I can get the parts," he said, chewing on his lip. "I'll call Ted. Tell him it's done for, time to bite the bullet and get a new one. Better all 'round. More efficient, less costly in the long run. It's long overdue."

"In the meantime," said Phyllis anxiously, "is there anything you can do so we can stay warm?"

"Yeah," added Lucy, in a hopeful tone, "a temporary fix?"

"Space heaters. That's what you gotta do," advised Seth. "They're on clearance this week out at the big box store. If I were you, I'd get out there before they're all gone."

"I'll go," said Lucy and Phyllis simultaneously.

"Maybe you should draw straws," suggested Seth, with a chuckle, pulling his cell phone out of his pocket as he marched toward the door. "Have a nice day," he said by way of farewell, and yanked the door open, once again jangling the bell and revealing Eileen Clancy, who was just about to enter.

"And a fine day to you, too," said Eileen, grinning broadly and speaking with a slight Irish accent. "Goodness, it's a mite chilly in here, is it not?"

"The furnace is broken," said Phyllis, pushing her chair back and giving Lucy a questioning glance. "I'm just off to buy a space heater."

"Get two while you're at it," suggested Lucy with a wan smile, watching enviously as Phyllis headed out to her car with its heated seat and working heater to make the toasty drive down the road to the gloriously overheated big box store. She rubbed her hands together, trying to restore her circulation. "What can I do for you, Eileen?"

"Mind if I sit down?" asked Eileen, eyeing the chair Lucy kept for visitors. She was a remarkably fit woman in her fifties, with fair skin, green eyes, and dark, curly hair, dressed in leggings, a puffy parka, and a tweed bucket hat.

"Oh, sorry. I didn't think you'd want to linger here in the Arctic. Please do."

Eileen perched on the edge of the chair, back straight and knees together, just as she'd been taught by Sister Angelique at school in her native Ireland. "As you know, I teach Irish dancing at my little school."

Lucy nodded, agreeing. She knew Eileen was being modest, her Clancy Academy of Gaelic Dance attracted students from far and wide. The walls in its lobby were lined with photos of her students along with the trophies they'd won in various competitions, sometimes even going to Ireland to compete. Eileen herself was a former Rose of Tralee winner, an annual talent competition in Ireland that attracted young women of Irish descent from all over the world.

"This year," continued Eileen, "I am very fortunate to have four absolutely darling graduating seniors who are all extremely talented dancers who are competing in an upcoming *feis* in Portland. They're lovely girls, and I believe each and every one has a very good chance of going on to the next level of competition, the *oireachtas*."

Lucy, who was jotting down the information, paused. "How do you spell that?"

Eileen obliged, then continued. "The *feis* is a regional competition, drawing dancers from southern Maine. The *oireachtas* will be in Boston and dancers from all over New England will compete. I expect my girls will do well at the *feis,* wouldn't be surprised if we had a few first-place wins, but it's going to be very tough for the judges to choose. So I was wondering, Lucy, if you might be interested in writing a little story about these beautiful and talented young ladies."

"I'd love to," said Lucy, who knew this week's news budget was overloaded with dry facts and figures in preparation for the annual town meeting where citizens debated and voted on various issues, including the all-important town budget. A feature story on these local girls would surely catch readers' interest.

"Would it be possible for me to interview the girls? Will their parents give consent?" asked Lucy.

"I thought ahead," confessed Eileen, producing

four signed parental permission slips. "For interviews and photos, too."

"Wow, you are way ahead of the game," said Lucy, taking the slips with an approving nod. After reviewing them, she pulled out her calendar. "What's a good time?"

"Well," began Eileen, "they have a class this afternoon at four."

"At your studio? I presume it's heated?"

"Quite cozy. I'll even give you a cup of hot Irish tea."

"It's a date."

"I'll have the kettle on the boil, Lucy," said Eileen, standing up and adjusting her hat and gloves.

"Sounds lovely," said Lucy with a sigh. She watched Eileen leave, then got up and went over to the coffee station, intending to make a pot. But when she went in the bathroom to fill the carafe with fresh water, she discovered there was none to be had; the pipes had frozen.

When the Willard clock announced it was half past three, Lucy was more than ready to escape the office, which was barely habitable thanks to the two space heaters, but it still had no water. After discovering that the pipes had frozen, she managed to get hold of Seth who returned with a gas-fired construction heater and a blow torch. The good news was that the pipes hadn't burst; the bad news was the weather prediction that promised frigid temperatures for the next few days. "Your best option is to drain the system," he had advised, "until I can get a new boiler installed. Otherwise they'll just freeze again in the night."

"That means no water, no bathroom, no heat?"

"Yup."

"You've got the space heaters," said Ted, who had returned later that morning to deal with the crisis. "You can bring coffee in a thermos and use the facilities at the library."

Lucy was dubious. "Really?"

"I think that's our best option. I don't want to close the office; people drop by."

"They could drop by in Gilead," said Phyllis, who was busy unboxing the heaters. "We could put a sign on the door."

"Folks are used to coming here," said Ted. "Those heaters will make a big difference. You'll see."

"I doubt it," said Lucy. "And doesn't the fire department warn about the dangers of space heaters every year?"

"It's just a temporary solution. The new furnace will be up and running in a few days," said Ted, turning on his heel and walking to the door. "This new furnace is costing me a bundle," he said. "I think you two could be a little more appreciative. And maybe you might hustle a bit for ads."

Lucy was quick to reply, "Not in my job description." But she was talking to a closed door and a pinging bell.

Ted's attitude still rankled when she was finally able to leave for the interview, already imagining herself tucked up in Eileen's heated dance studio with her hands wrapped around a mug of hot tea.

And when she arrived, Eileen was as good as her word and had an electric tea kettle steaming in a corner of the roomy dance studio. Soon Lucy was installed in a rocking chair, wrapped in a colorful crocheted afghan, and provided with the promised tea. As she fussed over Lucy, Eileen instructed the four girls to continue their warm-ups. It was only when Lucy was settled that Eileen turned on the music, a lively Irish jig, and the four girls lined up, linked arms and began to demonstrate the intricate footwork involved in step dancing, including high kicks. Lucy took advantage of the performance to snap some photos on her cell phone, catching the girls in action. When they finished, she gave them a hearty round of applause.

"That was fabulous," she said. "As I imagine you already know, I'm Lucy Stone from *The Courier* newspaper and I'm going to write a feature story about you all and your dancing. Now, can you introduce yourselves and tell me a bit about yourselves?"

They all seemed somewhat embarrassed and looked to their teacher for guidance. Eileen stepped right in. "Girls, why don't you all take a seat?" She pointed to the row of chairs that lined one wall of the mirrored studio. "Let's begin with you, Siobhan," she continued. "Siobhan Delahunt has had quite a bit of success in competition, now haven't you, Siobhan?"

Delahunt, thought Lucy, wondering if Siobhan was related to Deirdre Delahunt, who was the town's top Realtor and a big advertiser in *The Courier*.

"I've done all right," said Siobhan, blushing. "I

love to dance, but I have to study, too. I'm taking a couple of AP courses and have to get ready for the exams."

"You'll do fine," said Eileen. "You have a four-point-oh average, don't you? And you're going to Boston College next year." She turned to Lucy. "Early decision. And she's already qualified to go on to the *oireachtas* next month."

"Congratulations," said Lucy, who was writing it all down and thinking how much pressure these high school girls had to deal with. Not that Siobhan was showing any signs of strain; she was obviously fit and healthy in her practice leotard, and her freckled complexion was clear, her blue eyes bright, her blond hair neatly confined in a ponytail. The only sign of teen rebellion was a tiny little gold nose stud.

"Thank you," replied Siobhan, and Lucy was struck by her good manners which she hadn't expected. Maybe, she thought, she should have been tougher on her own four kids, now grown, and raised her expectations concerning behavior.

"Now I'd like you to meet Brigid Callanan," said Eileen, breaking into her thoughts. "Brigid is a talented dancer who has great discipline, and she also volunteers at the local food pantry."

"My mom is a board member," explained Brigid, who seemed a bit more mature than the others, maybe because she was the tallest. She had perfectly cut long blond hair, pearl studs in her ears, and a silver bracelet with a heart charm that Lucy happened to know came from Tiffany's, having seen it advertised in the *New York Times*. Her leo-

tard and tights seemed to have come straight from
their packages, and her dancing shoes were free of
the scuffs and nicks on the other girls' shoes. Brigid,
she guessed, came from a privileged background,
and Lucy wondered if she was related to the Dr.
Callanan who had a thriving plastic surgery practice in Gilead. She also understood from Eileen's
careful phrasing that Brigid wasn't as naturally talented a dancer as Siobhan but worked hard to
compete successfully.

"And how long have you been step dancing?"
asked Lucy.

"Oh, ever since I was four," she said with a shrug.
"We all have."

The other girls all nodded in agreement, and
Lucy was drawn to one girl who stood out from the
others with a head of wild, red hair and a huge
smile; she seemed to radiate energy.

"They start quite young," added Eileen. "That's
why I'm so fond of them all. I've seen them grow
up from adorable little tykes into beautiful and
accomplished young ladies. Speaking of accomplished," she continued, "Erin Casey is quite the
artist and made her own costume for competition."

"Really?" asked Lucy, thinking of the photos in
the lobby that showed the dancers togged out in
elaborate costumes and hairdos, complete with
tiaras. "Those dresses are very complicated, aren't
they?"

"My mom has a business, making the costumes,
and she's taught me. It's fun designing the patterns. I especially like the Celtic knots," volun-

teered Erin, who was the smallest of the four, and the slightest, but also seemed more comfortable about being interviewed. She had dark hair, pulled back into two braids, and revealed uneven teeth when she smiled, which actually added a charming quirkiness to her appearance. Her hazel eyes sparkled with mischief and she spoke right up. "It must be fun being a reporter and interviewing people," she said, making eye contact with Lucy.

"It is," admitted Lucy. "I love my job. Are you interested in journalism?"

"I'm not sure. I'm going to the community college next year; I want to help people but I'm not sure exactly how." She paused. "And I really love designing clothes, too."

"I'm sure you'll find a way," said Lucy. "Good luck."

"Thank you. I'll need it," said Erin, laughing.

"You make your own luck," advised Eileen, moving on to introduce Kelly Tobin, the redhead who had attracted Lucy's notice. "Kelly, now," Eileen continued, in a slightly mocking tone, "doesn't practice like the others, but manages to captivate the judges nevertheless. I can only dream about what she'd accomplish if she'd work a bit harder."

Kelly tossed her head and grinned broadly, a gesture that Lucy imagined would win over even the most hard-hearted judge, and laughed, untroubled by Eileen's critique. "I practice when I can," she insisted, "but I'm busy, busy. I'm on the student council, I'm on the yearbook committee, I'm making a commemorative video for graduation, and I'm a captain of the field hockey team."

"Wow," said Lucy, struggling to write it all down. "How do you have time to study?"

Kelly bit her tongue and smiled. "I don't sleep much."

"I guess not," said Lucy. "So tell me about this upcoming competition. A *feis*. Is that what it's called?"

"Yes," said Eileen. "It's the Gaelic word for festival and it's quite the affair. It will take place in the Tripletree Hotel in Portland next Saturday. Dancers from much of the state will come to compete and hopefully win a chance to advance to the next level, the *oireachtas*, which is the regional New England competition. After that are the nationals and a chance to go on to Ireland to compete in the world championships."

"It's not just competing, though," offered Kelly. "There's things for sale, and it's very social. We catch up with girls we know from other areas. It's a hoot."

The other girls all smiled and nodded enthusiastically in agreement, which gave Lucy an idea. "I'd love to cover it for the paper. Would that be possible?"

"Sure. It's open to the public, anyone can come," said Kelly.

"I'll give you the details," said Eileen, indicating that the interview was over. Lucy stood up, preparing to leave, when Brigid approached her.

"Can I see the photos?" she asked, somewhat hesitantly. "I know you took some while we were dancing."

"Sure," said Lucy, pulling her phone out of her

pocket as the girls gathered round. She displayed the photos, pleased to see that she'd caught their energy and enthusiasm. "Okay?" she asked.

"I guess so," said Brigid, chewing on her lip. Lucy noticed that unlike the other girls, Brigid rarely smiled, and guessed she was self-conscious about the braces on her teeth.

"You look great, Bridge," offered Kelly.

"I look fat. Look at my thighs," said Brigid, pointing to a photo in which her skirt had flown up during a kick.

"Not at all," said Lucy, suspecting that despite her enviable good looks, Brigid was suffering from some body image problems. "I'd kill for beautiful long legs like yours."

"Time's flying," reminded Eileen. "You girls can work on your set pieces while I give Lucy the information about the *feis*." She clapped her hands. "Chop, chop." Out in the lobby, she made a copy of the *feis* announcement while Lucy zipped and buttoned up, preparing to go outside. "We usually go the night before and stay in the hotel so everyone is fresh and rested," advised Eileen.

"Thanks," said Lucy, thinking this might be a good excuse for a little getaway. She could use a break, she thought, picturing herself soaking in a hotel hot tub. Plus, it would give her an opportunity to catch up with her youngest, her daughter Zoe, who had finally flown the nest and was living in Portland.

Ted, however, was quick to bring her back to reality when she pitched the story to him. "I like the story, but I can't swing the hotel. This new furnace is costing a small fortune; it's imported from Germany," he added, rolling his eyes. "Winkle says it's superefficient and will save money in the long run. If I live that long," he added, sighing, "or the darn thing doesn't bankrupt me first."

Realizing that her dreams of a hot tub were out of the question, she called Zoe and begged a bed for the night. Much to her surprise, Zoe was quick to issue an invitation. "That would be great, Mom. Charlie's been spending most weekends with his boyfriend, so you can use his room."

"Are you sure he won't mind?" asked Lucy, hesitant to invade Charlie's private space.

"Not at all, Mom, and he's, well, kind of obsessive-compulsive about cleanliness. You'll be right at home."

Now where did that come from? wondered Lucy, who could hardly be considered obsessive about cleanliness. *No matter,* she thought, quickly accepting the invitation. "I'll take you out to dinner Friday," she offered. "You choose the place."

"Okay, Mom," trilled Zoe. "See you then."

So Lucy quit work early on Friday and drove to Portland, where Zoe and Charlie shared an attic apartment on a side street near the medical center. There was plenty of parking since all the neighbors were at work, and after climbing two flights of stairs she found the key Zoe had left for her under the doormat. Stepping inside, she noticed a few recent improvements—an IKEA sofa and a bright new rug—but the retro red leatherette and chrome dinette set the landlord had insisted remain was still in place in the kitchen, cute as ever.

Charlie's room was every bit as neat and clean as Zoe had promised, and he had even left a welcoming note for her taped to the mirror above his dresser. She set her duffel bag on the bed, went into the bathroom to freshen up, and when she came out, she found Zoe arriving home from work. After hugs and greetings Zoe suggested a nearby brewery and off they went for a girls' night on the town.

Sitting at a table in the trendy gastro-pub, sipping on a foamy IPA, Lucy asked Zoe how she was getting on with her public relations job for the Sea Dogs Double-A baseball team.

"Fine, Mom. It's really a lot of fun. The guys are great. . . ."

"Any romance brewing?"

Zoe laughed. "I don't know. It's hard to take them seriously. They're mostly focused on the game, and their chances of making it to the majors." She paused. "I have been seeing a guy who works for the *Herald*."

"Oh no," moaned Lucy. "Not a newspaper man."

"Don't worry. I don't think it's serious." Zoe took a bite of her veggie burger. "You know what's really weird? Leanne and the gang got all friendly with me when they realized I was working for the team."

Lucy remembered how hurt Zoe had been when her best college friend, Leanne, backed out of their plan to be roommates and moved into a fancy loft reno with a couple of other girls.

"I suppose they thought you could help them meet some players?"

"Yeah, all of a sudden when they figured out I was working with an entire team of hunky baseball players they were able to overlook my status as a poor, scholarship kid whom they claimed couldn't possibly afford rent in the loft building. Not to mention my working-class background and unfortunate family connections."

"That's right," remembered Lucy, dipping a fry into ketchup. "They thought you'd reveal personal secrets that I'd publish in *The Courier*." She took a bite and chewed thoughtfully. "I wonder what secrets they were worried about."

"Not worried anymore, Mom. Leanne would love for you to let everyone in Tinker's Cove know that she's dating Bart Helmand, the team's top scorer."

"Her secret is safe with me. I wouldn't dream of violating her privacy," said Lucy, smiling. "So I guess all is forgiven and you're friends again?"

Zoe gazed off into the glassed brewing area containing the huge stainless-steel vats and grimaced, adding a little shrug. "It's a small world, I don't like to hold grudges, but we're not close like we used to be. I can't quite forget how Leanne and the others treated me."

"Well, I think you're wise to let bygones be bygones, but you now know that you can't rely on Leanne's friendship."

"Yeah," agreed Zoe. "What really still stings is

the hypocrisy, the way they all acted as if they were doing me a big favor, like it was in my best interest to be excluded from the loft, when they were really just being mean."

"I'm sorry you had to go through that," said Lucy.

"Well, it's worked out for the best," admitted Zoe. "Charlie's great. He cleans and cooks and he's gone on weekends. What more could a girl want?"

What indeed? thought Lucy, feeling a mite jealous. She'd married right out of college and never had a chance to spread her wings like Zoe. She'd made her choice, she loved Bill, but she realized she'd missed out on something, too. She'd never lived independently; she'd always had to consider others' preferences as well as her own.

Zoe was still sleeping next morning when Lucy headed out to the hotel to cover the *feis*. She slipped out quietly, leaving a thank-you note on the red Formica table, and drove the short distance to the Tripletree Hotel, where free parking was provided in an outside lot. The temperature had moderated somewhat, and it was a lovely, clear day; just her luck to be stuck inside when she could have been hiking with Zoe. But she'd asked for the assignment and was determined to make the best of it as she rode the elevator up to the ballroom. When the doors slid open, she found the girls had not exaggerated; she felt as if she was stepping into a huge Irish festival. The lobby outside the ballroom was packed with lots of kids, mostly girls and their moms, all perusing the various tables selling dance shoes, wigs, costumes, jewelry, sparkling tiaras, and other Irish items, such as sweaters and tweed caps. From inside she heard the strains of Irish music and the thumping of step-dancing feet.

"Ah, here you are," exclaimed Eileen, greeting her with a big smile and handing her a program.

"How's everybody?" asked Lucy. "Ready to win?"

"The girls are fine," said Eileen, rolling her eyes, "but the mothers had quite a donnybrook last night. Too much Irish coffee, if you get my meaning."

Chapter Two

"There's basically five categories," said Eileen, taking her by the arm and leading down the hall. "Reel, Light Jig, Slip Jig, Treble Jig, and Hornpipe," she rattled off, as Lucy quickly pulled out her phone to record it all. "The girls also have set pieces, individual dances, that they present. My girls are at the open championship level, which means they will compete in three rounds today, either Reel or Hornpipe, Slip Jig or Treble Jig, plus their set piece. They're about to do their set pieces. They drew those first, which is nice because they're always a bit nervous to begin and the set pieces are choreographed to showcase their strengths. Not to mention they practice their sets constantly; they can do them in their sleep."

"How much do they practice?" asked Lucy, a bit confused by all the details.

"Oh, every day," said Eileen. "For at least an hour.

We have class four days a week and they practice at home the other days."

Wow, thought Lucy, who hadn't realized the level of commitment the dancing required. "And these competitions? I assume there's quite a bit of cost to the families."

"Oh yes," said Eileen with a nod. "Travel and lodging, meals, not to mention the registration fees. And then there are the costumes and wigs. The wigs are required, you know. . . ."

Ah, that explained the elaborate hairdos she'd noticed on the older girls, thought Lucy, as Eileen continued. "And the shoes . . . it's quite a commitment. But," she added, pausing in front of a set of doors, "it's a way for the girls to connect to their Irish heritage, which is important to their families. Speaking of which, the step-dance community is really like one big family; everyone is very supportive." With that, she opened the door and Lucy stepped into a function room, a section of the huge ballroom, where the carpet had been covered with a plywood platform. An accordionist sat to one side, warming up, and chairs were provided for the audience behind the table that accommodated the three judges. Ten dancers were standing in a row at the back of the platform, waiting their turns, including Eileen's four darlings. Lucy noticed that three of the girls were wearing costumes slightly different from the other contestants, dresses that featured complicated appliqué in classic Celtic designs rather than the glittery jewels that studded the others. She assumed they were created by Erin's mom, and decided she preferred them to Siobhan's fancier, jewel-encrusted costume. As required, all four were wearing the wigs Eileen had mentioned, which were elaborate constructions complete with tiaras. "Ah, it looks like we're just in time," said Eileen. Getting a wave from one of the judges, she pointed out the four moms and made her excuses, slipping off to watch from the side.

The four moms, all familiar faces from Tinker's Cove, had been expecting her and greeted her with smiles. One, identified by the mop of curly red hair that matched her daughter's magnificent mane, waved Lucy over. "Hi, Lucy. I'm Kelly's mom, Tori."

"I've met you before," said Lucy. "You live next door to my friend Sue Finch." Lucy hoped to sit with the group but discovered that all the chairs in the row were occupied.

"Oh, gosh, we need to sit down. They're about to begin and the rules are quite strict. Let's go back a few rows," said Tori, popping up and leading the way. "Just as well," she said as they sat down side by side and, leaning in, Tori placed one hand on Lucy's arm. "This way I can give you the skinny, the real scoop."

This was an opening Lucy couldn't resist; she had to ask. "Eileen mentioned something about you moms having a bit of a donnybrook after drinking too much Irish coffee—her words—last night. What was that all about?"

The music was beginning and a very skinny girl stepped forward from the line of waiting dancers and began tapping and kicking her way across the platform, holding her back and arms perfectly rigid. Tori leaned even closer and whispered in her ear, "It wasn't so much the coffee as the chardonnay and cosmos that went before," she said, chuckling. "Only a bunch of Irish girls would think dumping whiskey into coffee would help them sober up. But," she added, with a shrug and a toss of that fabulous hair, "no real harm done. Just some venting."

The skinny girl had finished her set and returned to her place in the rear, replaced by a boy dressed all in black. While he danced, Tori launched into a lively description of the other moms. "Deirdre Delahunt—you must know her?"

"Yup, she's Delahunt Realty, a big advertiser at the paper."

"Right. She's Siobhan's mom and, not surprisingly considering her real estate success, is super competitive. Siobhan's really the best dancer— she's already qualified for the *oireachtas*—and I know Eileen has dreams that she can go all the way to the Worlds."

The boy had finished and was replaced by another, similarly dressed but with the addition of a sparkling green vest.

"Who's sitting next to her?" asked Lucy.

"That's Karen Callanan. Her husband is the plastic surgeon, and she's loaded. If money could buy first place, Brigid would be headed for the Worlds, but she'll be lucky to get the win she needs to go to the *oireachtas*. Don't get me wrong, she's a solid dancer. But her emotions sometimes get in the way."

"Yeah," agreed Lucy, remembering her concerns about Brigid. "She seemed quite anxious about the photos I took the other day and how she'd look in the paper." Lucy paused, watching as another dancer advanced to replace the boy in the green vest. This girl had a blond wig, unlike the other girls' darker wigs. "That leaves Erin's mom . . ." prompted Lucy.

"Right. Margaret Casey. Bless her. She's a single mom, works at the bank so it's really a stretch for her to afford Erin's dancing. Competing, like this, gets expensive. I think Eileen gives her a break on the lessons, and she makes custom dance dresses that she sells to make money. Erin does a lot of the sewing, too. They're a team, and the costumes are exquisite, as you can see. I think they gain the girls points for presentation."

Lucy agreed, noticing that Margaret's costumes were very flattering, tailored to each dancer, and classier than the others. Unlike the dresses that were spattered with gaudy fake jewels, Margaret's designs featured complicated white appliqué and embroidery in traditional Celtic patterns that contrasted with the emerald green of the dress. The designs varied, probably chosen by each girl: Erin's had the intricately twisted Celtic knots she loved, Kelly's had Irish harps, and Brigid's was a riot of shamrocks.

"They're beautiful," agreed Lucy. "Very elegant. But what about Siobhan?"

"I guess she wants to stand out from the others. Deirdre was saying that Siobhan had worked so hard on her dancing that she deserved something better than Margaret's dresses. She wanted her to sparkle, that's what she said. And that dress, well it delivers a lot of sparkle."

From her tone of voice, Lucy surmised that Tori thought the dress was a mistake.

"Oh, gee, just listen to me," continued Tori, laughing, "running off at the mouth again. I'll say anything. I've got no secrets."

"Well, I'm pretty sure my editor doesn't want to be slapped with a libel suit, so anything you say is just between you and me." Lucy watched as Kelly stepped forward and raised her phone to begin snapping photos. "Tell me about Kelly. She's such a lovely girl."

"People say she takes after me," said Tori, twisting a lock of her long, wavy hair. "She's not the best dancer, to be honest, but she makes up for it with her smile and flair."

Indeed, unlike the preceding dancers, who had maintained absolutely blank expressions, Kelly began with a toss of her wigged head, a wink at the judges, and a big smile. Then she was tapping and high kicking her way across the stage, clearly enjoying herself.

"I have to say, despite everything you've said, I was very impressed with the girls when I interviewed them," observed Lucy, snapping away. "They seem to see themselves as a team, even a family."

That sent Tori into peals of laughter, which prompted a few head turns and tut-tuts from neighboring audience members. "That's rich," she said, tossing her head. "They actually detest each other, especially Siobhan, whom the other three consider stuck-up." Now the neighbors were shushing Tori, and she nudged Lucy, indicating that Kelly had finished her set and was being replaced by Brigid.

Brigid was a stunning contrast to the other

dancers, taller and projecting an air of self-confidence that Lucy suspected she didn't truly feel, remembering her anxiety about the photo, but had learned to project. Lucy was relieved she was sitting a few rows back, so as not to distract the girl with her picture taking. Brigid's dancing seemed to Lucy to be perfect, if slightly hesitant and careful, and when she finished, she gave a visible sigh of relief before retaking her place at the back of the stage.

Next up was little Erin, in the beautiful dress she'd made herself and a huge wig that seemed in danger of slipping down over her eyes. *Probably secondhand and the best her mom could afford,* thought Lucy, checking the screen on her camera, but a clear distraction for Erin and anyone watching her dance. Lucy found herself holding her breath, fearing that the wig would fall and blind the poor girl. But Erin tapped and twirled and flew across the stage fearlessly, putting her heart into her performance. Lucy began to slap her hands together, wanting to applaud, but Tori grabbed her hands and shook her head no. Applause was forbidden, she whispered, until all the dancers had finished.

Finally it was Siobhan's turn, and there was a distinct change in the atmosphere in the room, as if everyone was suddenly ready to pay close attention to a dancer they remembered from previous contests as something special. Indeed, as Siobhan advanced to the front of the stage, her steps, the same steps that the others had used, seemed crisper and cleaner. She seemed to float above the scuffed plywood surface of the stage. Lucy snapped a couple of photos as Siobhan reached the front and gave a neat jump that levitated her entire body. Just then, as she landed, the jewel-encrusted skirt of her costume suddenly came loose, slipping down until it fell in a puddle around her ankles. Her face flamed scarlet and she burst into tears, standing there in her black panties with her bare legs exposed all the way down to her regulation poodle socks as the accordion music suddenly stopped. Her mother jumped up and ran to her, pulling the skirt back up. The two stood together, Deirdre's arms wrapped protectively around her daughter. Suddenly Siobhan whirled around and turned to face Erin. "You did it! Why? Why did you do this to me?" she cried, through her tears.

Erin's face crumpled. "I didn't. I never even touched your costume. I wouldn't do that. Why do you think I would?"

"It had to be you!" proclaimed Siobhan, gaining steam. "You've always envied me. You've always been jealous because I win all the time and you don't."

That's when Margaret, Erin's mom, joined the fray, defending her daughter. "Don't be ridiculous! This is what happens when you wear one of those overpriced dresses stuck all over with those heavy fake jewels."

"I'll have you know this dress cost more than you make in a week at that dumb bank," declared Deirdre, defending her daughter. "I'll have you know these so-called 'cheap jewels' are genuine Swarovski crystals!"

By now the judges were taking action, fearing the argument would descend into an actual physical fight, as the two parties were drawing closer.

One judge, the only man, had positioned himself
between Margaret and Deirdre, and another, a
rather chubby woman, was standing beside Deirdre and Siobhan, ready to block Erin should she
decide to respond with an attack. But neither Margaret nor Erin had any such intention: Erin was
sniffling and Kelly was holding her hand, whispering in her ear; Margaret reached out with her arm
but only, she said, to see if she could fix the dress.
"I have my sewing kit . . ." she began, only to be si-
lenced by Deirdre.

"Oh, you think you can make this better with a
stitch or two! You and your daughter have done
enough damage already, thank you." She turned
to the judge. "We're withdrawing from this pathetic excuse for a *feis*. Siobhan's already qualified
for the *oireachtas* and we don't need you!" With
that she dragged Siobhan off the stage, stopping
to retrieve her bag from a rather stunned-looking
Karen. Then, turning back and locking eyes with
Margaret, she announced, "This is not the end of
this. I will be contacting a lawyer." With that she
grabbed Siobhan's hand and marched out of the
room, leaving everyone shocked and silent.

"When you're ready," the third judge said, with
a nod to the accordion player, "we will continue."

There was a pause as the dancers resumed their
waiting positions, the judges returned to their
table, and the audience settled down. The strains
of a jig began and another boy dancer advanced,
doing his best to concentrate on the steps he knew
so well but faltering on a kick and missing a step.

"Well, that was quite a show," whispered Lucy.

"I suspect somebody had Irish coffee for breakfast," replied Tori.

"You mean Siobhan's mom? Does she have a drinking problem?"

Tori shrugged. "I'm an actress, I've even been called a drama queen, but even I thought that performance was over the top." She smiled. "Face it, it was funny. And even she admitted that Siobhan didn't need the win. There was no reason to accuse poor Erin, except for spite. I don't know what she's got against the poor child, or her mother. . . ."

What indeed? wondered Lucy, as the final dancer completed her set and the judges conferred at the table.

Chapter Three

Eileen hurried after Deirdre and Siobhan, looking distraught and no doubt eager to smooth things over. "Poor Eileen. She doesn't want to lose her best dancer," whispered Tori. "Deirdre's always threatening to take Siobhan to the school in Rockland. It's much bigger and the teacher was a world champion back in the nineties."

Lucy was thoughtful. "Doesn't all this competitiveness kind of take the fun out of dancing?"

"I think so," said Tori with a shrug. "But I'm not very competitive. I know I'm a B-list actor, and that's fine with me. I get enough commercials to pay the bills, and I've got plenty of time for myself. Kelly knows she's never going to go to Worlds—she'll be lucky to qualify for the *oireachtas*—but she loves the dancing. I'll find her tapping her toes and going through the steps when she's sitting at dinner or doing her homework. I think she finds it soothing in some weird way."

"I can see that," said Lucy, who remembered how her mother always rotated her foot when she was watching TV, and later, when her memory began failing, the way she rolled her thumb against her first two fingers. Sometimes, when she was stressed, she caught herself mindlessly doing the same thing.

The judges were now rising from their table, ready to announce the winners. There were three: third place went to the boy with the green vest, second to Erin, and first to Brigid. They all beamed, receiving their trophies, and Lucy snapped a photo. "Eileen did well. Two of her girls won," said Lucy, looking to see if the teacher had returned and discovering she had not.

She spotted Karen and Margaret, along with their daughters, gathered around Kelly, apparently consoling her. "Here we go," sighed Tori. "The pity party." She made her way to the little group, followed by Lucy, in time to hear Karen telling Kelly not to worry, she'd place next time. "Too bad, though, what with Siobhan out of the running, you had a good chance. I don't know what the judges saw in the boy."

"When there are boys, they always pick at least one," grumbled Margaret. "There aren't very many and I think they want to encourage them."

"They probably do have to put up with a lot of teasing, even bullying," said Karen thoughtfully. "People don't realize how physically challenging dancing really is. It's probably harder than playing baseball or football."

"Wasn't there some football player who famously took ballet lessons?" asked Tori, embracing her daughter. "You looked great out there."

"Thanks, Mom. I had a great time. Did you see that kick?"

"I did," laughed Tori. "Way high."

"But it cost you a misstep," said Karen, taking Brigid's trophy and admiring it.

"That kick was worth it," said Kelly, getting a squeeze from her mom.

"What next?" asked Lucy. "Are the girls dancing in more categories?"

"Oh yes," sighed Tori, as Eileen came bustling back.

"Congratulations, girls," she crowed. "I saw the listing in the lobby. Very nice work, Erin and Brigid." She turned to Kelly. "No excuses, now, Miss Kelly. The hornpipe is yours, if you concentrate and skip the theatrics."

"I will," promised Kelly, blushing, as the group broke up. Lucy remained with Eileen, who gave her the schedule for the remaining dances and suggested which ones she should watch. Lucy dutifully attended the slip jigs, reels, hornpipes and treble jigs, but found they all seemed to run together in her mind. Her ears were ringing with jaunty Irish tunes and her eyes were glazing over when the final note sounded and the last of the contestants began packing up and leaving. Erin was the only one of Eileen's dancers who had competed in that final dance, so Lucy accompanied her and her mom as they left the hotel, making their way through the carpeted lobby. "Were you pleased with the day?" asked Lucy.

"Yup. I picked up another first, so now I've qualified for the *oireachtas*," said Erin, "but I don't know if I'll go."

"Why not?" asked Lucy.

"It will be in Boston and might be too expensive," said Margaret. "I'm running out of vacation days, too."

"Eileen said I might be able to share with one of the other girls," said Erin, as they began walking through the parking lot. "Ms. Callanan asked if I was planning to go and said you should call her."

"We'll see. There's still the registration fee, and I'd like for you to have a new wig if you're going to compete," replied Margaret, giving her daughter a smile and pausing at a row of parked cars. "I think our car is down here."

"Safe home," said Lucy, pausing before heading off to the far reaches of the lot where she had parked. "Thanks for coming," said Erin. "I can't wait to see the story."

"I'll work on it tomorrow, it will probably be online Monday," said Lucy with a little wave. Mother and daughter headed off down a line of cars and Lucy continued on past row after row to her SUV. She took her time settling in, waiting a few minutes for the heater to kick in and for her seat to warm up. She was approaching the lift gate when she noticed a little Corolla stopped in the driveway with the hood up and saw Margaret peering into the engine block. She pulled up alongside and braked, rolling down the window. "What's the matter?" she asked.

"I don't know," admitted Margaret. "I only went a few feet before it stalled out."

"Maybe it's the battery," suggested Lucy. "I've got cables."

She climbed out, fetched the cables from the back, and soon had them clamped on Margaret's battery, but it was no-go. "It's not taking the charge," she admitted after a few tries. "You'd better call Triple A."

"I would if I could," said Margaret. "Maybe the hotel can call a tow for me."

"How will we get home, Mom?" asked Erin, looking worried.

"Don't panic," said Margaret, anxiously chewing her lip. "I'm sure it can be fixed. I probably just need a new battery. Or maybe the starter. I don't know."

"I have Triple A. I'll call."

"Can you do that?" Margaret was doubtful.

"Yeah. No big deal. I did it last month when my friend's car got a flat in my driveway."

"I don't want you to get into trouble. . . ."

"I won't. It's okay," said Lucy, pulling the card out of her wallet and dialing. "Half an hour," she reported, after giving her membership number to the automatic phone system. "Meanwhile, we can wait in my car to keep warm."

The tow truck came, the little Corolla was loaded on board, and Lucy followed with Margaret and Erin in her SUV to the garage. There the car was unloaded and examined by a mechanic while Lucy, Margaret, and Erin waited nervously for the diagnosis, seated on the battered couch provided for customers in the office. It seemed to Lucy almost as if they had accompanied a sick relative to the ER.

The afternoon sun was dimming when the mechanic returned, a sorrowful expression on his face. "Well," he began, shaking his head, "it's like this. The catalytic converter's shot, you had some coolant leaks . . ."

"So the battery's okay?" asked Margaret.

"Uh, no. It's dead, and while you're at it, you really need new tires, and the brakes don't look too good either. . . ."

"So how much are we talking?" asked Margaret, cutting to the chase. "Just so I can get going again."

"Well, the converter alone is about five hundred. . . ."

Margaret's face fell. "Really?"

The mechanic nodded sadly. "But honestly, your inspection sticker is out of date and right now your car won't pass. I can't put it back on the road without fixing the brakes and tires. It's not safe."

"Doesn't matter," said Margaret with a resigned sigh. "I haven't got five hundred dollars."

"So what do you want to do?"

"I don't know," said Margaret. "I need to go home, back to Tinker's Cove, and think about it. Can you keep the car for a few days? Work up an estimate?"

"Sure." The mechanic thought a bit, then gave her a smile. "I can probably find some reconditioned parts, help you out a bit. Here's our card. Call me on Monday."

"Thanks," said Margaret. "I really appreciate it."

"I'm sure you'll figure something out," said

Lucy, trying to be encouraging as they made their way to her car. "That mechanic was really nice."

"I get so tired of being a charity case," said Margaret. "I've got a full-time job at the bank and a side gig making the dance dresses, I ought to be able to afford a car."

"I'm sure it's not much comfort, but you're not alone," said Lucy, who'd only recently done an investigative piece about the county's working poor, folks who were caught between low wages and the ever-rising cost of living. "Meanwhile, what do you say to dinner at McDonald's before we head back to Tinker's Cove?"

"As long as you let me buy your dinner," insisted Margaret. "You've been so kind . . ."

Lucy was prepared to protest but held her tongue. She understood that Margaret's pride was wounded, and allowing her to buy the meal was a way for her to restore her sense of self-worth. "You've got a deal," said Lucy.

They all climbed into her car and Margaret got directions on her phone for the nearest McDonald's, which was only a few blocks down the road from the auto repair garage on the brightly lit miracle mile. "Bright lights, big city," mused Lucy, thinking of Tinker's Cove with its single traffic light.

"We're not in Tinker's Cove. That's for sure," said Margaret.

"You know, Mom," ventured Erin, "the car drove great coming down."

"It was on borrowed time, Erin," said Margaret. "I knew it wouldn't pass inspection. I'm surprised I didn't get stopped. I wouldn't be surprised if the local cops turned a blind eye. They know I'm struggling."

"I dunno," mumbled Erin. "Siobhan's mom was out to get us; she wanted to get me disqualified. Why else would she accuse me of sabotaging Siobhan's dress? If Siobhan couldn't dance, she wanted to make sure I didn't either."

"She was just upset," insisted Margaret. "Anyone would have been, if it happened to them. The way that dress just fell apart. It was a shame."

"You're too kind, Mom. I overheard Siobhan's mom last night, saying how she saw you using food stamps at the farmer's market, and how you should be buying food at BJ's where you'd get more for your government money."

"People who live in glass houses shouldn't talk," grumbled Margaret, rolling her eyes. Then she seemed to think better of whatever she was about to say concerning Deirdre and instead defended her fish purchase. "It was the end of the day and I got a good deal on that fish. But, believe me, I'm not too proud to pick up clothes at the thrift store and even go to the food pantry. I do what I gotta do, but sometimes I do like a bit of fresh fish." She fell silent for a moment, then added, "You know, I'd like to see some of those ten-percenters I see at the bank walk in my shoes for a day. I bet they'd change their tune real fast if their Amex got denied and they only had a hundred twenty-nine dollars and forty-one cents in their checking accounts to last five days until payday."

"Well, here we are," announced Lucy, turning in under the golden arches. "I don't know about you, but I'm starving!"

"Well, you get whatever you want, Lucy," said Margaret, walking alongside Lucy. "I don't think even Deirdre can fault us for eating at McDonald's."

"Are you kidding? As far as I'm concerned, if I don't have to cook it, it's fine dining!" proclaimed Lucy.

It had been a long day, so Lucy splurged a week's worth of calories on a Big Mac, fries, and a chocolate shake, which also happened to be featured as a combo for a reduced price. "Thanks, Margaret. This is a real treat," she said, as they settled in at a Formica table. "I love Mickey D's and I hardly ever get to go. Too fattening."

"It's a guilty pleasure," agreed Margaret. "Sometimes I just get the fries. They're so good."

"It's bad for the environment," grumbled Erin. "All this packaging, and the beef . . . they say it's a big reason for deforestation in the Amazon."

"Not to mention the methane gas the critters produce," offered Lucy with a sympathetic smile as she dipped a fry into a puddle of ketchup. "It adds to global warming."

"Well," said Margaret, "it's a good thing that this is a rare treat. I don't think we have to feel responsible for global warming if we only eat fast food once in a blue moon."

"I couldn't agree more," said Lucy, slurping up the shake through a straw and finding it delicious. "It really was too bad about Siobhan's dress," said Lucy. "Have you ever seen that happen before? Do you think someone really did sabotage her dress?"

Margaret was quick to answer. "I doubt it very much. I really meant what I said about those dresses.

The Irish ones are fine, but sometimes they sneak in ones made cheaply in China and Vietnam. When you start piling on a lot of jewels and heavy trim, you've got to reinforce the dress. Now that was a beautiful dress, and quite flattering to Siobhan, but it wasn't well made." She shrugged and chewed on a fry. "People get taken in by a pretty dress and don't bother to consider how it's constructed."

"Construction! You make it sound like a bridge or something," teased Erin.

"You can laugh, Erin, but you know what I'm talking about. There's a reason French seams and interfacing were created. It's a real challenge to create a dress that's both beautiful and will stand up to a lot of movement. I made a skating costume once and I got to say, it was a challenge to make something that looked like a bit of wisp but allowed the skater to move freely in those jumps and turns. These dancing dresses are almost as challenging. I always make French seams, I line the skirts, and I even add weights to the hems so they fall back nicely after the kicks."

"Well, Mom, everyone says your dresses are the best."

Margaret smiled and reached across the table to pat her daughter's hand. "I love making them, and it's a real joy to me to teach you. I love seeing you dance in a dress you made."

"That dress makes me feel special, Mom," replied Erin, withdrawing her hand and taking a long swallow of Coke. "It's too bad about Siobhan," she added with a sly smile, "but for once she got what she deserved."

Chapter Four

When Lucy got to the office on Monday morning she was relieved to find the heat was back on. She greeted Phyllis with a smile and a big sigh as she began taking off her coat. "Feels absolutely loverly," she sang, reprising a tune from the Little Theatre's recent production of *My Fair Lady*, directed by her good friend Rachel Goodman.

"Well, you're not going to sit 'abso-bloomin'-lutely still,'" chimed in Ted, who had arrived moments behind her and had also seen the show. "Don't take off your coat. We've got to get all this food over to the food pantry." He looked at Phyllis and added in a no-nonsense tone of voice, "It's all hands on deck."

"But my back . . ." began Phyllis. "I'm not supposed to lift stuff."

"Noodles are not all that heavy," advised Ted. "I

swear, I never saw so many macaroni and cheese dinners in my life."

"My kids used to love that stuff," said Lucy, thinking of her four kids, now flown and leaving her and Bill with an empty nest. "They liked it much better than the recipe I made from scratch with eggs and milk and four kinds of cheese."

"Kids!" muttered Phyllis, donning the bright pink Puffa jacket that intentionally clashed with her burnt orange leggings and matching hair; Phyllis loved bright colors and mixed and matched with abandon. "I'm glad I never had any. Ungrateful wretches."

"Not always," insisted Lucy. "I'm proud of my gang." She glanced out the window thinking of Toby and his wife, Molly, along with her precious grandson, Patrick, far away in Alaska. And Elizabeth, on another continent altogether, in Paris. Sara in Boston, and Zoe in Portland were closer to home, but too busy with their own lives to make frequent visits home. "It was great to see Zoe this weekend, but it just reminded me how much I miss them all. Nowadays the house is so quiet."

"You and Bill have a great family," said Ted. "But now I need your muscle, and your car, Lucy. Pam took my truck to pick up some firewood, so I'll need you to deliver the food in your SUV."

"I'm putting in for gas," said Lucy. "And for the trip to Portland on Saturday. It's a good thing I went, by the way. Margaret Casey's car broke down and she needed a lift home."

"That old jalopy looks as if it's held together

with chewing gum," said Phyllis, groaning as she picked up a box of ramen noodles. "Like me."

"She's waiting for an estimate to repair it," said Lucy.

"She should scrap it and get something newer and younger that's in better shape," observed Ted, narrowing his eyes and looking pointedly at Phyllis.

"Good luck, Ted," snapped Phyllis, catching his drift. "Nobody's gonna work for the pittance you pay me."

"And I don't think Margaret can afford a new car," said Lucy. "I doubt she can even afford the repairs. The mechanic said it needs a lot of work to pass inspection."

"Maybe the Hat and Mitten Fund can help," suggested Ted, naming the fund Lucy and his wife, Pam, along with their friends Sue Finch and Rachel Goodman had established years ago to provide warm winter clothing for local kids. Through the years the fund had grown and now provided holiday parties, back-to-school backpacks, summer camp scholarships, and even occasional emergency funds as well as the original gently-used cold-weather gear.

"I'll bring it up when we get together for breakfast," said Lucy, who always looked forward to the Thursday morning gathering at Jake's Donut Shack with her friends that had become a weekly event. She hoisted a shopping bag filled with canned goods and settled it on her hip, heading for the door. "Maybe Brendan at the food pantry can help, too."

Lucy's car was fortunately parked right out front

of the office, so it wasn't long before it was packed to the gills with all sorts of non-perishables, albeit with a strong emphasis on peanut butter, mac and cheese, and ramen noodles. Ted watched with a satisfied expression as Lucy reached for the button to close the rear hatch, then told her to wait. "We need a photo, to thank our readers."

Lucy obligingly got out her phone and snapped a photo of Ted and Phyllis standing on either side of the packed cargo area. "I think we've got a good chance of winning the contest," he said, smiling. "Won't it be grand? I can see it now. *The Courier's* banner right on the sign of the new food pantry building."

"It'll be a great use of that old warehouse," said Phyllis, who was making a big show of rubbing her back. The food drive, as they all knew, was only part of a yearlong effort to raise funds and awareness of the food pantry, which had outgrown its current facility in the basement of the Community Church. If successful, the pantry's board hoped to raise enough money to purchase an abandoned warehouse next to the former train station on Railroad Avenue that would also include affordable housing. As part of this effort, local businesses had been invited to take part in a friendly competition to collect the most unperishable food; the winner would get naming rights for the improved food pantry.

"It's awfully ambitious," cautioned Lucy, whose husband, Bill, was a highly regarded restoration contractor. "Even if they get a good price on the warehouse, it's going to need some serious renovation."

"Maybe your Bill could donate some time. . . ." suggested Ted. "Especially considering it's going to have *The Courier* as part of its name." He paused, adopting a dreamy expression. "Should it be 'Sponsored by *The Courier*?' Or maybe we just put the masthead up there, above COMMUNITY FOOD PANTRY."

"I wouldn't count your chickens before they're hatched," advised Phyllis, as she dramatically bent over to illustrate how much pain her back was giving her and shuffled back into the office. "Don't put that thermostat above sixty-eight!" warned Ted, heading down the street to his car.

Phyllis paused in the doorway. "Oh, right, Ted," she replied, giving Lucy a mischievous wink.

Lucy smiled to herself as she finally closed the hatch and started her car; she was pretty sure the office would be a comfy seventy-two degrees when she got back, maybe even seventy-four, which Phyllis favored but which she found a bit too warm. It was only a matter of a few blocks down Main Street to the Community Church, where she saw the OPEN flag was flying by the basement door. She parked as close as possible in the church's gravel driveway and was greeted by Brendan Coyle, who had observed her arrival and was already wheeling out a donated tea cart that had seen better days but was still useful for transporting foodstuffs. Lucy thought he looked a bit silly pushing the cart, considering he was a big man, well over six feet, and boasted a substantial belly that required belting his trousers beneath it.

"Ta-da!" said Lucy, who had hopped out of the car and clicked the button that raised the hatch. "Ted can't decide if he wants *The Courier* masthead above or below COMMUNITY FOOD PANTRY on the sign."

Brendan let loose with a hearty laugh, appraising the load. "Most impressive," he admitted, "but I suspect that Deirdre Delahunt has the lead."

"Really?" Lucy was disappointed. "Ted will be crushed."

"She doesn't like to lose, you know. And what with that real estate business of hers, she's got all her agents collecting for her. She's got a sign and a basket at every open house, and I heard she's even got them going door to door, begging for anything folks can spare."

"Our readers were very generous, and so was Tony Marzetti at the IGA," said Lucy, grabbing a case of rice pilaf mix and dropping it on the trolley.

"Eileen Clancy is doing very well, too, at the dance school," said Brendan, hoisting a heavy shopping bag filled with canned goods. "She stopped by this morning with a load and promised more to come."

"I was with her at the *feis* in Portland this weekend; I did a photo-essay that's already online. You ought to take a look at it." Lucy grabbed another bag, this one containing several boxes of breakfast cereal.

"I saw Margaret at church Sunday and she told me that there was a bit of an upset. Siobhan withdrew and Brigid Callanan won first place for her set piece and Erin placed second, but went on to get a first in the jig."

"Yeah, Siobhan's dress kind of deconstructed right in front of everyone. I didn't put that in the story."

"What a shame for the poor girl." Brendan added one final box to the pile on the trolley and began pushing it inside; Lucy picked up a couple of shopping bags and followed him into the pantry. "It's sad for Siobhan, of course, but I have to admit I'm especially happy for Erin. Her mom's a client here and I know what a tough time she's having. Margaret is a genuine good soul, always thinking of others before herself. She'll never take more than a bare minimum. Says there's others that need it more."

"She could use some financial help now; her car broke down in Portland."

"And Margaret told me how kind you were to use your Triple A card and give them a ride home."

"It was nothing," said Lucy dismissively. "I was there. What else was I going to do?"

Brendan looked at her over the stack of boxed food he was building. "Not everyone would help. You'd be surprised how blind people can be to the needs of others. That said, I have to admit that people in Tinker's Cove are really rallying to our cause. Look at all this food. The generosity is amazing, and it couldn't come at a better time. The end of winter is usually a low point for us. Folks give at Thanksgiving and Christmas, but come March, they're often tapped out themselves."

"I know you also get cash donations," said Lucy, taking in the extraordinary amount of donated food that was overflowing the shelves and covering the floor. "And since you're not having to buy food, thanks to all these donations, I wonder if the pantry might be able to give Margaret some money, to help with her car?"

Brendan sighed. "No can do. We have a strict policy. Food only." He scratched his beard thoughtfully. "Karen Callanan might be able to help. She's one of our biggest supporters. She doesn't just donate money, much as that's appreciated, but she volunteers one afternoon every week to work here in the pantry, and she's also on the board of directors. She's one who's always ready to pitch in. I bet she'll come up with something."

"I don't know her well, but she does seem to have a kind heart. Erin said Karen might be able to take her to the *oireachtas*. Her mom can't get time off or afford the cost."

"That doesn't surprise me at all," said Brendan. "That's just the sort of thing Karen would do."

"It's hard for Margaret and Erin, too," continued Lucy, resting her bum on a table and settling in for a bit of a gossip. "I think they feel defensive about being strapped for cash. Eileen told me the moms had a bit of a brouhaha the night before the *feis*. She tries to pretend that they're all one big happy Irish family but . . ."

"Trust me," said Brendan with a smirk, "there's no such thing as a happy Irish family. If they're not at each other's throats, they're certainly not Irish. It's just the way we are."

Lucy laughed. "Not only Irish families. My kids never get together without some sort of squabble; they can't seem to resist going after each other. I guess you never quite outgrow sibling rivalry."

"Too true," agreed Brendan. "And when you get a bunch of Irish 'tiger moms' together, they all want their little cubs to win."

"All moms, I guess. Eileen blamed it on the Irish

coffee they drank. Says it's become a tradition with the moms, along with plenty of cosmos and chardonnay."

"Ah, the drink, the curse of the Irish, they call it. But for myself, I do enjoy a wee drop now and then."

"I guess as long as it's wee, you're fine," said Lucy, thinking she really ought to skip the glass or two of wine that had become a daily ritual. "Well," she sighed, pushing off from the table, "I guess I better get back to work. The town meeting warrant's out and I'm sure the good people of Tinker's Cove are counting on me to explain it to them." She paused, thinking of the task ahead. "In detail."

"Better you than I," said Brendan, as a large white Ryder truck pulled in front of the pantry and braked hard, followed by a caravan of cars. "What . . . ?" he asked, wondering aloud and staring out the open doorway.

They watched, open-mouthed, as the truck driver's door opened and Deirdre Delahunt hopped down from the cab. "I hope you've got plenty of room," she yelled, "because I've got a big load for you. And plenty of helpers," she added, indicating the caravan containing half a dozen agents from her real estate business. All were dressed, Lucy noticed, in matching green Delahunt Realty blazers as they assembled beside the truck.

Lucy and Brendan quickly stepped outside and followed Deirdre to the back of the truck, where she gave the lever a big yank and the door rolled up, revealing cases and bags and boxes of food.

The agents, apparently prepped by Deirdre, all cheered and clapped.

"My goodness, where did it all come from?" asked Lucy.

"I hope you left something in the store," said Brendan.

"Never fear. Most of it came from clients' pantries; everybody's got something they can donate. And my agents, they were great. They all volunteered to make calls and collect the food. And I owe a big thank-you to the folks at Cali Kitchen. They put me in touch with some wholesalers who supply local restaurants, and they were very generous. Some of it is past the sell-by date, but they've assured me it's still perfectly good. So here we are." Deirdre swung her arm in a gesture of presentation, getting another round of applause. "And what good timing, catching Lucy. How about a picture for the paper, before we unload the truck?"

Lucy thought of the photo Ted had insisted upon, and how pathetic *The Courier*'s carload would look in comparison to Deirdre's truckload, along with her small army of "volunteers" who had no doubt been pressured to give up their time or face retaliation. Lucy knew how real estate worked, how the agents all worked on commission, and had to compete with each other for listings, open houses, and advertisements, all of which Deirdre controlled.

"Sure thing," she said, reluctantly producing her phone. Deirdre grabbed Brendan and placed him at one side of the open truck rear. Then she arranged the agents, placing herself front and center, waiting for Lucy to raise the phone. When all was ready, she yelled, "Cheese!" then erupted into laughter. "That's funny! There's actually a ton of mac and cheese in here!"

"I guess we can start unloading," said Brendan. "Let me check with the reverend. I think we're going to have to use the fellowship room, at least temporarily."

"Take your time," said Deirdre. "We're all yours."

"Then I'll be right back," he said, going inside to find Reverend Marge.

"While we wait, Lucy and I can discuss how the sign should look," said Deirdre, giving Lucy a triumphant smile. "You know. The sign for the Delahunt Realty Food Pantry."

This got yet another cheer from the agents, which Lucy found rather irritating. She knew when she, and more importantly, Ted, were beat, and she didn't feel like sticking around while Deirdre rubbed salt into the wound. "Well, I wish I could stay and help, but I've got to get back to work." She gave Deirdre a weak smile. "Well done. Thanks to you, a lot of tummies are going to be full."

"I'm all for charity. Those of us who are fortunate should give back," said Deirdre, as if delivering a sound bite. "From those to whom much is given, much is expected, and I most certainly appreciate the fact that I'm in a position where I can help those who are less fortunate." She paused and lowered her voice, speaking into Lucy's ear. "Of course, charity should be entirely voluntary. What I don't like is this entitlement culture. All this gimme, gimme. Nobody deserves reparations for stuff that happened hundreds of years ago and college loan forgiveness and free childcare. If you want it, you ought to be prepared to work for it or do without. That's the way I was brought up." She gave a knowing nod. "You can't tell me these child tax credits aren't going for booze and drugs."

Best not to disagree, thought Lucy, who knew only too well that hard work didn't guarantee a commensurate paycheck. "Well, see you around," she said, giving a little wave and heading to her car. It was too bad Deirdre couldn't simply be happy with her winning donation, but had become a sore winner. She wasn't just making a generous gesture; she had turned the food drive into something more than a friendly community competition. Her conspicuous generosity was really messaging the notion that she was so successful, she had more than anyone else and therefore could give more, at the same time demeaning those who needed help. The folks who weren't rich and successful like her had only themselves to blame for their failure, and in her eyes they had indeed failed. They were losers and she was a winner. It was that simple.

Lucy started her car and exited the lot slowly, careful to avoid the Delahunt Realty agents who had formed a bucket brigade of sorts and were unloading the truck under Deirdre's direction. Thinking back to the *feis*, it was no wonder the other girls hadn't been terribly sympathetic when Siobhan's dress had fallen apart. That was the problem when you always won, especially if you weren't an especially graceful winner, or if you had a mother like Deirdre. Sooner or later people began rooting against you and looking for your weak spot. All too often, thought Lucy as she turned onto the highway and picked up speed, it turned out that what appeared to be great success was actually nothing more than a false front.

Chapter Five

Lucy hadn't got very far before her phone sounded off and, figuring it might be Ted with a breaking news assignment, she pulled to the side of the road and dug her phone out of her bag. Checking the display, she saw she was right. "What's up?" she asked, awaiting orders.

"I picked up something on the scanner," he said, referring to the device that monitored the public safety dispatch system. "Seems there's been some sort of emergency at 43 Parallel Street."

"That's next to Sue's house," she said, feeling her chest tighten with worry for one of her oldest and dearest friends. What if the dispatcher got the number wrong and it was 45? "You're sure it's 43?"

"That's what I heard, but you better check it out."

"Right. I'm on it."

She dropped her phone into her bag and pulled

into the road, forgetting to check for oncoming traffic and getting an angry horn blast from an aged Subaru that had swerved to avoid hitting her. "Sorry, sorry," she muttered, tapping the brakes and trying to stick to the speed limit. If only she could fly, she wished, or had second sight. It wasn't far. Aptly named, Parallel Street ran parallel to Main Street, connected by a short bit of School Street, but even that short distance seemed to take forever. Even worse, she had to pull over for the rescue squad, which sped by with siren blaring and lights flashing, making her heart race. Finally reaching the turn onto Parallel, she saw the ambulance, as well as a couple of squad cars, all gathered together by Sue's house.

Of course, that's where they would be, filling the street in front of 43 and its neighbors. Who lived at 43? Wasn't Tori Tobin Sue's neighbor? Lucy knew they were chummy, but which side did Tori live on? Was she at 47? Tinker's Cove was a small town and house numbers were an afterthought; people tended to geolocate using landmarks, like "the big old pine tree that was hit by lightning," "behind the post office" or "next to the Daleys' old house, the one on Depot Street." Lucy parked in front of 37 and took a deep breath, bracing herself for whatever was coming, and climbed out of the car. She hoofed it down the bumpy sidewalk, which lurched this way and that due to tree roots and frost heaves, and was immediately hailed by Sue, who was standing on her front porch.

She stopped for a moment, letting out a huge sigh of relief and taking a few deep, calming breaths. Her heart rate restored to something approximating normal, she continued on and joined her friend, giving her a hug. "I was afraid it was you," she said, giving Sue's hand a squeeze.

Together, they observed the house next door, where the open door indicated something was going on inside. Lucy knew the rules; as a reporter she wouldn't be welcome inside where she'd only be in the way. She would have to wait for whatever was happening to happen before she could approach a first responder and get the story. "Any idea what's going on?" she asked Sue.

"I don't know. The rescue squad came, and then the cops. I hope Tori's okay."

"So it *is* Tori's house. I wasn't sure." Lucy fell silent, sending up a little prayer for Tori before her mind began filling with questions. "What's the deal with the husband? I heard they got divorced?"

"A while ago. But it's amicable."

"Does he live there?"

"Comes and goes. He's close to the daughter." Sue paused. "They have shared custody. Kelly often spends weekends with him."

"He's an actor like Tori?"

"Finn Tobin. He's away a lot. He gets a lot of work playing tough-guy gangster roles. I'm sure you've seen him. It's kind of funny, because he's actually the sweetest guy. Sid and I were just over there weekend before last. Finn cooked up a big pot of chili and they had the basketball game on the TV. It was fun, real relaxed. A lot of laughs." She crossed her arms over her chest and massaged them. "I hope everything's okay."

"I don't think so," said Lucy, spotting the white medical examiner's van approaching on the street with a feeling of dread. That meant somebody had died, and she hoped against hope it wasn't Tori, or Kelly. Turning back to gaze at the open door, they spotted Officer Sally Kirwan stepping out and marching down the path, supposedly to meet the ME. Reaching the sidewalk, however, she turned and came toward them. Lucy and Sue stepped off the porch to greet her, wondering what she wanted.

Meeting them, Sally cut right to the chase. "This is off the record, right?" she demanded, speaking to Lucy.

Unusual, thought Lucy, *even kind of weird.* Certainly not what she expected, but she was willing to play along. Sally, who was a member of the large Kirwan clan that filled most town jobs, occasionally provided Lucy with story leads. Today, however, was not one of those days. "No problem," said Lucy, more than willing to cooperate with a valued source. "What's going on?"

"An unattended death. Tori Tobin, discovered by her daughter, Kelly."

Reeling with shock, Lucy and Sue reached for each other's hands and held on tight, struggling to understand. *What could have happened?* wondered Lucy. Tori had been just fine at the *feis,* she remembered, picturing Tori smiling and laughing, tossing her head and flipping back her fabulous red hair. *And poor Kelly,* she thought, feeling her heart tighten. What an awful thing to happen to a young girl, to come home and discover her mother's body. It was incomprehensible. But Sally was still talking so Lucy concentrated on listening to what she had to say.

"So I'm asking you for a big favor," she was saying, speaking to Sue. "We haven't been able to contact family. Would you mind if Kelly stayed with you for a bit?"

"Of course not." Sue let go of Lucy's hand and stood up a little straighter. "I'm happy to help. I'll do anything for Kelly."

"Yeah." Sally gave a grim little nod. "It's pretty terrible. She says she spent the night with her father. He dropped her at school in a hurry this morning because he had a plane to catch. She got through a couple of classes, then felt ill and asked to be dismissed. When she got home she found her mom in the bathtub."

"In the bathtub?" exclaimed Lucy.

She immediately got a warning look from Officer Sally. "Off the record, right?"

"Absolutely," vowed Lucy. "But what happened? Did she fall? Hit her head?"

"Possibly," said Sally. "There will have to be an autopsy. Hopefully that will give us a cause of death. But meanwhile, I've got the living to think of and Kelly needs some TLC in a safe place."

"Bring her right over," said Sue.

"As soon as *she* skedaddles," said Officer Sally, with a nod toward Lucy. "I don't want her pumping the poor girl with questions."

"I would never," protested Lucy, feeling rather hurt. She had standards and tried to remember that no matter how sensational and newsworthy a story might be, it was always about real people who were dealing with difficult situations. Unfortunately, Ted didn't always appreciate her kid-glove approach, but she'd just have to be firm with him.

Kelly was only a kid who had tragically lost her mother and Lucy was not going to hound her with questions. "I'm going, I'm going," she said. "But keep me posted, okay?" She paused, turning to Sally. "You know this is going to be all over town. But they won't be getting it from me."

"I know," said the officer, with a sigh. "And there'll be a lot of nasty gossip. You know how it goes. An ordinary slip and fall turns into an overdose, even murder. It's going to be tough for Kelly."

"I'll do everything I can to protect her," promised Sue, brushing away tears and preparing to greet Kelly. Confident that the bereaved girl couldn't be in better hands, Lucy gave a little wave and headed back to her car, obeying Sally's directive to make herself scarce. She had the basic facts, an unattended death at 43 Parallel Street, and knew that Ted would want her to immediately post that much as breaking news on the online edition. The police chief would most likely be issuing a statement before the day was out, which they would use as an update, and she had a couple of days for the story to develop before the Wednesday deadline for the printed weekly.

She was confident she had the story well in hand as she got back in her car and started driving down the street, rolling slowly past the house and the police cars, the ambulance, the ME's white van. As she went, she saw Officer Sally walking to Sue's house, one arm wrapped protectively around Kelly's shoulders. There was no sign of the confident dancer today; Kelly was walking blindly and stumbled on the uneven sidewalk, caught by Sally before she could fall. The sight made Lucy's heart lurch, and she was overcome with sadness for the unfortunate girl.

When Lucy arrived at the office, she was relieved to discover that Ted was absent; she would have a reprieve before he began asking questions that she couldn't answer. Phyllis, however, had heard the scanner and wanted to know what had happened.

"Tori Tobin is Sue's neighbor, right?" she asked, peering over the polka dot cheaters that often dangled on a gold chain to rest on her ample bosom but now were perched on her nose. She was wearing a black sweater with enormous white polka dots, continuing a theme, but her shiny leggings were bright red. "So what's going on?"

"Tori Tobin is dead," said Lucy. "I don't know much more than that," admitted Lucy. "So far it's an unattended death. I saw the ME's van. That's public knowledge. I can't even use her name until we get a statement from the chief."

"Ted's not going to be happy."

"I know." Lucy paused, struggling with her promise to Sally and her desire to share what she knew with Phyllis.

"What does Sue have to say?"

This seemed a safe topic of discussion, so Lucy opened up. "She says that as far as she knows, the Tobins are a happy couple. They're divorced, but the husband . . ."

"He's an actor, right?"

"Yeah. He's away a lot for work, but it's a friendly divorce, and he and Tori shared custody of the daughter."

62 *Leslie Meier*

"That's right. There's a daughter!" Phyllis sighed. "Poor kid."

"Yeah," said Lucy, biting her tongue hard. She was saved by the ring tone of her phone, but when she pulled it out of her bag and saw that it was Ted, she knew she was in for a grilling.

"So what's going on?" he demanded.

"An unattended death at 43 Parallel Street. That's all I've got."

"Well, you better get some more!"

"I've got more," admitted Lucy, feeling defensive, "but it's off the record. We'll just have to wait for the chief's statement."

"Tell me what you've got and I'll decide if we can use it."

"I can't. I promised."

"I know you and Sue are best friends, and Sue lives next door. What did Sue tell you?"

"Sue told me that she and Sid had a lovely evening at the Tobin house a few weekends ago watching a game on TV and eating chili that Finn Tobin made."

"Ha-ha," said Ted, clearly not amused. "Tori has a kid, right? One of those Irish dancers you covered?"

"Yes. Kelly Tobin is a student at Eileen Clancy's step-dancing academy and she competed in a *feis* on Saturday in Portland."

"Well, I heard she discovered her mother's body in the bathtub when she came home this morning after a weekend with her dad," said Ted.

Wow, thought Lucy. So the news was out already.

"People will talk," said Lucy. "Doesn't mean it's true."

"Maybe you could call the chief and ask for a

confirmation," said Ted. From his tone Lucy knew it wasn't a suggestion; it was an order.

"I can do that," said Lucy.

"Well, get on it!" snarled Ted. Before cell phones, when he had a desk model, he would have slammed it down, thought Lucy. But nowadays he was limited to punching the little red dot, which Lucy knew wasn't nearly as satisfying.

Still holding her phone, Lucy walked over to her desk and put it down, then set her big African basket bag on the chair she kept for visitors. She shrugged out of her barn coat and hung it on the coat tree, then ambled into the bathroom. That mission completed, she poured herself a cup of coffee from the pot Phyllis had made earlier and carried it over to her desk. She sat down, powered up her computer, and sipped some coffee. The PC was old and slow, so she watched as the blue circle went round and round and was eventually replaced with three alternating blue dots. She watched them skipping across her screen, struggling with the fact of Tori's death. With death, period. How could someone so lovely, so vivacious, so alive, be gone in an instant? She'd heard people say nobody gets out alive and she knew it was true. She'd lost her parents and Bill's father, but they were old. As a reporter she'd also covered plenty of deaths, but she'd been able to preserve a professional distance. Those deaths were stories; they weren't personal. This one, somehow, was different.

She'd just about finished her coffee when her e-mails appeared and she scrolled through them, saving a few announcements of upcoming events and deleting everything else. That task completed, she sighed, and called the police department. Not surprisingly, the chief was unavailable. Anticipating Ted's reaction, she also called the district attorney's office, and the medical examiner's, too. All were unavailable, but she left voice messages to please call her back, messages that she figured would be relegated to the virtual trash bin.

The best thing, Lucy decided, would be to get out of the office, conveniently forgetting her phone. But where could she go? She checked the news budget for the week, spotting a notation for the fish ladder with a question mark. Perfect, she decided. She'd take some photos of the fish ladder, which enabled alewives to make their annual spring migration from the ocean to the ponds where they spawned. It was a bit early for the alewives, also known as herring, but readers would want to know if the fish ladder, which had recently been restored, was still in good condition. And she could get some quotes from the fish warden to round out the story. Her phone was sounding off, but suspecting it was Ted, Lucy ignored it. She got up, grabbed her coat and bag, leaving her phone on the desk. It fell silent as she made her way to the door, but Phyllis's went off.

"I see you're out to cover a story," said Phyllis.

"Yes. If that's Ted, tell him I'm at the fish ladder."

"Will do," said Phyllis, grinning wickedly. "I think you forgot your phone."

"Oh, dear," sighed Lucy. "I'd forget my head if it wasn't attached."

"Hi, Ted," said Phyllis, answering the office phone as Lucy stepped out, leaving the little bell on the door jangling behind her.

Watching for the return of the herring was a traditional spring activity in Tinker's Cove, and when Lucy arrived at the Herring Brook, she wasn't surprised to see a man and a woman standing by the fish ladder. "Hi!" she said, joining them. "Any fish yet."

"I didn't see any," said the man, who had a pair of binoculars dangling from a cord around his neck. "But the birds are gathering." He indicated the bare trees around Herring Brook, where numerous cormorants were roosting. A handful of herring gulls were circling high above, calling impatiently to each other as they waited for the tide to turn, bringing in the coming feast.

"Do you mind if I snap your photo for the paper?" asked Lucy, producing the little digital camera she always carried in her bag as backup for her cell phone.

"Okay," said the guy, calling the woman over, who happened to be his wife. They posed together as Lucy snapped the picture and took down their names: Phil and Esther Murphy. The couple had served on the fish ladder restoration committee and had come to check it out. "It looks good," said Phil, nodding approvingly.

"Funny you're out here," said Esther, who had a head of curly white hair. "Isn't the big story in town?"

"Yeah," agreed Phil. "I heard some woman on Parallel Street committed suicide."

"Discovered by the daughter, just a little girl," added Esther, tutting and shaking her head. "How terrible. I don't know why people do it."

"Depression, I guess," said Phil, raising his binoculars. "Bald eagle."

"Oh!" Esther also raised her glasses. "Beautiful."

They all watched as the eagle circled low over the fish ladder, then soared up, up, and away.

"Nature. That's the answer," announced Phil. "When folks feel down, they ought to get out and look around. See God's beautiful creation."

"So true," agreed Esther.

"Just so you know," said Lucy, feeling a responsibility to do what she could to halt a particularly nasty rumor before it gained any more traction, "there's no word yet as to the cause of that death on Parallel Street."

"Do you know who it was?" asked Esther.

"Not officially," said Lucy. "But the house belongs to Tori Tobin, and she does have a daughter who is a high school senior. That's all I know so far."

"A sad situation, to be sure," said Phil, shaking his head sadly and staring down into the fish ladder.

"I think we'll know more later today. So, whatever you might hear is only speculation until we get an official statement."

"Ooh, there's a fish!" exclaimed Phil. "First one I've seen."

"There's a couple more. Look, one leaped!" exclaimed Esther.

"Maybe I can catch one on my camera," said Lucy, stepping closer.

* * *

By the time Thursday rolled around, the Tinker's Cove rumor mill was in full swing. The print edition of *The Courier* was already out in stores and would arrive in mailboxes during the day, but Lucy's fact-based reporting was limited to recounting Police Chief Jim Kirwan's statement that Tori Tobin's body had been discovered in her home and the cause of death was undetermined awaiting the results of the medical examiner's autopsy. She had not even been able to write an obituary since efforts to contact family members had been unsuccessful, but she had been able to lard her story with a few quotes from friends and neighbors. Eileen Clancy had mentioned Tori's positive attitude, Sue Finch recalled frequent gatherings at the Tobins' fire pit, and Dot Kirwan, the cashier at the IGA, said she would miss Tori's warm smile and big laugh.

Those were the quotes she was able to print; she'd soon discovered that everybody in town had something to say about Tori's death, but it was all based on rumor and innuendo. Word had leaked out that Tori had died in her bathtub and that had led most everyone to assume she had killed herself. "What an awful thing to do to her daughter," sniffed a young mom, stroking her little one's silky head, conveniently located beneath her chin in a Snugli baby carrier. "It must have been the divorce. She couldn't cope as a single mom," observed a busy soccer mom, interviewed at a practice. Even Reverend Marge, who was generally discreet and circumspect, suggested that loss of faith often left people adrift and depressed, even suicidal.

When Lucy joined her friends at Jake's Donut Shack for their weekly breakfast, she found they pretty much agreed with the general consensus that Tori had killed herself. Lucy had just seated herself at the group's usual table when Norine, the waitress, thunked down a mug of black coffee in front of her. "The usual?"

Lucy started to nod, agreeing to the hash and eggs she always had, then shook her head. "I'll have an everything bagel, toasted, with butter, please."

Norine began crossing out the notation she'd already made in her order pad and the others all dropped their jaws. "What's up?" asked Sue, raising her delicately arched brows over her eyes. "Are you sure you want a bagel?" asked Pam Stillings, Ted's wife, tossing the ponytail she'd worn since college. "Is everything all right?" asked Rachel Goodman, reaching for her hand. Rachel had majored in psychology in college and never got over it. "Are you feeling down? A touch of depression?"

"Just want a change," said Lucy, surprised at their reaction. "It's a female prerogative, right?"

"If you say so," muttered Norine. "What about the rest of you? Are you asserting your female pre-whatsits?"

"Muffin for me," said Rachel, shaking her head.

"Yogurt parfait for me," said Pam.

"Don't even bother," said Norine, glaring at Sue. "Just more black coffee, right?"

"You don't happen to have cappuccino, do you?" inquired Sue, adopting a questioning expression and tucking one glossy lock of hair behind her ear with her perfectly manicured hand.

Norine gave her a look that indicated she surely should have known better.

"Never mind," said Sue, laughing. "Just teasing."

Norine turned on her heel, snorting in disgust.

"I'm serious, Lucy," continued Rachel. "I know that covering Tori Tobin's suicide must be very stressful. It would get anyone down."

"We don't know it was suicide," asserted Pam, who had heard Ted's frequent complaints about how long it was taking the medical examiner to release autopsy results. "It could've been an accidental overdose. There's a lot of that going around." She took a sip of coffee. "Seems likeliest to me. I don't think she would kill herself knowing her daughter would discover her body."

"She enjoyed a good time, for sure," said Sue, "but I don't think she used drugs. Pot, maybe, but nothing stronger."

"What about alcohol?" asked Pam. "That can get you in trouble. I saw her out with some girls at the Cali Kitchen a while ago and they were very merry indeed. They'd started with cosmos and knocked off a couple of bottles of wine with dinner and then wanted Irish coffee, but Matt wouldn't serve them, which caused a bit of a ruckus. They only settled down when he threatened to call the cops."

"I really don't know what to think," said Sue, staring into her coffee cup. "She always seemed so bright and cheerful, but I see now that she was probably just covering up her depression. I know she did like a glass of wine, but she could make one last all evening."

"That's what serious drinkers do," said Pam.

"They're moderate in public in order to hide their alcoholism and hit the sauce in private."

Sue looked stricken, unnecessarily stirring her black coffee with a spoon. "I was her neighbor, her friend. I should have picked up on the signs, I should have sensed her desperation and reached out to her."

"There were no signs," said Lucy, giving Sue an encouraging smile. "Nothing to feel guilty about. I saw her at the *feis*, I spoke to her at length. She was a hoot; she was fun and full of life. I don't think she was an alcoholic, or abused drugs, or took her own life. I think it was an accident, a slip and fall. That seems the most likely to me."

Norine arrived with their meals and returned with a fresh pot of coffee, which she used to top off everyone's mug. Lucy bit into her crunchy bagel, savoring the melted butter, and repelling all thoughts of guilt over the calories.

Pam dug into her yogurt and Rachel broke off a bit of Sunshine muffin but set it down instead of popping it in her mouth.

"Suicide often takes family members and close friends by surprise. They didn't see it coming and feel a mixture of guilt and confusion," said Rachel. "And remember, Tori was an actress. She would have been quite skilled at concealing her depression. Think about it. She was all by herself, her daughter was with the divorced dad, it was a Sunday night and that's a real low point for people, worrying about the week to come. And we know the challenges a single mom faces," she continued, picking up the chunk of muffin. "I think she probably did kill herself," she finished, popping the bit of muffin top in her mouth.

Later, when they were leaving, Lucy walked with Sue along the street to the office. "I didn't want to bring it up with the others, but how did things go with Kelly? Did she say anything?"

"No." Sue shook her head. "I gave her some tea and offered breakfast, but she didn't want anything. She said she'd got her period and was having cramps, that's why she came home from school. I gave her a heating pad and told her how sorry I was and that she'd get a lot of support, to not be afraid to ask for help, and she said thanks for the heating pad and it seemed to be a nice day and that spring was her favorite time of year. I took that to mean she was in shock, so I sat with her and she sipped her tea and a few minutes later her dad arrived. He said his plane was delayed and he was finally just about to board when he got the call and rushed back to be with Kelly."

"How was he?" asked Lucy.

"Real upset, a bit angry. He muttered something to me about how he couldn't believe Tori would do something like this. Then he saw Kelly and gave her a big hug and they left."

"So he seemed to think it was suicide?" asked Lucy, pausing in front of *The Courier*'s front door, with the gold letters inked on the glass.

"Yeah." Sue nodded.

"What a waste."

"Yeah," agreed Sue with a sigh, before continuing on down the street, leaving Lucy to get on with her job.

But Rachel and the others, including Lucy herself, and even Finn Tobin, were all wrong, as she discovered when she opened her e-mail the next morning and discovered the ME's report. The autopsy had revealed signs of struggle; the cause of death was drowning, and Tori's death was ruled a homicide.

Chapter Six

"Oh my God," exclaimed Lucy, her jaw dropping to the floor. "The ME says Tori's death was a homicide. There were signs of struggle and she was drowned."

"Whuh?" Phyllis was similarly shocked, and she pressed her hands over her heart. "In her own house? In the tub? Gives you the creeps, doesn't it? I mean, a woman all alone . . ."

"She wasn't alone," said Lucy, the wheels grinding in her head. "She was with someone, someone she was intimate with. Someone she allowed to see her bathing."

"Why do you think that, Lucy? Maybe it was a home invasion, a robbery gone wrong."

"Because that's the stuff of movies," said Lucy. "It's a fact that almost all murder victims are killed by people they know, people they know well."

"A boyfriend? Did she have a boyfriend?"

"I don't know, but I do know she had an ex-husband, and they were on friendly terms."

"But they were divorced," said Phyllis, with a prim little sniff. "I think that means it's hands off, if you get my drift."

"Not always," said Lucy. "Old habits die hard. Maybe the issues that drove them apart weren't sexual. It could've been money, or maybe their work commitments got in the way, maybe they wanted more variety . . ."

"You have a filthy mind, Lucy."

"I just think that people have physical needs and it's easier with someone familiar, someone you've already been intimate with. No unpleasant surprises. It's like slipping on an old shoe. Comfy."

"If that's what happened, there must've been a pebble in that old shoe, 'cause she ended up dead."

"Yeah, I don't like the way this is going. . . ." Lucy already had a horrible feeling that the police were probably thinking along the same lines she was.

"So you think that Finn Tobin killed her," said Phyllis, voicing Lucy's unspoken thought. "They must have had some serious disagreements. They were divorced, after all."

"I'm not saying he killed her," said Lucy, backtracking. "I'm just saying that the husband, especially if he's an ex, is always the prime suspect. That puts Finn front and center."

"Absolutely awful for the daughter," said Phyllis. "Who's taking care of her? She isn't staying with her father, is she?"

"I hope not," said Lucy, as her phone sounded

off. Grabbing it, she saw the caller was Brendan Coyle, from the food pantry.

"Hey, it's Brendan." She sighed. "Probably announcing Delahunt Realty as the winner of the naming contest."

Phyllis gave a shrug and returned to the stack of mail she was sorting, and Lucy swiped up to take the call. "Hi, Brendan. What's up?"

"I've got a correction for the press release I sent you guys the other day."

"Okay. What was it about?" asked Lucy. "Was it an e-mail?"

"Yeah." His tone was curt, even depressed.

"Okay," said Lucy, opening her e-mails and searching for the file. "Here it is. The one for the gala auction?" The auction was part of the year-long fundraising effort for the food pantry.

"That's it." She heard a long sigh. "You see, Tori was going to be the emcee. . . ."

"Oh, I see. I can change it."

"I just can't believe it," he said, his voice breaking. "She was so beautiful, with that fabulous head of red hair and that gorgeous smile. How could this happen? People are saying she overdosed or killed herself. I can't stand it. She wouldn't do that. Why would she do that? She had so much to live for. I always thought she was one of those people who was high on life. She didn't need drugs. And she had a daughter! How could she be so desperate, so selfish, to do that to Kelly?" He gave an enormous sniff and Lucy pictured him wiping his eyes. The very thought of a big man like Brendan crying made Lucy tear up, too. She had to tell him the truth of Tori's death, but she knew he would take it hard.

"Brendan," she began, her voice soft. "I've seen the medical examiner's report and it's going to be difficult to hear."

She heard another, massive sniff. "I'm ready."

"It was a homicide; someone drowned her."

Lucy heard a sound like someone getting punched in the gut. A wail of genuine pain. "That can't be true."

"There didn't seem to be any question at all. The report was very clear-cut."

"I can't stand it," he moaned. "Who would hurt Tori? She was kind and good . . . a beautiful person." He paused, and Lucy tried to think of something comforting to say, but found herself at a loss for words. Brendan, however, had found his voice. "It must have been some psychopath, or maybe it was a thief, some intruder after money or cash who found her taking her bath . . . oh, my God, maybe he tried to rape her and they fought and she drowned?"

Even though Lucy thought that was extremely unlikely, she understood why people often clung to the idea that a terrible crime must have been committed by a bogeyman, an evil stranger. It was certainly preferable to thinking that one of your friends or neighbors, even your nearest and dearest, might have done something terrible. "I'm sure the police are investigating all the possibilities," said Lucy, thinking it was time to change the subject. "So who is replacing Tori at the auction?"

"Oh, fortunately for us, her husband, Finn Tobin,

has agreed. He's taking a break right now and he said that it was what Tori would want, that she was a big supporter of the pantry, she really believed in the work we're doing here. Of course, it won't be quite the same. Tori had a wicked sense of humor and she was planning a sort of roast, jokes about the local big shots, you know. She thought a little laughter at their expense might shame them into donating more generously." He sighed. "It won't be quite the same with Finn."

Lucy was once again speechless. What could she say? "Uh, Brendan, don't you think people might be put off by seeing Finn? It might make them feel uncomfortable."

"I think it will be good. Seeing Tori's bereaved husband being so brave and stepping forward despite his grief, I think it will open their hearts and their pocketbooks." He sighed. "In the end, it might be a good thing."

It was hard to believe that a person could be so naïve, so pure of heart himself, that he couldn't see what was obvious to everyone else. "Brendan, Finn Tobin is the prime suspect. The police are probably already questioning him."

"That's crazy. It's wrong. He wouldn't hurt Tori. He loved her. He was her husband."

"Divorced husband."

"Not in the eyes of God," said Brendan, clinging to his faith. "And I believe that in their hearts Tori and Finn knew that. They'd been joined until . . ." Lucy heard a major sniff and his voice quavered as he reached the inevitable end of the phrase. ". . . until death parted them."

"Well, just in case he's not available, maybe you should think of someone else, as backup," suggested Lucy.

"No." Brendan's voice was once again firm. "No. I'm not making any changes. We'll simply have to hope and pray for the best."

"Okay," said Lucy, smiling in spite of herself. "You got it. I'll make the change, but if I were you, I'd make sure to get—"

"Thanks for the advice, but I'm sure it won't be necessary," he said, cutting her off, and the screen went black.

Lucy went ahead and deleted Tori's name, replacing it with Finn's in the announcement, which would run in the coming events column. When she'd finished, she decided to give Sue a call; she would want to know how her neighbor died.

Sue wasn't home when she answered the phone; she was checking out the spring arrivals at the town's newest and trendiest boutique, Raggtime.

"Lucy, you gotta see these velour tops, so comfy for our chilly weather, but in lovely spring colors."

"I will, I will," promised Lucy, thinking that she'd actually be choosing her spring clothes at the hospital thrift shop. "But I've got to tell you something serious. Can you talk?"

"Yeah. It's just me and the associate at the moment."

"Brace yourself, it's bad news. Awful news."

"Oh no."

"Tori was murdered."

There was a long silence, as Sue processed this information. "Oh, my," she finally said.

"I thought you should know."

"Do you think there's a predator, some sort of sex maniac? Is that what the police are saying?"

"They haven't said anything yet. It was in the medical examiner's report. There was a struggle and she was drowned."

"That is so creepy," said Sue. "You know, people are always trooping along my driveway taking that shortcut to Main Street. If it was some perv or something, he could've come that way."

Lucy reconsidered, wondering if maybe, just maybe, Tori had been killed by a psychotic serial killer. "Have you seen anyone lurking around her house? A Peeping Tom?"

"No, but I only glance out the windows to check the weather and the bird feeder, not to monitor people's comings and goings."

"Is there anyone who does? Do you have a busybody?"

"Not that I know of. All the close neighbors work. That's one reason why Tori and I became friends. We were the only ones at home during the day. But I'm sure the police will want to question everyone on the street."

"They'll go through the motions, but I don't think they'll investigate very hard. They've already got a suspect. . . ."

"Finn," said Sue, finishing her sentence. "That movie clip of him drowning the lady is trending on the Internet."

This was news to Lucy. "What clip?" she asked.

"It's from a movie he made years ago. It shows him drowning a woman in a bathtub. It's all over social media. Millions of hits."

"Not what you want to be famous for," said Lucy,

thoughtfully. "What do you think? I'm sure the police have already decided he's suspect number one. Do you think he could have done it?"

Sue let out a long sigh. "Of course not. They were divorced but they'd remained friends." She paused, then continued. "Of course, you never know what goes on in a relationship. Feelings get hurt, some new issue comes up. He might've been having a bad day, she might have said something that sent him over the edge. It happened to me—in a small way. One night I used nail polish remover when I was in bed, and Sid went bananas. I didn't know he hated the smell."

"But Sid didn't kill you."

"Not that time, but believe me, now I make sure to remove my polish in a well-ventilated space when he's not around." She was quick to add, "Don't get me wrong. I'm not afraid of him. But if it upsets him, if he's sensitive to the smell for some reason, I don't want to cause him discomfort." She paused. "It's like never, ever serving brussels sprouts for dinner."

"You're a good wife and very considerate," said Lucy. "But speaking of Finn, did you see him afterward? How was he? And what about Kelly? Is she with him?"

"Well, Finn picked her up the morning of the, you know, when she found her mother. He seemed stunned, in shock like, but he was very concerned about Kelly. Gave her a big hug, told her everything was going to be all right, that he was there for her. She got kind of hysterical, said she didn't want to go back to the house, and he said she couldn't go home anyway because of the, you know, the yellow tape and all. His place is real small so he said that Tori's mom, her grandma, was coming and they'd figure something out. I think she lives in Rockland, so that's probably where Kelly is."

"It's lucky the grandma lives so close, but far enough to give Kelly some distance," said Lucy, thinking of the media attention that such a sensational murder would attract.

"You know, I've kind of lost my enthusiasm for a new outfit," admitted Sue. "I think I'll go home and check my locks. Just in case."

"Couldn't hurt." Ending the call, Lucy's thoughts turned to Finn Tobin. She knew that he had been attracting media attention even before the ME's report came out and Tori's death was officially a homicide. Reporters and camera crews had wasted no time setting up watch outside his condo in a trendy rehabbed motel on the outskirts of town. And now, Lucy discovered, checking her phone, there was this grainy footage of a much younger but clearly identifiable Finn Tobin drowning a woman in a scene from a B movie.

Finn, she saw, had been quick to address the matter, posting that he'd made the movie years ago, playing the role of a psychotic killer, and going on to say he had a terrific relationship with his ex-wife and was devastated by her death. He ended the post writing, "I'll love her until the day I die."

Finn wasn't the only one hounded by reporters; they'd even tracked down Kelly. When Lucy tuned into the noontime local news on her laptop, she saw video of Kelly leaving the Tinker's Cove High School, driven in a car by an older woman Lucy assumed was her grandmother. She lowered the window as the car rolled by, yelling that her father was innocent, he was with her all night. "I told police it must have been . . ." The rest was unclear, but Lucy thought she picked up something that sounded like "one of the dance moms."

Lucy was mulling this over when her phone sounded off and she saw Ted's name on the screen. He got right to the point, immediately demanding, "What have you got?"

"School board meeting, finance committee, and the town meeting preview . . ."

"Very funny. You know I mean the Tori Tobin murder."

"I saw the ME's report, I talked to some neighbors, but they didn't see anything unusual. . . ."

"You talked to Sue. Anybody else? What about the other neighbors? What about Finn Tobin?"

"You know how I feel about hounding people. He's bereaved; he deserves to be left in peace."

"He's suspect number one, Lucy, and you need to talk to him before the cops arrest him."

"I'll see what I can do," said Lucy, half-heartedly.

"I'll expect an update by five o'clock," said Ted, speaking in no uncertain terms.

"Right," said Lucy, somewhat sarcastically, but he had already ended the call.

Lucy didn't have Finn's number, so she couldn't call him. She could probably get it from Sue, but when she called her friend, she learned that Sue only had Tori's number, not Finn's. She sat at her desk, staring at the Willard clock on the wall, assessing her options. The more she thought about it, the less likely it seemed that Finn would answer his phone, even if she could dig up his number. And besides, she didn't really want to bother the guy. Calling him seemed like harassment. Reluctantly, she got to her feet, put on her jacket, and headed to the door.

"Where are you off to?" asked Phyllis.

"I'm going to check out Finn Tobin's condo, see if there are any developments."

Phyllis was surprised. "Really? You want to be part of that zoo out there?"

"No. But Ted wants an update, and the media attention itself is a story, right?" She picked up her bag. "And I might get lucky. If he's there, Finn might take pity on me."

"If you say so," admitted Phyllis, clearly disapproving.

"And one more reporter is hardly going to make a difference," said Lucy with a shrug.

So Lucy drove on out to Route 1, where the rehabbed motel, advertised as offering luxury condos, sat right by the road. Reporters weren't allowed in the parking lot, or on the landscaped lawn, so they filled the grassy verge along the busy road with satellite trucks, set up mics and lawn chairs, and gathered in groups drinking take-out coffee and chatting to pass the time. She had to park some distance and walked back, pasting a smile on her face as she approached a familiar face from a Boston news station. "Hi, I'm Lucy Stone from the local paper. Anything happening?"

"No." The guy, whom Lucy guessed to be in his thirties, with short hair, a bit of fashionable beard stubble, and wearing a red windbreaker with the network's logo, shook his head. "Tobin is lying low. If he's home, he isn't coming out."

"So why are you all here?" asked Lucy.

"Good question," he replied, laughing. "In case the cops decide to arrest him. That's about it. Have you heard anything?"

"Nope. I thought the chief would have put out a statement by now, but no such luck." She chuckled. "Us locals have been getting the news from you."

There was a bit of a flurry as a police car approached, lights flashing, and cameras were trained on it, ready to record whatever happened. But the unit slowed and pulled onto the verge, just ahead of the gathered news crews, and parked. The lights continued flashing, and it became clear that the car was there to warn oncoming motorists and to protect the gathered crowd of reporters.

"He's just keeping an eye on us, keeping an eye on Tobin," laughed one reporter.

Lucy got that reporter's name and snapped her photo. She got a few more quotes and took more photos, even catching a familiar face from CNN, then headed back to her car. She had a lead that they didn't have and she was going to follow it, she decided. She was going to talk to Eileen Clancy and ask her about Kelly's accusation. Could one of the dance moms be Tori's killer? It was a reach, but given the friction among the women, it was a question worth asking.

It was early afternoon and Lucy doubted Eileen would be at the dance academy, so she went instead to her house, where she'd interviewed her a year or so previously when Eileen was in the running for grand marshal of the St. Patrick's Day parade. She hadn't won then, and this year's winner was the area's newly elected state rep, Liam Maloney. Eileen's car was in the driveway when Lucy arrived, and she answered the door promptly when Lucy rang.

"Well, what brings you?" asked Eileen with an amused smile. "Following up on the *feis*?"

"I wish," said Lucy, letting out a huge sigh. "I'm looking for background on Tori Tobin."

"Well, come on in. I can give you a cup of tea and a chat, but I don't have any inside information about poor Tori."

"Tea would be lovely," said Lucy, thinking it was just what she needed and wondering why she never thought of it herself. She followed Eileen into her kitchen and settled herself on a stool at the island. The kitchen had been newly renovated with white cabinets and granite countertops, but the island was Irish pine, topped with a thick slab of richly grained wood. She watched as Eileen filled an electric kettle and switched it on, then busied herself spooning loose tea in a pot, placing some cookies on a plate, and collecting a couple of mugs. By the time she was ready, the kettle was whistling.

"Here you go, a nice cuppa Irish breakfast tea," said Eileen, joining her on the other stool.

Lucy helped herself to an oatmeal cookie and nibbled it, waiting for her tea to cool. "This is off the record, but I have been worried about Kelly. How's she doing?"

"She skipped class, so I called her. She's got a

phone of her own, all the kids do, but her grandma answered. She said Kelly's with her and the
best thing would be for Kelly to go to school and
follow her usual routine, but it's impossible because of the reporters. She said she can't bring her
to dance class either—that when she took her to
pick up her books and assignments at the school,
they were mobbed. It was even on the news."

"I saw," said Lucy.

Eileen nodded. "She made me promise to keep
her location a secret."

"I know she lives in Rockland," said Lucy, sipping her tea.

"So do a lot of people," said Eileen. "Kelly deserves to grieve in peace."

"I agree. I'm certainly not going to dig up her
grandma's address," promised Lucy. "What I really
wonder is, if Finn Tobin is innocent, as he claims,
who else might have wanted to kill Tori?"

Eileen threw back her head and laughed.
"Don't tell me you're thinking of the other three
moms? Do you really think their little spats led to
murder?"

"You're the one who said they had a donnybrook. What was it about?"

"What it was always about," said Eileen, rolling
her eyes. "They were thrown together a lot, but I
think they tried to make the best of it. They
weren't women who'd naturally become friends, if
you know what I mean. Tori was madly attractive,
which I'm sure the others found off-putting. And
Karen, with her plastic surgeon husband and big
house and fancy car and big bank account, well
that sort of thing can cause a lot of jealousy. Deir-

dre's a workaholic, thinking of nothing but her real estate business, and Margaret struggles to keep her head above water. They're all really different. They don't have anything in common except their Irish heritage and the step dancing, and as you've seen, step dancing isn't exactly a team sport. There was a lot of rivalry and they got increasingly catty with each other as the girls got older and the competitions got more serious. The drinking certainly didn't help matters, but the Irish coffee became a ritual. I imagine it smoothed over the rough edges a bit, but it also loosened their tongues."

"So you don't think it's at all possible that one of them might've killed Tori?"

"Absolutely not. And she was killed in her bathtub, right?" Eileen shuddered. "It reminds me of that movie *Psycho*. I think it must've been some crazy weirdo."

"If that's the case, we may never know what happened," said Lucy, sipping the tea, thinking of the unsolved murders, cold cases, that filled police files. Sometimes the killer was identified years later, thanks to a deathbed confession, or a convict sharing information in hopes of getting a shorter sentence. But, she thought with a sinking heart, there were also cases where innocent people were convicted and spent decades in prison.

"Is everything all right?" asked Eileen, noticing her downcast expression.

Lucy looked up and, remembering the tea, took a big swallow. "Nice and strong," she said with a little smile. "Hits the spot."

Chapter Seven

Lucy's brain was awhirl when she left Eileen's. She shared the dance teacher's concern for Kelly and swore to herself that no matter how much Ted pressed her, she was going to leave Kelly and her grandma alone. The last thing they needed was to have to fight their way through a scrum of reporters every time they stepped outside. She wondered if Finn was actually at home, or if he'd managed to sneak out and find shelter someplace far away. Maybe he'd gone to the police voluntarily, figuring that since he was virtually imprisoned in his home by the media, he might as well present himself for questioning and hope to convince investigators of his innocence.

Driving back to town, she remembered Kelly's assertion that her father was home with her all night and wondered if it would hold up. It was a flimsy alibi anyway since he could have slipped out while she was sleeping. On the other hand, she remembered being rather surprised at how upset Brendan Coyle had been about Tori's death. And that bit about Tori and Finn being married forever in God's eyes . . . what was that all about? She knew he was a man of faith, but always thought he was on the progressive end of the spiritual spectrum. More of a faith-in-action kind of guy. Was he protesting a bit too much? Could he have been in love with Tori himself?

That was an interesting idea, thought Lucy, wondering if Brendan and Tori had been involved in a relationship. Brendan was single and lived alone, and Tori was free on Sunday nights when Kelly was with her dad. Maybe they were in the habit of getting together, perhaps initially to work on issues concerning the food pantry, but gradually growing closer. It could happen, thought Lucy. Tori was very attractive and Brendan was a big, healthy fellow, brimming with energy. She could imagine it all too clearly, recalling a romance novel she'd been reading last night before falling asleep. In her mind, she pictured Brendan slipping into the house, making his way up the familiar stairway to the candlelit bathroom, where Sting was singing about golden fields of barley and Tori awaited him in a tub full of bubbles. And then, she continued, improvising, what if Finn had come back for something he forgot, and realized what was going on? He wouldn't have confronted them directly. Brendan was enormous, for one thing. No, he would have held the betrayal close to his heart, nursing it. He would have waited, feeding his hurt and letting it grow, until one night he decided to confront Tori, killing her in a jealous rage.

Or, remembering how heartbroken Brendan had been over Tori's death, perhaps he'd been expressing his own guilt and remorse. If he and Tori were having an affair, perhaps he'd been so consumed with guilt that he ended up killing her, blaming the woman who had enticed him, seduced him, and caused him to sin.

By now Lucy had almost reached the office, but fired up by the steamy scenario she'd created in her mind, decided it needed to be investigated. Who could she ask about Brendan and Tori? Of course! Karen Callanan was a big supporter of the pantry and as a volunteer she worked closely with Brendan, and she also knew Tori. Karen was the one she needed to talk to, and it was only a short drive out to Shore Road where Casa Callanan was perched on a cliff high above the ocean with a million-dollar view.

Gulls were wheeling in the sky above the crashing waves below, calling to each other, as Lucy turned into the driveway. Unlike the gulls, who seemed to be reveling in the wind that allowed them to soar so high in the sky, Lucy found herself bending against the freezing blast that blew off the ocean and forced her to fight her way to the sheltered side door. Karen answered the bell, admitting her to a mud room straight out of a design mag complete with a row of Hunter wellies lined up beneath a couple of Barbour jackets. "Breezy out there," she observed, as Lucy caught her breath.

"Oh, my, storm must be brewing," said Lucy, rubbing her arms.

"That sky does look ominous," said Karen, casting her eyes upward. "What brings you here?" she asked, obviously surprised by her unannounced visit.

"Oh, I know I should have called first, but I was passing by and it happens that I have a few questions about the, uh, food pantry gala," began Lucy, fudging about the true reason for her visit. "So I thought I'd take a chance and stop by," she continued. "Do you have a few minutes?"

"Sure. Can I take your coat?"

Lucy shrugged out of her barn coat and Karen hung it on a free hook, then led the way into the enormous kitchen, where carrots and onions were arrayed on a cutting board, along with a chef's knife. The delicious scent of browned meat filled the air. "I've just been putting a stew together. This weather calls for something hearty."

"I don't know if spring will ever come," said Lucy, noticing the kitchen's generous supply of white custom cabinets, Carrara marble countertops and backsplash, and the runway-sized island.

"This, too, will pass and summer will be here," said Karen, looking on the bright side. And why shouldn't she, thought Lucy, as she was certainly one of the world's more fortunate citizens. "So what do you want to know about the gala?"

Lucy seated herself on one of the stools at the island and pulled her reporter's notebook out of her bag. "Well, Brendan called and told me that Tori was slated to be the emcee, but now Finn is taking her place. . . ."

"That's right," said Karen.

"Do you think that's a good idea?" asked Lucy.

"What do you mean?" asked Karen, pausing before slicing into an onion. "I realize Finn doesn't have Tori's sense of humor, but that might be a good thing. She was planning to do a roast, make jokes about people, and I was worried it might backfire."

"It's not that Finn wouldn't do a good job, Karen. The fact is, he's the prime suspect."

Karen furrowed her brow and looked doubtful. "Really? Why is that?"

"Haven't you seen the video?" inquired Lucy, amazed at her reaction.

"No. I really limit screen time for Brigid. She gets an hour of PBS and that's it." She cut the onion into big chunks, adding them to a Crock-Pot. "And I'm too busy to bother with all that social media. I don't care what Meghan and Harry are doing, or what paint colors are trending. I've got a life, in three dimensions."

"I feel the same way," said Lucy, "but my job requires me to keep abreast of developments, and it just so happens that Finn played a psychopathic killer in a movie he made years ago and there's a clip of him drowning a woman in a bathtub that is playing on screens everywhere. If you turn on the news you can't escape it."

"But it's an old movie," said Karen with a dismissive shrug. "He was acting."

"Right. But these days it seems a lot of people are having trouble telling the difference between fiction and reality."

"So what exactly are you asking me?" demanded

Karen. "Do you want to know if I think we should choose another emcee?"

Lucy hesitated. Karen was a tougher nut than she'd expected from Brendan's glowing description of his favorite volunteer. "Actually I'm wondering if you've considered postponing the gala?"

"Off the record, we are looking into it. Brendan wants to go ahead, but some of the other board members aren't so keen. We have contracts with vendors, however, so we'll just have to see," said Karen, clearing her cutting board with the chef's knife and setting it in the farmhouse sink. She rinsed off her hands, dried them on a fresh tea towel, and checked the setting on the Crock-Pot. "If we do make a change, you'll be the first to know. So if that's all, I've got a busy day."

"Oh, well," stammered Lucy, getting the message that it was time to leave, "there is one other thing I was wondering about." It was now or never, she decided, so she would simply have to ask the question she'd really come to ask. "It's about Brendan and Tori. He seems so broken up about her death and I wondered if there was some sort of romantic relationship there."

Karen stared at her, open-mouthed in disbelief. "You've got to be kidding."

"No. I'm serious. He was really broken up about her death and went on and on about how fabulous she is, I mean, was."

"I'm not surprised," said Karen, in a gentle voice. "Brendan's a very emotional guy. He feels deeply about everything. He can be a bit obsessive."

"So you don't think . . ."

"No, Lucy." Karen shook her head and an amused smile played on her lips. "For someone who keeps abreast of developments, I have breaking news for you: Brendan is gay."

Now Lucy was the one open-mouthed in disbelief. "Really?"

"Really." She put her hands on her hips, gave Lucy a look that indicated it was time to move along, and opened the door to the mud room. "Now if that's all, I think I heard the school bus. I'm in a bit of a rush as I've got to take Brigid to the orthodontist."

"Well, thanks for your time," said Lucy. "I'll be looking for that press release."

Karen was already taking Lucy's jacket off the hook and handing it to her. "Have a nice day."

"You, too," said Lucy, who hadn't finished zipping up when the door closed behind her. She was standing on the millstone that served as a stoop when she noticed Brigid coming up the long driveway, so she walked slowly to her car, intending to meet her.

"Hi!" Brigid said, with a questioning look.

"I was just interviewing your mom about the gala."

Brigid didn't seem interested in chatting. "Mom will be waiting for me." She gave a rare smile that revealed a mouth full of wire. "I'm finally getting my braces off."

"I won't keep you," promised Lucy. "But I have been wondering how you're all doing. Has Kelly been coming to class?"

"No, she's taking some time off. It's been hard. It's not as much fun without her."

"I imagine everyone must be pretty upset."

"It's awful. Siobhan has a big chip on her shoulder about the *feis*. Erin's mom offered to make her a new costume, but Siobhan refused. She won't even talk to Erin and . . ." She paused, as if realizing she was saying too much. "Well, it's horrible," she concluded. "I wish things could go back to the way they were before."

"So do a lot of people," said Lucy, giving her a sad sort of smile. "Good luck with the orthodontist."

"Uh, thanks," said Brigid, hurrying up the driveway to the Range Rover, where her mother was waiting impatiently for her.

Lucy figured she'd better get on out of the driveway, as she was blocking it. She was feeling a bit as if she'd been expelled from the UK as she drove down the driveway, leaving the vine-covered Tudor-style mansion on Shore Road behind and turning onto River Road, where folks had boats and RVs parked beside their modest houses, many equipped with satellite dishes that delivered hundreds of TV channels, and porches occasionally sported a defunct washing machine or sofa. She was fretting a bit about her faulty gaydar, wondering why she hadn't realized that Brendan was gay, and she'd almost reached town when she switched on the radio and flipped through the stations until she got the one that offered news all day. While she'd been out chasing hares, it seemed she'd missed the big story of the day: Finn Tobin had been arrested for his ex-wife's murder.

Chapter Eight

Ted was not pleased that Lucy missed the DA's press conference announcing Finn Tobin's arrest when she arrived in the office. "About time!" he yelled, by way of greeting, his voice exploding and filling the office. "Where were you? I've been trying to reach you for hours."

Lucy reached for her phone and saw that the battery was dead; she'd forgotten to charge it the night before. She should have noticed, she realized guiltily, because she usually got lots of calls, but instead she'd let her imagination run wild and had been wandering about in la-la land, like a stray dog that broke its chain and ran off or a cow that wandered out of the pasture and on to the road where it had no business to be. "I'm sorry," she said. "I forgot to charge my phone."

"Well, you better do it now!"

"Right." Still wearing her jacket, she rummaged in her bag until she found the charger and got the phone plugged in. "I suppose there's a press release," she said, starting to unzip her coat, "or would you rather I try to talk to Aucoin myself."

Ted narrowed his eyes at her. "What do you think? I think a phone call would be preferable, since you missed your opportunity to ask him questions at the press conference."

"He took questions? He doesn't usually," said Lucy, putting up a weak defense.

"Well, this time he did. They had him live on NECN."

Lucy suddenly realized what was really bothering Ted. "So I blew a chance for some regional exposure. . . ."

"Yeah, would've been nice to hear your voice saying 'Lucy Stone from *The Courier,*' followed up by a penetrating question. Something like 'What evidence did you uncover that links Tobin to the murder?' or 'Did the drowning video influence your decision to charge Tobin?' or maybe 'What was Tobin's motive?' But instead of hearing your dulcet voice, I heard George Dundee from *The Commercial Fisherman* and Deb Hildreth stringing for *The Boston Globe.*"

"Well," said Lucy, hopefully presenting him with her rather pitiful bit of breaking news, "I got a lead from Brendan Coyle that Finn will emcee the food pantry gala, but," she belatedly realized with a feeling that she was digging herself in deeper, "of course, actually now he won't."

"Unless he gets bail," offered Phyllis, in a bright

tone that matched her hot pink sweatshirt. Lucy knew she was only trying to help, but Ted seized on that thought to continue berating Lucy.

"Oh, ba-ai-ail," scoffed Ted, drawing out the word. "Now there's a question you could've asked. Like will the DA oppose bail at the arraignment which"—he paused to check the Willard clock on the wall—"oh, yeah, the arraignment that you've already missed."

Lucy was wondering how long she was going to have to endure this abuse. Except that it really wasn't abuse; she deserved it. She should've been at the press conference; in fact, she really wished she'd been there. She was every bit as angry with herself as Ted was and was eager to redeem herself. But how? She was painfully aware that she had messed up and she wouldn't blame him if he fired her, except of course, he wouldn't, because he'd never find anyone to replace her at the pitiful wage he paid her.

"I'll get right on Aucoin," she promised, finally shrugging out of her coat and sitting down at her desk. She reached for her desk phone and placed the call, but it was answered by the DA's secretary. Aucoin was in a meeting, she said, but she'd be sure to let him know Lucy had called. Hanging up, Lucy knew she was beat. There was no way Aucoin was going to return her call today.

It wasn't until Monday morning that she got a chance to redeem herself. She was sitting at her desk, about to dial the DA's number, a number she knew by heart, when the little bell on the door jangled and an older woman with a round, pleasant face entered.

"Hi," said Phyllis, greeting her. "How can I help you?"

"Um, I'm dropping off a funeral notice," said the woman, who had a head of curly white hair and was wearing a handknit Aran sweater and green tweed slacks. Her plump, rosy cheeked face crumpled as she continued. "It's for my daughter, Tori Tobin."

Suddenly, it was as if electricity surged through the dusty old office and attention was focused on the woman.

"Let me help you with that," said Lucy, rising and hurrying across the scuffed wood plank floor. "I'm Lucy Stone. Notices are my department." She took the proffered sheet of paper and issued an invitation. "Won't you sit down? Perhaps you'd like some coffee, or tea," she said, giving Phyllis a look.

"A cuppa would be lovely," admitted the woman, with a little shiver.

"Well, sit right down and my assistant, Phyllis, will fetch it for you." She watched as Phyllis somewhat grudgingly pulled on her neon green jacket and shuffled out the door, heading for Jake's. *The Courier*'s refreshment options were limited to bad coffee, made fresh in the morning, and very bad coffee, which was whatever remained of the morning's bad coffee that had been sitting in the pot all day, along with a few stale donuts left over from the weekly news budget meeting.

Lucy led the way across the office to the corner where her desk was located along with the chair she kept for visitors. As they went, Lucy introduced herself and also Ted, who was already on his feet, heading for the morgue where the old papers were stored and a large table provided conference space. Lucy knew he was hoping that in his absence she might be able to encourage Tori's mom to open up and provide some inside information.

"I'm Kitty Carney," said the woman, seating herself. "Like I said, I'm Tori's mom. I've been taking care of my granddaughter Kelly."

"Well, we're all really sorry for your loss," said Lucy, "and we'll do whatever we can to make this easier for you. I met Tori and Kelly when I wrote a feature about step dancing, and I immediately liked both of them."

"That was you?" exclaimed Kitty, her eyebrows shooting up. "I saw it online. You wrote a beautiful story, made me feel as if I were right there seeing the girls dance." Her face sagged as she continued. "Tori would have loved it but never got the chance. . . ." She turned her head when the door on the bell jangled and Phyllis returned with a carry-cup of hot tea. She took it in both hands and carefully set it on the corner of Lucy's desk. "Well, as you can see, we're holding the funeral next weekend . . ." began Kitty, who was prying the flap on the carry-cup cover open and taking a tentative sip of the hot liquid. "We need to move on, you know. Kelly needs to get back into her routine. She's been out of school, staying with me in Rockland, you know, and she misses her friends and the dancing, too."

"Are you going to bring her back to Tinker's Cove?"

"That's the plan. I want her to finish up and graduate with her class, but we have to wait until we get the all clear from the police so we can get back into the house."

"How is Kelly doing?" asked Lucy, genuinely concerned.

Kitty let out a big sigh. "It's been hard, especially now that her dad's been arrested. We knew it was coming. Finn presented himself for arrest, but that doesn't make it any easier for poor Kelly." She glanced at the clock, then picked up the cup and took a longer swallow. "She's helping out at my friend's knitting shop this morning, so I could run a few errands, but I need to get back to her."

"Do you think he's guilty?" asked Lucy, aware that time was running out and wanting to get Kitty's reaction. Would she lash out angrily? Or throw Finn to the sharks?

She did neither but simply shrugged. "No. He's innocent. I've always liked Finn. I was sorry when they divorced, but he stuck around. He's been a good father to Kelly. I always thought he and Tori handled the situation very well." She began to stand up, preparing to leave, saying, "Well, you've got all the information about the funeral, so I won't keep you any longer."

"You know, I could use some information for the obituary . . ." began Lucy, hoping to forestall her departure.

"Oh, the man at the funeral home said they'd take care of that."

"They do. They do a good job with the basic facts, survivors and all that, but I can make it more personal if I have a quote or two about—" She paused, about to say "the deceased," but instead using Tori's name.

Kitty sat back down. "That would be nice," she said, as a cloud seemed to pass over her face, erasing her bright and sociable aspect and replacing it with the stunned look of a survivor. "Tori was always a free spirit, even as a child. And always an actress. She loved to show off, staging little shows." Her face had grown softer, livelier, as she recalled Tori's childhood.

"I think everyone who knew her thought of her as a free spirit," responded Lucy. "And she was so generous, so full of life, I think that's how people will remember her."

Kitty had wrapped her hands around the paper carry-cup, warming them, and then remembering it held tea, she raised it to her lips and drank. "She was harmless, you know. Wouldn't hurt a flea. Many's the time I saw her carefully lift a spider and carry it out of the house, setting it down on a branch or flower. I don't understand why anyone would kill her, and certainly not Finn, not if he was in his right mind. The only thing that makes sense is some crazy nutter, a serial killer out for thrills. And Tori, she wasn't cautious, you know. Not a fearful bone in her body. She wouldn't have locked the door. She would have invited the killer in, yelling that she was in the bath and would be down in a sec." Maybe sunlight coming through the blinds had shifted, but Lucy now saw every line, every wrinkle, every sag on Kitty's face, and she reached out, covering Kitty's age-spotted hand with her own.

"Murders are usually committed by someone the victim knows, usually an intimate, like a husband or lover, or an ex," she said softly.

"Nope." Kitty shook her head decisively. "I don't

see it. Not unless Finn has suddenly changed. The Finn I know has an ugly mug and he's played lots of bad guys in the movies, but he's really the kindest, gentlest man. If you could have seen him when Kelly was born, the man was over the moon. Couldn't get him to put the babe down. He'd just sit and hold her for hours, gazing at her little face."

Sensing that Kitty was close to breaking into tears, Lucy turned to the notice she'd brought and reviewed the times and dates of the observances, fact checking. Then she opened her e-mail and saw the funeral home had sent the obit, so she went over it with Kitty, who added a few corrections. Then they were done and Kitty got to her feet. "Thanks," she told Lucy, taking her hand. "I feel better knowing you'll do right by Tori."

"Of course I will," promised Lucy. "You take care now, and give my love to Kelly."

Kitty smiled, knotted her plaid scarf, and headed out. "Bye now," said Phyllis, as she passed her desk, but Kitty didn't respond, didn't notice, lost in her thoughts.

"Poor woman," noted Phyllis, after the door closed behind Kitty. "Imagine having to be mother to a teenager at her age. I wouldn't want that."

"People do what they gotta do," observed Ted, emerging from the morgue. "Kelly's fortunate to have her."

"It would be better if she had her dad," said Lucy, clicking away on her keyboard to finish up the obit. "Grandma sure doesn't think he did it."

"But the DA does," said Ted, grabbing his jacket. "I'll be at the Gilead office if you need me."

Lucy's and Phyllis's eyes met. This was too good to pass up. "Need you?" they chorused together.

"Ha-ha," he said, pushing the door open and letting the wind slam it shut behind him. Lucy got on the phone and finally managed to speak to Aucoin, but he had little to say except that he was surprised she wasn't at the press conference. "It was on NECN, you know," he said, perilously close to actually bragging.

"I missed it," said Lucy.

"I'm pretty sure they'll show it again today. You know how they recap the big stories. Probably a clip, anyway."

"Any particular part?"

"Why don't you watch for yourself?" said Aucoin, ending the call.

"Can you believe it?" exploded Lucy. "Now the DA thinks he's some sort of celebrity just because NECN ran his stupid press conference."

"Face it, Lucy," advised Phyllis. "Tori's murder has all the ingredients for a sensational story. She was beautiful, she was naked, she was killed, she and Finn were both in the movies and on TV, which makes them almost celebrities. You might as well just go with it."

"I can't," confessed Lucy. "I don't see Tori or Finn or Kelly as characters in some salacious made-for-TV movie. They're real people caught in a tragedy."

"And you want to get to the truth. I get it." Phyllis riffled the stack of press releases on her desk. "It's not going to be easy."

"Well, at least I've got Kitty Carney. That ought to keep Ted happy. For a while, anyway."

"You never know what tomorrow will bring," said Phyllis, glancing at the clock. "I've got to go. I've got a mammogram appointment."

"Lucky you," said Lucy sarcastically.

She spent the rest of the day plugging away on her story about the proposed town budget, finally wrapping it up around four, when she decided to call it a day. Putting on her jacket, she found a list in the pocket and remembered she needed to pick up salad and a loaf of French bread for dinner.

While she was perusing the salad cooler in the IGA it occurred to Lucy that she'd used up the last of the oatmeal and needed to buy some more. She was cruising into the cereal aisle when she spotted Margaret, who was standing transfixed in front of the Raisin Bran.

"Hard to choose," she said, stepping beside her.

"Can you believe these prices?" she asked, looking worried.

"The store brand is on sale."

Margaret was doubtful. "Is it good?"

"Almost as good," said Lucy. "How did you make out with your car?"

"I had to junk mine, but Brendan knew about an old woman who died over in Gilead and somehow managed to get her car for me. He said the family didn't want it, was happy to get rid of it. He actually made it seem like I was doing them a favor, taking it off their hands."

"That's Brendan for you," said Lucy, watching as Margaret dropped the box of store brand cereal into her cart, preparing to move along.

"How's Erin doing, after the fuss at the *feis* and all?"

"Sounds like a bad mystery," laughed Margaret. "The Fuss at the *Feis*."

Lucy found herself laughing and struggled to control herself. "It has a ring, that's for sure," she finally said.

"It does," agreed Margaret, "but it's not actually all that funny. Siobhan and Brigid have ganged up against Erin, and Kelly hasn't been coming, so it's two against one."

So that's why Brigid was suddenly tongue-tied, thought Lucy, remembering the awkward conversation in the Callanans' driveway. "They still think Erin sabotaged the costume?"

Margaret shrugged. "It's kind of gotten beyond that. There's lots of whispers, giggles behind her back, that sort of thing. And Erin's self-conscious to begin with, because we can't afford the cool stuff that Brigid and Siobhan have." She sighed. "I tell her, 'cause I see it at the bank all the time, that a lot of folks driving brand-new cars and wearing Apple watches don't have two cents to rub together. It's all on credit. But that doesn't make it any easier for her. And Eileen's made it worse because she's arranged for the girls to put on a special performance at the food pantry gala. It's going to mean extra rehearsals and Erin will have to spend more time with Siobhan and Brigid." She screwed up her face and shook her head. "Erin's about had it with the others. She's been begging me to let her quit."

"After all these years? Maybe you could switch to another school?"

"Eileen gives me a break on the tuition. I can't afford to switch."

Lucy thought of Zoe's confession that she was still bothered about her "best friend," Leanne, who dropped her in favor of another group of girls, and how she'd moved on from that devastating experience. Zoe had been transitioning from college to her first job, which made the breakup easier. Both girls were in Portland and occasionally ran into each other where it seemed they were somewhat tentatively resuming their friendship. "Girls can be so mean," said Lucy, attempting to offer encouragement, "but they often make up in the end."

"Erin's already moving on. She's got herself a boyfriend," whispered Margaret, rolling off down the aisle.

"Well, that explains it then," said Lucy, turning back toward the bakery section and calling over her shoulder. "They're jealous."

What with Finn Tobin's arrest and a whole week before Tori Tobin's funeral, there was a welcome pause in the news coverage of the murder and the reporters and camera crews drifted away, giving everyone a bit of breathing space until the weekend, at which time they would certainly return. The annual town meeting was approaching, and Lucy focused on that, interviewing department heads about their budget requests, and writing an in-depth analysis of a proposed zoning change that would allow accessory dwelling units such as in-law apartments.

Brendan Coyle was a supporter of the ADU by-law, and when Lucy interviewed him, he told her that affordable housing was in short supply in the region as home prices had steadily risen in recent years, becoming out of reach not only for low-wage workers but for middle-class folks like teachers. He explained that the new quarters for the food pantry in the old warehouse on Railroad Avenue would also provide low-cost housing. "It was moving full-speed ahead," he told her, "but now I've been informed by the community preservation committee that citizen concerns about the project are on the agenda for their next meeting." He shook his head, expressing puzzlement. "I don't get it. I've been working with various churches and community organizations. It's a county-wide project that will benefit the entire region. Right now, it's an empty shell of a building and it will eventually fall down if it's not put to use. It would be a huge waste."

Back at the office, Lucy called Ruthann Schweitzer, chairman of the community preservation committee, and asked her about the objections to the project. "Well," began Ruthann, "I've been hearing from some business owners in the area who are worried about bringing low-income people into the area, especially the food pantry clients. They say that could draw a criminal element. They're worried about shoplifters, street crime, that sort of thing."

"Really? This is Tinker's Cove. These folks work hard, sometimes at two or three jobs, and we need them. Who's going to deliver the oil and paint the houses and teach the kids?"

"Lucy, I entirely agree with you. We're losing young people, school enrollment is down, and you see HELP WANTED signs everywhere. There's a short-age of available housing, and what little there is costs too much. Used to be you could buy a house for seventy thousand dollars. Now they're only put-ting up these five-hundred-thousand-dollar con-dos that sit empty except for a week or two in the summer. It's hollowing out our community."

Lucy thought of the area around the defunct rail line, where the old warehouse stood. It was oc-cupied by small businesses that included an auto body shop, a landscape company, and a feed store. "I'm a little puzzled," she began. "You said it's busi-ness owners who are worried about shoplifters and street crime, but these aren't exactly high-end re-tailers like jewelry stores or designer boutiques. Do you think the concern is genuine?"

Ruthann snorted. "Personally, I think it's just NIMBY. You say low-income, and a lot of people automatically think the worst. But as committee members we have a responsibility to hear them out, give them a chance to say what's bothering them, and hope that's the end of it."

"Well, I'll be sure to cover the meeting," prom-ised Lucy.

"Good. We need to get this out in the open, so people can see it for what it is."

"Righto," agreed Lucy, but as she ended the call, she wondered what exactly *it* was. What was really going on?

Chapter Nine

Instead of eating lunch, Lucy decided to take a drive out to Railroad Avenue and see the disputed area for herself. The old railroad station that once stood about a mile from Main Street was now defunct, and the tracks had been torn up, but the line had skirted the river, taking advantage of the gently graded riverbank. The warehouse in question was a reminder of the time when the railroad had been an economic lifeline transporting goods and passengers to and from Portland, Boston, and beyond. Now, however, it loomed above its neighbors, with boarded-up windows, peeling paint, and sagging clapboard siding. Despite its present shabby appearance, Lucy knew the building had once been the pride of the town and the envy of neighboring villages as the tallest and largest structure in the county.

As she turned onto Railroad Avenue she slowed

and took a long look at the gray warehouse, admiring its simple, elegant architecture with its peaked roof and precisely arranged rows of windows. It had been built to last back in the nineteenth century, and Lucy had seen the town building inspector's report that certified it was still structurally sound. It seemed a perfect choice for affordable housing, as well as the food pantry. It was easily accessible, there was plenty of parking, and would no doubt attract new businesses to the area. She was thinking along these lines when she parked in front of the Seal Island Lobster Company, a modern steel building that contained huge tanks where lobsters were stored awaiting shipment. She got out of the car and walked through the open garage door, spotting owner Jim Riordan in his tiny cubicle office.

"Hi, Jim!" she called, and he looked up from the papers he was studying and greeted her with a smile.

"Hey, Lucy, what can I do for you? A couple bugs for dinner?"

Lucy hated the way lobstermen called the creatures bugs; it reminded her all too well that they did indeed resemble large insects, what with their hard shells and long antennae. They were delicious, but she'd rather not think of their evolutionary connection to the creepy-crawlies. She preferred her lobster already cooked, shelled, mixed with a dab of mayonnaise, and tucked into a buttery grilled bun. "Not today," she said. "I'm here about the upcoming community preservation committee meeting. I understand you got yourself on the agenda."

Jim, a long, tall guy with a full beard, who was wearing rubber boots and a couple of sweatshirts under his waterproof Grunden overalls, leaned back in his black leatherette desk chair. "Well," he began, "you know this old warehouse is a local treasure, and it seems kinda dumb to fill it up with a lot of down-at-the-heels pantry clients who are most likely druggies and alkies. Mebbe we oughta think about upgrading it, using it for something better."

"What have you got in mind?" asked Lucy. "Some kind of fancy mall or something? This isn't exactly Fifth Avenue, you know."

Jim laughed. "Yeah, it's zoned commercial and industrial, but there's a lot of leeway in those categories. And I know I'd feel a lot better if we had condos instead of apartments, homeowners instead of renters."

Lucy was puzzled. This neighborhood didn't seem appropriate for upscale development. "Condos?"

"Yup. Condos. People who are invested in the area, not renters."

"What's the problem with renters?" asked Lucy.

"Not stable, not reliable. I know Rob at the auto body shop says he's already had problems with addicts stealing his tools, and the plumbing supply place has had to hire a night watchman. They were losing copper pipe faster than they could replace it." He leaned forward, making eye contact. "And the food pantry is gonna attract a lot of down-and-outs, looking for more than a bag of groceries. And whadda we got here?" He generously included the entire neighborhood in a big wave. "A lot of stuff they can sell for good money."

Lucy furrowed her brow, troubled by what he was saying. "Brendan vets the food pantry clients very carefully. They're actually people working hard at low-wage jobs, single moms, folks who've hit hard times due to sickness and medical bills."

"Ah, Brendan," said Jim, shaking his head sadly, "he's a soft touch. He'll fall for any hard-luck story."

"Sometimes people need a bit of a helping hand. That's nothing to be ashamed of." Lucy heard the constant hum of the filters on the lobster tanks and noticed a definite, fishy smell. "Do you really think a fancy condo development is a viable option here? I'm doubtful that people with hundreds of thousands of dollars to invest are going to want a lumberyard, a plumbing supply outfit, an auto body shop and, no offense, a lobster pound for neighbors."

"Riverfront property, Lucy," he said, with a knowing nod. "We can fix ourselves up, y'know. Some grass, fences, shrubs, all that'd make a big difference. That's what that Deirdre lady told me, when she was collecting for the pantry."

What on earth? wondered Lucy. "What was Deirdre saying?"

"Quite a lot. Getting donations and talkin' 'bout our responsibility to the less fortunate, even though they have a lot of problems with drugs and booze. Can't help themselves."

"So she was collecting food for poor folks, at the same time saying they're drug addicts and alcoholics?"

"Well, the two go hand in hand and we shouldn't judge, but there are limits, right? And like she said, it makes good sense for the pantry to stay in town, where the police can keep an eye on things, and if there's an overdose, well it's just 'round the corner from the rescue squad at the fire station. They don't have to come all the way out here." He paused and shook his head sadly. "From what I hear, this Oxy stuff is causin' a lot of grief. And it's just about impossible to get clean. These users come out of rehab and go straight to their dealer. I got that on good authority from my buddy who's an EMT."

Lucy straightened up, looked him in the eye, and gave it to him straight. "That's true enough. And from what I hear, folks in condos are just as likely to be addicted to OxyContin as homeless people, even more so, because they can afford it. The street people have mostly switched to heroin."

"Heroin! Well, we sure don't want that stuff around here!" exclaimed Jim. Seeing that Lucy was turning to leave, he made a last-ditch offer. "I can give you some lobstahs for five bucks a pound. Sure you don't want any?"

"I'm sure," said Lucy, smiling and giving him a wave as she left the building. She had an uneasy feeling as she walked to her car, suddenly aware that a lot had been going on in Tinker's Cove that she'd missed. She wasn't as on top of the town's currents as she thought. It was that darn social media, she decided, that allowed people to spread rumors and false information. When she wrote a story, she found out very quickly from readers if she'd made a mistake, and was quick to write a correction. But there was no check on social media

where people could post any fool thing, no matter
how crazy, and somebody would believe it. It
would be great if *The Courier* could monitor social
media and check facts, but that would be a huge
job and they were already short-staffed.

She was thinking along those lines, maybe a hu-
morous weekly column about the most outrageous
lies recently seen on social media, when she
climbed into her SUV and started it. Her phone
went off and she grabbed it, seeing it was a call
from Ted. "Hey, glad I caught you. Aucoin is holding a press conference. . . ."

"He is?" she asked, incredulous, aware that the
DA was notoriously closemouthed. If he was holding a press conference, it must mean something
big was unfolding. "What's happened?" she asked,
expecting to hear there had been a bank robbery
or a police shooting.

"He's providing an update on the Finn Tobin
case."

This was unusual. It must mean a huge development. "He's dropping the case?"

"No. There's new evidence linking Tobin to the
crime."

Lucy turned off the engine; no sense wasting
gas while she sat there trying to grasp this amazing
development. DA Phil Aucoin never released information about evidence before going to trial; he
was known for holding his cards close to his chest.
"You're telling me that Aucoin is going to put his
evidence out there? Isn't that going to contami-
nate the jury pool, or something?"

"If you ask me," explained Ted, "he's discovered
that he likes the attention. His pretty face was all

over the TV and reporters were hanging on every word that fell from his lips, but once Tobin was arraigned, the media dropped the story in favor of rumors that Tom Brady was coming out of retirement, and nobody was calling him anymore."

"Except us," said Lucy.

"Clearly we can't compare with CNN and *People* magazine."

"Okay," sighed Lucy. "When is this media event? And do you think they'll come?"

"It's five o'clock today, which is short notice, but they've all got stringers who are dying to get a scrap of breaking news."

Lucy knew that was true; mass-media outfits were able to respond to breaking news anywhere in the country in minutes. "At his office?"

"Uh, no. He's expecting a crowd. It's in the Gilead municipal building."

"Well, I hope he's not disappointed," said Lucy, who knew that Gilead, as the county seat, needed a building large enough to house county-wide departments as well as town offices that also had a large meeting room. "It's awful to throw a party if nobody comes." She paused, thinking. "Do you think he really has new evidence?"

"Maybe. That's why I'm sending you."

"Well, I'm on it, boss. In fact, I think I'll do a bit of digging and see what I can turn up."

Ending the call with Ted, she dialed Officer Sally Kirwan's number. Officer Sally was her favorite inside source at the police department, but unfortunately, it was her day off. She also called her old buddy Officer Barney Culpepper, but he was out on assignment and unavailable. Stymied in that direction, she decided to follow a different trail and started the engine. It was time to catch up with her neighbor Frankie La Chance, who just happened to be a real estate agent. The town's top agent, in fact, before Deirdre Delahunt opened her office.

Frankie lived on Prudence Path, a small cul-de-sac lined with modest homes that had sprung up a few years before, off Red Top Road, next to Lucy's old antique farmhouse. When she drove down the little road, she immediately noticed that Frankie's Cadillac SUV was in the driveway, which meant she was home. She pulled in next to it, hopped out, and knocked on the back door.

"Lucy!" exclaimed Frankie, greeting her with a big glossy-red-lipstick smile. She still wore her black hair long, and dressed to kill in clingy wrap dresses and high heels. "Long time no see. Come on in. I just put the kettle on."

"Yeah, it has been a while," agreed Lucy, following her into the kitchen, where an electric kettle was already steaming. "How's Renee?" she asked, naming Frankie's daughter who had been friends with Zoe and Sara in high school.

"She's gone back to school," said Frankie, beaming as she collected a couple of mugs. "She's going for a master's in public health policy at BU. Herbal or Tetley?"

"Tetley, thanks," said Lucy, thinking she'd want to be wide-awake at the press conference. "That's a great field. Good for her," she added, climbing onto a stool at Frankie's kitchen island.

"What about your girls?" Frankie set the mug of hot tea in front of Lucy, then sat beside her.

"Sara's in Boston, you know. She works at the Museum of Science."

"They should get together," said Frankie. "I know Renee's a bit lonely."

"Sara, too, I think, though she has been getting to know more people." Lucy took a sip of tea. "You know, I've been covering the food pantry expansion project out at that old warehouse. . . ."

"You mean, Deirdre's condo?"

"Yeah. That was a surprise to me. What do you know about it?"

"It's a bit of a magic trick. Now you see affordable apartments, then presto change-o, it's luxury condos."

"But that whole area is zoned commercial-industrial, isn't it?"

"And she wouldn't be able to build a residential project there at all, except that the planning committee gave a variance for the much-needed affordable housing. We have a crisis in town. Young families are getting priced out of the housing market and moving away. Plus, we can't attract the workers we need, like teachers and cops, because they can't find a place to live."

"So she's outbidding the pantry for the warehouse?" Lucy wrapped her hands around the mug, finding its warmth reassuring and comforting as she contemplated Deirdre's outrageous behavior. "Isn't that kind of hypocritical?"

Frankie shrugged. "Deirdre's profit driven. The variance has been approved, she sees an opportunity to cash in, and instead of affordable units, the town gets another fancy-dandy luxury complex occupied for a few weeks in summer by people who have two or three other homes."

"But the committee specified that the variance was for affordable housing."

"So what? They'd have to go to court to enforce it, and the town doesn't have the money they'd need to hire top-notch real estate lawyers."

"Isn't that unethical?" Lucy wanted to believe there was a way to make sure the rules were followed. "What sort of financing is she getting?"

"I don't know. But even if it's government financed, they're probably just grateful when a developer actually builds something instead of grabbing the dough and running off to the Cayman Islands."

Lucy took a long, restorative swallow of tea. "This is unbelievable. She actually won naming privileges for the food pantry, but she's scuttling the expansion."

"Well, in her defense, she's in a tough spot. That strip mall she built out on Route 1 is still vacant, and there's little chance she'll be able to find renters. Retail is dead. I heard she's in the hole with a big balloon payment coming due, so she needs to raise money fast."

"And if she got approval for the condo, she'd be able to get financing?"

"You got it."

"But how can she use the condo money to pay off the strip mall?"

"It'll just get rolled into the new loan. Happens all the time."

Lucy thought of the numerous times she and Bill had refinanced their house, pulling money out as their equity rose to pay for improvements, or the kids' college expenses. But that wasn't quite what Deirdre was doing. "Isn't that fraud?" asked Lucy.

"That's up to the bank to determine, and it's part of the reason she's got everybody thinking she's a big supporter of the pantry. It's sleight of hand, like a magician who distracts and draws your eye away from what they're actually doing. She wants people to think of all the food she collected and donated. Of course she supports the pantry. She just doesn't see any need for the food pantry clientele with their old cars and thrift shop clothes to move into a building she could use for her expensive condos."

Lucy glanced at the kitchen clock and started, realizing it was almost five. "Oops, gotta go. I've got to be over in Gilead for a press conference."

"It was great to see you, Lucy. We should do this more often."

"Absolutely," promised Lucy, as she dashed for the door.

It didn't take long to cover the ten miles of winding two-lane roads that led to Gilead, where a couple of white TV trucks with satellite dishes from regional stations were parked outside the municipal complex. The large parking lot was unusually crowded with cars and Lucy had to park in a distant spot, which made her a bit late when she reached the meeting room. Phil Aucoin was just entering as she edged down to the front of the room, aiming for the last empty seat in the front row. Once seated, her notebook in hand, she took in the room as he went through the usual intro-

ductions of state police, local police, and his assis-
tants.

The conference had attracted a goodly assortment of reporters, and a couple of camera crews
were recording everything. Turning her attention
back to Aucoin, she noticed he was wearing a new
suit, had gotten a fancy haircut, as well as a mani-
cure. Looking closer she thought she detected a
light application of foundation on his face. Aucoin
had indeed gone Hollywood.

But that wasn't the story she was covering, she
told herself, focusing her attention on the state
police detective who had taken the mic. "We have
evidence that Finn Tobin was in the victim's home
on the night of the murder," she was saying. "Two
mugs containing the residue of Irish coffee were
found in the kitchen, and DNA from the mugs was
identified as belonging to Ms. Tobin and Finn
Tobin. We believe that after consuming the coffee
the couple moved to the candle-lit bathroom for a
romantic rendezvous that went terribly wrong."

Hands popped up and questions were shouted,
which Aucoin was surprisingly willing to answer.
"Is there further evidence that Finn Tobin was actually in the bathroom?" demanded the guy from
NECN.

"We have absolutely found DNA evidence that
Finn Tobin was in the bathroom," said Aucoin,
looking rather smug as he shoved the female officer aside and took the mic.

Lucy saw her chance and raised her hand. "Tobin
and his ex-wife were on friendly terms, so wouldn't
you expect to find his DNA in the house?"

"We also have evidence from the autopsy," said Aucoin.

"DNA? Finn Tobin's DNA was found on Tori Tobin's body?" demanded Lucy.

"I'm not going into detail about the autopsy," said Aucoin, shifting his eyes. "You've all seen the medical examiner's report, and he will be testifying at the trial."

"But there was no . . ."

"Did I miss something in the report?"

"There was nothing about DNA . . ."

Aucoin ignored those questions, instead turning to the state police captain standing beside him. "I want to commend the hard work and diligence of the state police in this matter, led by Captain Laurie Cunningham. It's cooperation like this, among various law enforcement departments, that has enabled us to identify a suspect and build a case that we believe will result in justice being done. . . ."

The rest of the conference was more of the same, as the various participants congratulated each other. When it was finally over, and people were leaving, Lucy noticed a small crowd had gathered in the hallway around Finn's lawyer, Gerald Fogarty.

Fogarty, who sported long white hair and a mustache, had a round belly and a rumpled appearance that belied his sharp mind. He was known as the state's top defense lawyer and was determined to maintain that reputation.

"My client Finn Tobin is innocent, and if what I heard today is any indication, I have every confidence that a jury of twelve fair-minded citizens will have no trouble at all reaching that verdict. Finn

Tobin has admitted that he and his ex-wife had Irish coffee that night, while they waited for their daughter to return from a day spent with friends. Tori Tobin was alive and well when they left."

Lucy lingered, hoping to grab Aucoin for more information, but he didn't show. Fogarty held forth for a while, pretty much repeating the same theme and insisting on Finn Tobin's innocence, and the media crowd began to disperse. Spotting her leaning against the wall, writing in her notebook, Fogarty greeted her.

"Hi, Lucy. I hope you got down everything I said."

"Absolutely," she replied, smiling at him. "But off the record, are you really as confident of Finn's innocence as you claim?"

"I dunno," he admitted. "This thing has all the features of a bad movie, and Aucoin is hoping the jury has seen the murderous husband plot a dozen times and will convict based on an unfortunate old movie and circumstantial evidence. What I need is a witness, someone who saw Finn leave, or even better, saw somebody else arrive."

"If there was a witness, wouldn't they have come forward by now?"

Fogarty raised an eyebrow and shrugged. "That's what's got me worried."

Chapter Ten

Fogarty's statement that he needed to find a witness stuck in Lucy's mind as she drove back to Tinker's Cove. Fogarty had said that Tori was alive and well when Kelly and Finn left together, so that must mean the DA believed that Finn had returned to the house. But where was Kelly all day? Fogarty said she had been out with friends, but could she have been involved in something that precipitated the murder? She was old enough to have a driver's license, but Lucy didn't know if she actually had one. But even if she did have a license, that didn't mean she had a car to drive. And she knew from her own experience raising four teens that they often drove around together in groups, but depending on the activity sometimes still got rides from parents. What was Kelly doing on that Sunday afternoon and who was she doing it with? She didn't have Kelly's phone number, but she did have her grandmother's, so as soon as she got back to the office, she gave Kitty Carney a call.

It was early evening, so she had the place to herself as Phyllis had already gone home and Ted was in the Gilead office, awaiting her account of the press conference. She put that thought out of her mind while she tapped out Kitty's number. It rang and rang but there was no answer, so she left a message requesting a call back, and then got busy on the press conference story. "DA Phil Aucoin held a press conference promising new evidence in the Tori Tobin murder case, but defense lawyer Gerald Fogarty says Aucoin was merely . . ."

She paused here, struggling to complete the sentence, when her phone rang; she saw Kitty Carney's name on the screen.

"Hi, Kitty. Thanks for returning my call."

"No problem, Lucy."

"I know it must be very hard. How is Kelly doing?"

"Not well. She misses her mom, of course, and her dad, too. She's furious that he's been accused of killing Tori; she gets real emotional. I don't know how to help her. I just keep saying that it will be okay, but I know that's not what she needs and I'm not even sure I believe it myself."

"Funny thing," began Lucy, "but I was at the DA's press conference today and Finn's lawyer gave a statement. He said that Finn and Tori had Irish coffee while waiting for Kelly to come home. Do you know what she was doing that day and who she was with?"

"I do. She was out with Siobhan Delahunt collecting goods for the food pantry."

"Were they driving around together, or was one of the moms driving them?"

"Siobhan's mom was driving and the girls hopped in and out of the car, collecting the food."

"And Siobhan's mom drove her home?"

"That's right."

"Just dropped her off?"

"I think they all went in the house. Siobhan's mom had some petition or something she wanted them to sign. Kelly told me her mom refused to do it. They had an argument. Kelly said Siobhan's mom got real mad about it."

Lucy thought that was very interesting and that maybe Deirdre had a motive for killing Tori. But then realized that even if she had a motive and means, she lacked opportunity. "But Siobhan's mom left the house along with Siobhan?"

"Yeah. Left in a huff. And then Kelly and Finn left, too. Finn said Tori was planning a quiet evening. She was going to have a tray dinner and watch some TV, have a bath, and get to bed early." Kitty paused a moment, then asked, "Why do you want to know all this?"

"Oh, like I said, the DA had this big press conference and it just got me wondering. Kelly is absolutely sure that her father was with her all night?"

"That's what she says and since she was sleeping on the sofa, it's unlikely he could leave without waking her."

"So the killer must have come back later, while Tori was in the bath."

"Yeah. But the police questioned all the neighbors and nobody saw a car, or a person sneaking around. The street was completely quiet. Even that woman walking her German shepherd said the dog didn't pick up on anybody prowling around, and there were no cars parked on the street."

So she'd come to a dead end, thought Lucy. There was no witness who could clear Finn. "Well, thanks for calling."

"No problem, Lucy. Believe me, I've gone over all this a million times." She paused. "If I think of anything more, I'll let you know."

"Thanks."

Lucy finished up her account of the press conference and left the office, heading for the little shared lot behind *The Courier* office where she'd parked her car because there was no room on the street. It wasn't an official parking lot, just a bit of unpaved ground occasionally used by neighboring businesses, which included an insurance agency, a consignment shop, and an acupuncturist. The rear border of the area was lined with trees, but they were still bare, and she noticed she could see Sue's house and backyard. She could also see Tori Tobin's house. There was even, she remembered, a little path that ran through the woods and led to Sue's driveway. Such little shortcuts were common in Tinker's Cove; this one gave residents of Parallel Street quick access to Main Street, as they didn't have to go all the way around the block. Sue never minded if neighbors made use of her driveway, especially since they often stopped to chat, or dropped off some homemade muffins or a plant cutting, by way of thanks. But, thought Lucy, studying the little path, it could have been used by

Tori's killer, who would have been able to park unnoticed and stealthily approach her house with its unlocked back door.

But surely the police had discovered the path and thoroughly searched it, and the parking lot for clues. Footprints could be matched. Maybe the killer dropped something. Of course, she told herself, searching now would be pointless because the area had certainly been covered by the police, and if it hadn't, any footprints would have been washed away by rain. Anything dropped by the killer, if paper, would be a soggy mess. Nevertheless, she decided it was worth taking a look, and since daylight was fading, she grabbed the flashlight she kept in the car and followed the path, eyes peeled.

It was just a narrow track with brush and trees on both sides, and even though she kept her eyes wide open and cast the light from side to side, she didn't find anything. Not a scrap of wool or thread caught on a twig, not a footprint, not even a candy wrapper or plastic water bottle. Reaching Sue's backyard, she saw she had a clear view of Tori's house, and the upstairs bathroom window, which would have been alight. A clear indication to the killer that Tori was most likely vulnerable and defenseless, she thought with a shudder.

Shaking her head, she turned back, realizing she needed to get home and start supper. She was feeling dejected, her head hung down a bit as she kept her eyes on the uneven surface of the path and dodged muddy patches in the parking lot. Even so, she stumbled a bit going past a trash can, and grabbed it for support, and that's when something lying on the ground caught the beam of her flashlight and sparkled. Picking it up, she discovered it was a black ball of a button, perhaps three-eighths of an inch in diameter, adorned with a tiny little bit of crystal. She held it in her hand, thought about tossing it in the trash can, but instead tucked it into her pocket.

Caught up in a busy week, she forgot all about the button which remained in the pocket of her barn coat along with a couple of lucky pennies she'd collected. She always picked up pennies she spotted on the ground, even though Bill and the kids teased her about stubbornly clinging to the belief that they would bring her luck.

Back at work a few days later, she made a few phone calls in preparation for covering the community preservation committee meeting scheduled for that evening. Deirdre Delahunt brushed aside Lucy's questions and argued that converting the warehouse to condos would boost the town's tax base, while Brendan Coyle said he'd been rallying folks in favor of the pantry expansion and affordable housing option. When she arrived at the basement meeting room in the town hall, she discovered that he was as good as his word and the room was packed with locals: fishermen in boots, moms with kids on their laps, and gray-haired retirees. Deirdre was there, too, along with a couple of professional types in suits and a number of Delahunt Realty agents in matching blazers. Spotting Margaret Casey, Lucy recalled her difficulties with Deirdre and thought she might get a good quote from her about the condo plan. There was no sign of the committee members yet, and there was an empty seat next to Margaret, so Lucy took it.

"Hi! Should be an interesting meeting," she began.

"I should think so. Brendan asked me to come. . . ." said Margaret, glancing uneasily at Deirdre.

Remembering how Deirdre had talked up her condo plan with the warehouse neighbors, Lucy wondered if she had attempted to sway some of the pantry clients as well. "Did Deirdre ask you to join her campaign?" she asked.

"Um, well," began Margaret, looking absolutely miserable, "I did something I shouldn't have, and Deirdre knows. And if she tells my boss at the bank, I could lose my job."

"So she wants you to speak in favor of the condo project?"

"Yes."

"Even though you don't want to."

"Right."

Lucy felt a surge of sympathy for poor Margaret who, being human, had made a mistake. Most likely something small that Deirdre had blown into something much bigger. "Margaret, I know you. You're a good person. What could she possibly hold over you?"

"It was at the *feis*. I drank too much and I was mad at Deirdre and repeated something I heard my manager say." She rolled her eyes. "It's very important to maintain client confidentiality at the bank—you can imagine it's rule number one—and I broke it."

"So that's what the donnybrook was all about?"

"Oh, it was quite the scene," admitted Margaret with a tiny little smile. "We'd all had too much to drink, including Deirdre. She really let go."

"I bet she was going on about 'entitled people getting stuff for free,'" began Lucy. "I've heard it all from her before."

"I just wanted to take her down a peg," said Margaret with an apologetic shrug.

"So you probably said something about her not being as rich as she pretended? Maybe she was even overdrawn?"

"Something like that," said Margaret, looking at her with a puzzled expression.

"I wouldn't worry, Margaret. It's not a secret that she's up against it. I heard it from a friend who's in real estate who said she needs the financing for this condo project to cover her losses on that strip mall."

Margaret's eyes widened, and she was about to say something when Ruthann Schweitzer banged her gavel and called the meeting to order. While they were talking, the committee members had filed in and taken their places at the long table on a raised platform.

"First on our agenda is the public comment portion of our meeting, and I see we have a number of people here tonight eager to comment on the proposed conversion of the old railroad warehouse building. I think we will begin with Deirdre Delahunt, who is the applicant."

"Thank you, Madam Chairwoman," began Deirdre, rising to her feet. "If you don't mind, I have an architectural rendering of the proposed conversion."

"I see no objection. . . ." said Ruthann, checking with the other committee members.

"Thank you," said Deirdre, stepping to an easel

in the front of the room and flipping the foam
board around, revealing the rendering that had
been hidden on the reverse side. As she maneu-
vered the foam board into place, the buttons on
the sleeve of her black turtleneck sweater caught
the light and sparkled.

Slipping her hand into her pocket, Lucy felt the
button she had found in the parking lot and drew
it out. Looking at it, she saw it was identical to the
buttons on Deirdre's sweater; in fact, there was a
gap in the row of buttons on the cuff. She had the
missing button, she realized, as the hairs on the
back of her neck rose. The button was proof that
Deirdre had been in the parking lot, the lot behind Tori's house, the lot that provided cover for a
murderer's car.

Get a grip, she told herself. Sure, she didn't much
like Deirdre, but that didn't mean the woman was
a murderer. What reason could she possibly have
for killing Tori? She started thinking, putting together scraps of information. According to Kelly,
Tori and Deirdre had argued the day Tori was
killed. Deirdre had wanted Tori to support her
condo plan. Was that it? And Tori had refused, in
no uncertain terms. And Tori was known for being
outspoken; hadn't she been planning to roast a
few local celebrities when she emceed the food
pantry fundraiser?

But was that a motive for murder? *Maybe,* thought
Lucy, remembering her conversation with Renee.
Deirdre was facing real financial pressure and needed
the condo project to go through. She thought of
how Deirdre flaunted her supposed wealth and
wondered how she would deal with bankruptcy.

Not well, she decided, remembering how angry she'd been about Margaret's slip of the tongue, even threatening to get her fired from the job she desperately needed. Deirdre's very identity depended on being a winner, not a loser.

Lucy focused on Deirdre's presentation, as she stood at the easel, pointing out the various features of the proposed conversion. She'd missed most of it, she realized, looking at her blank notebook. Luckily, she reminded herself, the meetings were videotaped and she could watch Deirdre's presentation. Deirdre was sitting down, now, and Ruthann was checking her list, calling on Brendan Coyle.

Brendan spoke eloquently in favor of the original plan for affordable housing and the expanded food pantry. He was followed by Kelly Tobin, who had slipped in unnoticed while Lucy was talking to Margaret, along with her grandmother. Everyone hushed, recognizing the grieving teen as she rose to her feet and began speaking in a hesitant tone. "Um, I'm just here because of my mom. She would have been here for sure because she was a big believer in treating everyone as she'd like to be treated. She often said that she and my, um, my dad, were only able to buy our house because real estate was in a slump. Nowadays, with prices so high, they'd never have been able to do it, and she worried that the town was changing, becoming too expensive for regular folks." Having said what she came to say, she sat down and got a hug from her grandma and an approving smile from Brendan.

Next up was Jim Riordan from the lobster company, who spoke in favor of the condo project and so it went, as pro- and anti- forces made their arguments. After an hour or so, Ruthann called for the end of the public comments, saying the committee was grateful for the high level of community interest and would carefully consider all the views presented. The committee, however, had other matters on the agenda, which they would take up after a short break and she banged down her gavel, temporarily suspending the meeting.

Most everyone got up and began making their way to the exits. Lucy spotted Deirdre gathering up her notes and putting them in her briefcase, so she approached her, holding out the button. "I found your button, Deirdre."

"Thanks, Lucy," she said with a smile. "Where did you find it?"

"In the parking area, behind *The Courier* office."

Deirdre made a quick calculation. "Oh, I must have lost it when I had an appointment for acupuncture."

"When was this appointment?" asked Lucy, recklessly pressing the point. "Sunday night, the night Deirdre was murdered?"

Deirdre grew rigid and raised her eyebrows. "What do you mean? The acupuncture place is closed on Sunday."

Spurred on by Deirdre's reaction, Lucy continued. "But you were there, in the parking lot, weren't you? You used it to access Tori's house from the rear, right?"

Deirdre glared at her. "You're out of your mind!" She grabbed her coat off the rack and marched past Lucy, only to be confronted by Kelly Tobin.

"You're unbelievable!" declared Kelly. "You're

such a hypocrite. I spent an entire afternoon collecting food donations with you, and now you're against the food pantry! I believed you, I thought we were helping hungry people, but it was all a big fake so you could get your stupid condos!"

Kelly's voice had risen, and people were starting to notice, pausing to watch this dramatic confrontation.

Deirdre narrowed her eyes. "Hypocrite!" She laughed. "You're calling me a big fake. Well, what about your mother? She thought she could make a laughingstock of me when she was the real fake! All the time tossing around that big head of fabulous red hair? It wasn't real! It was a wig! She was bald as a bat! Tori Tobin was bald as a bowling ball and she thought she could make a fool of me!"

Kelly's jaw dropped as she realized what Deirdre's accusation meant. "There's only one way you would know that," she said, eyes fixed on Deirdre. "She never took that wig off, not ever, *except in the bath.*"

People were really starting to pay attention now, and Officer Sally Kirwan was keeping a watchful eye on the crowd.

Deirdre's eyes darted around the room, looking for an exit. "Uh, no," she said, picking up her briefcase and edging toward the door. "She showed me one time when it slipped a bit, made a joke about it."

"Never happened," insisted Kelly. "That wig never slipped, not ever. I never saw her without it. Neither did my dad. She had a disease, alopecia, and she said it would end her acting career if anybody knew. She only took it off when she was in the bathtub, and that's where you saw her. . . ."

"That's ridiculous!" declared Deirdre, moving a little faster.

"But you were in the parking lot. That's where I found the button," said Lucy.

"I told you, I was getting acupuncture . . . I had a sore shoulder from carrying all that donated food around." She'd worked her way through the crowd and was almost at the doorway, which was blocked by Officer Sally Kirwan.

"Pardon me . . ." she said in a hopeful little voice.

"I think you better come to the station with me," said Officer Sally. "I have a few questions I'd like to ask you."

"Right now? I need to . . ."

"I don't want to have to arrest you, but I will," said the officer.

"Okay," said Deirdre, attempting a nonchalant shrug, "but you're making a big mistake."

Everyone followed as they climbed the stairs to the parking lot, where people gathered in little knots and watched as the two women made their way along the sidewalk to the police station.

"Do you think she really did it?" asked Jim Riordan, looking doubtful.

"We'll know soon enough," said Lucy, thinking that if Deirdre was charged, this was one press conference she didn't want to miss.

A few days later, Lucy was front and center at 9 a.m. when DA Phil Aucoin announced that Deirdre Delahunt had been charged with the murder of Tori Tobin, and all charges had been dropped against Finn Tobin. Asked what new evidence had been found that resulted in the charges against Deirdre Delahunt, Aucoin cited fibers found under the victim's fingernails that appeared to match one of Deirdre Delahunt's sweaters and had been sent to the state crime lab for examination. "There was also a button found near the crime scene . . ."

Lucy smiled to herself, pleased that she'd helped solve the crime, and possibly saved an innocent man from a lengthy prison sentence. But as she listened to Aucoin's self-congratulatory description of the new development in the case, that sense of satisfaction soon passed and she thought of the waste. Not only Tori's terrible death but the damage to so many lives, including Deirdre and her family. And it all began, she thought, when a few too many Irish coffees loosened tongues and tempers flared.

DEATH OF AN IRISH COFFEE DRINKER

Lee Hollis

Chapter One

"Oh, Randy, that's delicious," Hayley moaned as she sipped from a mug while perched atop her usual stool at her brother's bar, Drinks Like A Fish.

Randy beamed while wiping his hands with a towel behind the bar. "The secret ingredient is the freshly whipped cream, plus the top-shelf Irish whiskey I use, a new brand I just discovered, shipped directly from Cork, Ireland."

"Well, don't keep me in suspense. What's the brand?" Hayley said, slurping some more, her eyes closed, a warm tingling feeling coursing through her body.

"I'm not telling you. That's why it's called a *secret* ingredient. But everyone I've tested it on has given it an unqualified rave, so I'm going to roll it out as my 'Month of March' drink special all the way to St. Patrick's Day."

"I'm sure it will be a huge hit," Hayley assured him, checking her watch. "Liddy was supposed to be here a half hour ago. I have to leave soon. I need to stop by the restaurant to check on things, and then Bruce and I are staying for dinner."

"I saw her running into the Criterion Theatre a couple of hours ago," Randy said, glancing out the large picture window at the front of the bar, which was directly across the street from the historic building.

"She had a meeting with her entertainment committee. They're trying to finalize their spring events schedule," Hayley said, swallowing the rest of her Irish coffee.

Randy grabbed her empty mug. "Another one?"

Hayley slid off the stool and removed her coat from the hook underneath the bar in front of her. "No, I've had enough. I really better get going. Tell Liddy I waited as long as I could." She wriggled into her heavy burgundy down hooded L.L. Bean coat and grabbed her bag off the floor just as the door flew open. And like a gust of cold wind, Liddy blew into the bar, shedding her black Harris Wharf London draped wool coat, which Hayley guessed cost about five times more than hers.

Liddy tossed it on the empty stool next to her and called out to Randy, "A bottle of your finest champagne! We're celebrating!"

"Liddy, I was just on my way out," Hayley said apologetically.

"I'm sorry I was running late, but as chairman of the Criterion Theatre entertainment committee, I couldn't just run out to meet a friend for happy hour, now could I?"

"No, but I have a restaurant to run so—"

"*Please*! Hayley's Kitchen can survive five more minutes without you. You've trained that staff so well, they're now like a well-oiled machine. You need to stop working so hard!"

Hayley sighed, wriggled out of her coat, and slid back up on her stool next to Liddy just as Randy arrived with a bottle of champagne.

Liddy eyed the label. "Dom Pérignon?"

"How about Cook's, five bucks a bottle? This isn't Le Bernardin in New York, it's Drinks Like A Fish in Bar Harbor. We don't have fancy champagne."

Liddy impatiently waved him off, anxious to get to her exciting news. "Yes, fine, whatever. Just hurry up and open it!"

Randy bowed like a *Downton Abbey* manservant. "Yes, m'lady." Then he chuckled and set about popping open the cork, which dislodged from the bottle so fast, it ricocheted off the Amstel beer tap and nearly took Hayley's eye out.

Randy licked the overflowing champagne from the side of the bottle before pouring what was left into two champagne glasses and handing them to Hayley and Liddy.

Hayley raised her glass. "Okay. Now, what are we celebrating?"

"Me!" Liddy cooed.

"You?"

"Yes, me and my astounding brilliance!"

"And modesty," Randy tossed in.

Liddy gave him a quick sideways glance, grimacing slightly, before breaking out into a wide smile as she returned her attention back to Hayley. "It's been a horrifically long dreary winter and people are desperate for some entertainment. I know we usually try to book the big acts at the Criterion during the summer season when there are so many tourists in town, but this year I decided the year-round residents of Bar Harbor deserved something special to look forward to before things start to warm up in late April, early May."

Hayley's eyes widened, full of excitement. "Who? Wait, don't tell me. You got Wade Springer! My favorite country singer of all time! He's finally coming back to play the Criterion!"

"No, not him. He's in Nashville until September appearing at the Grand Ole Opry. But I'll give you a hint. He's a very funny stand-up comedian."

"Jim Gaffigan! I love him! He's so funny."

"No."

"Dave Chappelle? His material might be a little too R-rated for the Criterion, don't you think?"

"It's not Dave Chappelle."

Randy took a stab at it. "Bill Burr?"

Liddy shook her head. "No! I don't even know who that is! I'm talking about Jefferson O'Keefe!"

"But he's a local," Randy muttered, disappointed.

Liddy shot him another annoyed look. "A local boy done good! Come on, he's a huge, successful talent. Jefferson has played clubs in Boston and New York, and don't forget his appearance on *Stephen Colbert* a few years back! He killed with that set and he got to meet one of the *Harry Potter* kids, the ginger, all grown up now, backstage!"

She was right.

Jefferson O'Keefe had been a hilarious cutup since they had all gone to high school together.

Jefferson had then gone on to Emerson College in Boston, studying Dramatic Arts. But he knew early on his destiny was stand-up comedy. He had spent years trying to make it in the clubs in New York, but it had been a constant struggle. Only after returning to Portland and honing his act to reflect more of his background, the absurdities and oddities of growing up in quirky Down East Maine, did he finally achieve some meaningful success as a humorist and storyteller. Now he was appearing regularly at sold-out shows all over New England as well as joining a few tours of other, more well-known, comedians.

Hayley had to admit, Jefferson was the perfect choice to appear at the Criterion, a cinema and live-show venue, a beautiful Art Deco theater built in the 1930s that was now a registered historic landmark in town.

"You have no idea the hoops I had to jump through to get him," Liddy declared, downing her champagne. "I had to deal with Jefferson's detestable hard-nosed business manager, some ornery disgusting fellow named Cal Lions. He rejected the first four offers, laughing at me as I tried negotiating with him, warning me that I was never going to be able to close the deal so I might as well give up. Every time I made a serious offer, he'd just pile on more demands, making it impossible for me to book his client."

"So how did you finally do it?"

Liddy fluttered her eyes coquettishly. "I went straight to the source. After all, I happened to be Jefferson's girlfriend during junior year in high school, if you recall."

"One of them anyway . . . *as I recall*," Randy joked, tossing the dish towel over his shoulder.

"Every girl was after him. But he chose me. Jefferson was the most handsome boy at Mount Desert Island High School."

Randy shrugged. "Really? He always looked to me like a stoned Muppet."

"Don't you have other customers to serve?" Liddy fumed.

Randy glanced around the mostly empty bar. "Nope."

Liddy ignored him and turned to Hayley. "Yesterday I finally sent Jefferson a direct message through his Instagram account and told him what I wanted and the brick wall I was running into with that hideous manager of his. Well, he responded almost immediately and said he would help me cut through the red tape, and by dinnertime last night I had booked him for our St. Patrick's Day show."

Hayley raised her champagne glass. "Liddy, that's fantastic!"

"I'm surprised he still remembers you since he's become so famous," Randy said, before noticing Liddy glaring at him. "I really can't believe I just said that out loud."

"I don't have to remind you that I am somewhat famous too, so it should come as no surprise that Jefferson still knows who I am even after all these years!"

"Actually you do have to remind me," Randy said, grinning. "How are you famous?"

"I'm quite well-known in New England real estate circles at least, and I have a handful of awards and certificates to prove it!"

"I'm sorry, Liddy, I'm just joshing you," Randy laughed. "I tell you what, to make up for my boorish behavior, why don't you let me host an after-party here at the bar following Jefferson's show?"

Liddy's whole face lit up. "Really? Are you being serious with me right now? You would do that?"

"Sure, I'll put a sign out that says CLOSED FOR PRIVATE EVENT. It can be by invitation only. I'll do a signature cocktail, maybe my Irish coffee, we'll serve some tasty appetizers, we'll make it real nice."

"Oh, Randy, how wonderful. I take back all the terrible things I've said about you over the years!"

Hayley snorted, then took one last sip of her champagne.

"And Hayley can cater it!" Liddy cried.

Hayley choked on her champagne, almost spitting it out, but then managed to swallow it. She cleared her throat. "I beg your pardon?"

"I suppose Randy could serve what's on his bar menu, but honestly, other than his fried clams, there's really not much to write home about. Your restaurant has a much better selection."

"Wow, I'm standing right here," Randy scoffed. "Can you see me? Am I invisible? Because otherwise it makes no sense that I just offered my bar for a party and you're dissing my food right in front of me."

"Your food is just fine, Randy, I promise. But let's face it, everyone in the bar is usually blotto when they eat it, so it's not exactly memorable. You can barely get a reservation at Hayley's, even in the winter, so it only makes sense that she be the one to cater the food for such a big high-profile celebrity like Jefferson."

Randy stared at her, incredulous. "It's amazing. She just keeps going on and on."

"Please, Hayley, will you do it?" Liddy begged.

"Yes, please, sis. You're our last hope to save the party from my apparently bland and boring fried appetizers!" Randy said with a healthy dose of snark.

"Things are pretty busy at the restaurant. The staff is so overworked as it is, I'm not sure I can ask them to help me with this party too."

Liddy shrugged. "You can always hire some temporary help. There are countless people in this town looking for part-time work. And don't worry. I will help out moneywise so you don't get stuck paying for everything."

There really was no way for Hayley to squirm out of this one, and so she simply nodded as Liddy called for another bottle of champagne before remembering the cheap brand and then requesting a simple Pinot Grigio.

That evening, after she and Bruce arrived home from dinner at the restaurant, Hayley emailed her replacement as office manager at the *Island Times* an advertisement she wanted put up on the website and for the next issue of the newspaper. She was looking to fill three temporary positions to help plan, organize, and work a very special St. Patrick's Day private party in honor of Jefferson O'Keefe, whose show had already sold out by the time she started meeting with prospective employees two days later.

Although her restaurant manager, Betty, and her chef, Kelton, had both kindly offered their time and services, Hayley stressed to them that they could best help her by keeping things running smoothly at Hayley's Kitchen. Instead, she lucked out during her first round of interviews, hiring her three local helpers on the spot in one afternoon. There was seventeen-year-old high school student Cody, an aspiring chef, who had impressed Hayley with a series of YouTube videos he made in his mother's kitchen that had already amassed quite an impressive following. He could help with the cooking. Then there was a retired grandmother and self-proclaimed Jefferson O'Keefe superfan, Mabel, who had spent years on the janitorial staff at an assisted-living facility just out of town. She could help with the cleanup. And finally, there was Cassie, a cashier at a chain store, Cost-Less, looking for something more exciting to do in her life. Working a private party where the guest of honor was a famous comedian definitely fit the bill. In her words, "Walking around with a plate of canapés at a fancy party is certainly more appealing than doing a price check on toilet paper." Hayley had liked her immediately. In fact, she liked them all. And with her temporary staff in place, it was time to start planning the menu, consulting with Liddy who remarkably had a clear memory of all of Jefferson O'Keefe's favorite foods.

Chapter Two

When Hayley breezed through the front door of Liddy's real estate office, ready to get her approval on the final party menu, she was suddenly taken aback by a man's booming angry voice shouting at the top of his lungs.

"What kind of amateur operation are you running here, Miss Crawford? We have a contract, and if you can't meet the requirements set forth, then you're in breach and we can just go home!"

"Your client showed up two days earlier than expected, Mr. Lions," Liddy growled.

"He wanted to spend time with his family before the concert. You should know he has a few cousins who still live in Bar Harbor," the man huffed.

Hayley remained in the small reception area. Liddy's assistant was obviously out to lunch. She didn't want to eavesdrop, but the door to Liddy's office was open halfway so there was no avoiding it.

"Well, nobody bothered to tell *me*. I wasn't prepared."

"A good concert producer learns to anticipate any scenario and is always ready for it!"

"Well, excuse me, Mr. Lions, but I'm not exactly used to booking A-list acts at the Criterion. This isn't Madison Square Garden. I'm not dealing with Beyoncé or Adele or Ed Sheeran, and let's face it, your client is not on *that* level!"

"You better watch what you say, Miss Crawford, because I am well within my rights to walk away right now, leaving you high and dry tomorrow night."

"Are you threatening me?" Liddy gasped.

"All I'm saying is, you should really start to think about meeting the demands of our rider as soon as possible or risk having an empty stage for your St. Patrick's Day show."

"I have tried making sure everything you requested was in the hotel room when I got word at the last minute that Jefferson was arriving early."

"You obviously didn't try hard enough. There were only six bottles of still water at room temperature, not twelve per the contract."

"That's an easy fix. I can bring over more—"

"I'm not finished! There was no assortment of chewing gum, no box of toothpicks as requested, and no hot sauce for his food. He likes to douse his food with a lot of spice!"

"But I *did* put a bottle of hot sauce in his room!"

"Tabasco, yes. But we specifically asked for Dirty Dick's because it was developed by a Massachusetts horticulturist and former competitive BBQ cook who also happens to be a friend of Mr. O'Keefe's."

"How was I supposed to know that?" Liddy sighed.

"You could have just reviewed the contract. It's right there in plain black and white!"

"Forgive me for thinking a hot sauce is just a hot sauce!"

"I have just sent you an email with all items in the rider that are currently missing. I will give you until three o'clock this afternoon to get everything to Mr. O'Keefe's hotel room or we are out of here. Understood?"

There was a long painful pause before Hayley could hear Liddy uncharacteristically mutter in a defeated tone, "Yes."

Hayley took a step back as the man marched out of Liddy's office. He was balding with a bulbous nose, a bit heavy, but full of pentup energy as he barely acknowledged Hayley with a nod and stormed out the door. Hayley watched him hustling across the street to his parked Porsche before poking her head in Liddy's office to see her at her desk, her head buried in her hands.

"Well, he certainly seems like a breath of fresh air," Hayley cracked.

Liddy raised her head, grimacing. "I had no idea what I was getting into when I hired Jefferson. They arrived yesterday and it's been unbearable ever since, one complaint after another."

"Is it Jefferson? Or his business manager?"

Liddy shrugged. "I'm not sure. I haven't even seen Jefferson yet. I've just been constantly harassed by that awful ogre Cal Lions! But I have to assume Jefferson must feel the same way."

"Not necessarily. Where's he staying?"

"At the Cleftstone Manor. They're usually closed for the season but they opened back up just for Jefferson. He and his entourage are their only guests."

"Hey. We're old friends with Jefferson. There is no rule that says we can't stop by his room and say hello. And as the chairman of the Criterion Theatre entertainment committee, it's also incumbent upon you to personally welcome him."

"You're right. I want to see for myself whether or not fame has really gone to his head!"

When Liddy drove them to the Cleftstone in her Mercedes, she confessed to having butterflies in her stomach about a reunion with Jefferson. She wasn't sure what to expect. But she needn't have worried because when the manager of the Cleftstone called Jefferson's room to announce who was at the front desk, they were immediately escorted to the most expensive deluxe estate room, the Joseph Pulitzer, where he was staying. After the manager knocked lightly on the door, it immediately flung open and Jefferson whooped with delight at the sight of Liddy, grabbing her in a big bear hug. He did the same with Hayley.

"How nice of you two to stop by and say hello!" Jefferson said, smiling sweetly. "I was going to try and get in touch with you today before meeting up with my cousins, but here you are! You haven't changed a bit, Liddy. You're just as gorgeous as ever."

Liddy blushed. "Oh, you were always such a smooth talker, Jefferson. Stop it. Actually don't stop. I have no idea why I even said that!"

He turned to Hayley. "And I hear you married Bruce Linney? You two were like oil and water back in high school!"

"I never would've believed it myself," Hayley chuckled.

Liddy tried to adopt a more serious tone. "Jefferson, the reason we dropped by, besides officially welcoming you to town, of course, is that I may have dropped the ball on a few of the items in your rider. . . ."

"And Cal is playing hardball?" Jefferson asked.

Liddy nodded. "I'm working as hard as I can to make sure you have everything you want, but this is a small town and our stores can have a very limited supply—"

"I grew up here, remember? I know you might have to find a few substitutions. Don't sweat it."

"It's just that Cal is making it very difficult—"

Jefferson placed his hands on Liddy's shoulders. "I'll talk to him and get him to lay off, okay? You have enough on your plate getting everything ready for tomorrow night."

"I will try my best to get everything possible. . . ."

"Forget the rider. That's for the bigger venues, not my hometown theater. I should've told Cal to scratch all those demands from the outset. I just need one thing."

Liddy braced herself. "What?"

"You," he said with a wink. "I haven't seen you since high school. We have a lot of catching up to do. I'm having dinner with my cousins at McKay's at six. Why don't you stop by here for a drink afterward, say around nine?" He suddenly noticed Hayley standing right there in front of him. "Oh, and you too, if you want, Hayley. And Bruce, of course."

She knew he was just being polite.

He was much more interested in some alone time with Liddy.

"Thank you, but no. I have too much work to do preparing for the after-party. I will have to take a rain check."

She could see the relief on both their faces.

Liddy checked her watch. "I have a showing in twenty minutes. I better get going. I will see you this evening, Jefferson."

He gave her a warm, inviting smile. "Looking forward to it, beautiful."

Liddy turned to Hayley. "Let's meet at Drinks Like A Fish first thing tomorrow morning to discuss the final menu."

"But I need you to sign off today so I can go shopping for all the ingredients I need. . . ."

"We don't have to discuss this in front of Jefferson. It's time to go, Hayley," Liddy chirped.

They said their goodbyes and hurried back outside the Cleftstone to Liddy's car.

"Drinks in his room at nine o'clock? You know what that means, don't you, Liddy?"

"Yes. Two friends having an innocent drink and talking about old times."

"There is nothing innocent about it and you know it! Are you sure this is a good idea? He's only in town for a couple of days and I don't want to see you getting hurt."

"Hayley, I appreciate your concern, but you have nothing to worry about. Despite how incredibly handsome he still is, not to mention charming, and sweet, and did you get a look at those muscles? What was I saying? Oh, right! Despite all that, I have no intention of rekindling *anything*."

"I don't believe you."

"You're my best friend! You *have* to believe me!"

"Well, I don't."

"Why not?"

"Because you always say that right before you go to bed with one of your old boyfriends!"

Liddy took a deep breath and exhaled. "Read my lips. I am *not* going to bed with Jefferson O'Keefe."

The following morning, at nine o'clock, a half hour later than when Hayley and Liddy had agreed to meet at Drinks Like A Fish, Liddy Crawford burst through the door and declared, "I went to bed with Jefferson O'Keefe!"

She did not get the reaction she had expected from the only two people in the bar—Hayley on her stool and Randy behind the bar polishing shot glasses. Mostly because neither of them was even remotely surprised.

"Well, aren't you even going to ask how it happened?" Liddy huffed.

"Why? We know how it happened," Hayley said flatly. "You went to his room for a drink, you shared memories from high school, and then . . ." She turned to Randy. "Should we say it together?"

Randy nodded and then in unison they both crowed, "One thing led to another."

Michelle, Randy's devoted bar manager, wandered out of the kitchen after hearing voices. Michelle had started out as a waitress, but was sharp and good with the customers, and had a business administration degree so she could help out paying the vendors and keeping the books. Randy quickly had promoted her to manager. She was also easy on the eyes with her stunning dark features and long raven hair, so the local fishermen, who made up a good chunk of Randy's clientele, certainly appreciated her presence.

Michelle went to pour herself a glass of soda from the fountain. "Whatever you all are talking about sure sounds juicy!"

"Liddy slept with an old high school boyfriend last night," Randy said. "I will give you a hint. He's sort of famous."

Michelle curiously cocked an eyebrow. "I'm a terrible guesser. Plus I'm ten years younger than all of you, so I hardly know anyone in your graduating class."

"Jefferson O'Keefe," Randy said.

Michelle's hand continued gripping the fountain lever and sticky soda began pouring over the sides of her glass and onto her hand. She quickly dropped the glass and it clattered into the metal sink. She snatched up a towel to wipe off her hand.

Randy noticed her fumbling.

Her face was ashen.

Randy put a hand on her arm. "Michelle, is everything all right?"

"Yes, yes, I'm fine. Excuse me!"

Clearly upset, her eyes brimming with tears that she tried to hide by quickly turning away from them, Michelle suddenly fled back into the kitchen, leaving Hayley, Randy, and Liddy staring at each other, utterly dumbfounded.

Chapter Three

Before Hayley, Liddy, or Randy had time to re-act to Michelle's dramatic exit, the door to the bar burst open and Cal Lions roared in, red-faced, eyes bulging out, and as Bruce often liked to say about his boss at the paper, the short-tempered Sal Moretti, "You could almost see the steam coming out of his ears!" He charged up to Liddy, poked a pudgy finger in her face, and screamed, "What the hell did you say to my client?"

Liddy, feigning ignorance, stared at him doe-eyed and gave a slight shrug. "I am sure I have no idea what you are talking about." She then turned and smirked at Hayley and Randy, which unfortu-nately was not lost on Cal.

"Don't give me that innocent look. I know you went behind my back and complained about me!"

"How did you even know I was here?" Liddy asked.

"I showed up at your real estate office and your secretary told me where you were! A cheap, dingy bar in the middle of the morning! Color me surprised!"

Randy held up a finger. "I can live with cheap—our prices are very reasonable—but *not* dingy! I have been here since six this morning cleaning tables and mopping the floor."

Cal ignored him, his blazing eyes focused squarely on Liddy. "Imagine my shock when I showed up at Jefferson's room at the Cleftstone this morning to go over the rest of the summer's touring schedule, and before I even had a chance to take one sip of my Bloody Mary, he told me in no uncertain terms that if I didn't shape up, I was out. At first I thought he was making a wisecrack about my weight. I've told him a hundred times I'm way too busy managing his career to spend much time at the gym, but then I realized it wasn't about my size at all. *You* had somehow gotten to him!"

"I can't imagine it had anything to do with me. I haven't seen Jefferson since high school," Liddy declared, coquettishly batting her eyes, relishing every moment of Cal Lions's obvious discomfort.

Sweat beads started dribbling down both of Cal's rosy round cheeks. "Don't play games with me, Miss Crawford! I saw the look on Jefferson's face when he opened the door to let me in. I'm *very* familiar with that look."

"And what look would that be, Cal?" Liddy asked innocently.

"You know the one I'm talking about! The flushed

face, the constant grinning, the strutting around like a rooster! And then, on top of all that, there was the faint odor of perfume in the air . . ." He took a step closer to Liddy, breathing in a big whiff. "Exactly like the one I can smell on you right now!"

As hard as she tried, Liddy could not stop herself from emitting a girlish giggle, which only managed to further enrage Cal Lions.

"I'm warning you, Miss Crawford, Jefferson O'Keefe is my biggest client. I cannot afford to lose him, so I'm warning you right now, I will not stand for you causing a rift between us and turning him against me!"

Liddy folded her arms. "If that's the case, then my advice to you, Mr. Lions, is perhaps you should stop being rude and yelling at the one person he appears to trust . . . intimately."

Cal sputtered a bit, realizing she had a point, and then he spun around and stormed back out the door.

Liddy turned to Hayley and Randy, an ebullient, triumphant look on her face. "I can't see how this day could get any better. See you kids later. I have some work to do at the office and then I'm meeting Jefferson for lunch." She floated out the door as if on a cloud.

"I'm going to go check on Michelle," Randy said, heading for the kitchen.

Hayley followed behind him through the swinging doors where they found Michelle dabbing at her cheeks with a dishrag.

"Michelle, what's wrong?"

She slowly turned around, slightly startled that Hayley was there as well as her boss.

"N-nothing," she sputtered.

"Come on. We've known each other too long. I know when something's bothering you. Does it have anything to do with Jefferson O'Keefe?"

She hesitated, keeping one eye on Hayley, and then shook her head. "No, why would you say that?"

"You seemed to get upset when Liddy mentioned that she had spent the evening with him at the Cleftstone."

"That's *not* the reason!" Michelle insisted.

"Then what?" Randy pressed.

Michelle motioned with her head toward Hayley. "It's her."

Hayley gasped. "*Me?* What did I do?"

"When I heard Randy offer to host the after-party, I was hoping he might hire me to do the catering."

"Oh, Michelle," Randy moaned. "I am so sorry. I didn't even think about . . ."

"It's okay. I know I don't have a lot of experience," she whispered, eyes downcast.

"Michelle, I didn't even know you had your own catering company," Hayley said.

"I don't. Not really. But Randy knows it's been a lifelong dream of mine and I've been working really hard trying to perfect a few signature recipes."

Randy turned to Hayley. "She practices here in the kitchen all the time. She's really good. I've gained ten pounds since she started."

Hayley felt terrible. "Michelle, if I had known

you wanted to do it, I never would have accepted the gig when Liddy asked me to take it on. I only said yes because I knew Liddy would never take no for an answer."

"It's okay. I'm sorry I even said anything. There will be other parties. Besides, I'm sure I couldn't do as good a job as you anyway," Michelle said, resigned.

"Nonsense! Let me talk to Liddy. I'm sure she won't mind you taking over. And I know you will do a bang-up job."

Michelle lit up. "Really?"

"Absolutely. It's done."

"This is so exciting! My first job as a professional caterer. Oh my God, there is so much to do. I need to put together the menu, shop for the food, call all my friends who I promised I would hire as cater waiters." She glanced over at her boss. "Randy, I'm going to need the rest of the day off, tomorrow too. You'll be okay running things on your own, right?"

Before he could answer, she bolted out of the kitchen.

"Are you sure Liddy is going to be okay with a last-minute switch with the catering?"

"No. I mean, come on, it's Liddy. She'll explode, but I'm hoping the mitigating factors will help alleviate the level of her freak-out."

"What mitigating factors?"

"Jefferson O'Keefe, for one," she said with a wink. "As long as he's around, she won't stay mad about anything for too long." Hayley checked the time on her phone and groaned.

"What now?" Randy asked.

"I just remembered I'm meeting my new catering staff at the restaurant in ten minutes to go over the plan for the after-party. I just hired them and now I have to fire them."

"Maybe Michelle could use them."

"No, you heard her. She's got her own people in mind. I'm sure they'll understand."

Hayley was right.

They did understand.

When she arrived to find all three of them, high school chef Cody, retired grandmother Mabel, and Cost-Less cashier Cassie waiting for her in the parking lot of Hayley's Kitchen, she immediately felt guilty for wasting their time. She invited them inside where she served them key lime pie and coffee and regrettably explained the whole situation. All of them were visibly disappointed, but none of them could argue with Hayley's compassionate reason for stepping away from the catering gig.

"I promise you, when something like this comes up again, and I'm sure it will, you will be my first three calls."

"When will that be? I'm eighty-six," Mabel cracked.

Hayley guffawed. "Soon, Mabel. But I'm not worried because I have a feeling you're going to outlive us all."

"Don't wait too long, Hayley," Cody said. "Pretty soon you won't be able to afford me."

"I have no doubt about that, Cody," Hayley chuckled.

"I'm going to stick around just so I can have

more of this key lime pie. It's out of this world, Hayley," Cassie gushed.

"Mine's better," Cody sniffed.

They all laughed, and Hayley had a strong feeling that although she had just lost a catering gig for a famous stand-up comedian, she had most likely gained three new good friends.

Chapter Four

Later that afternoon at Hayley's Kitchen, as her staff prepared to open for the dinner rush, Hayley sat in her office going over the previous evening's receipts on her computer when she received a frantic call from Liddy.

"You will not believe the day I've had," Liddy cried.

"I'm a little busy right now. We're just about to open and Betty overbooked—"

Liddy did not seem at all interested in hearing about Hayley's problems at the moment and just plowed full steam ahead. "I am close to closing escrow on a house and suddenly at the last minute the buyers want to pull out after an inspection turned up an electrical issue in one of the guest rooms! It's a five-hundred-thousand-dollar house and they're worried about something that will cost two hundred bucks to fix! I tried to explain it to them—I even offered to pay for the repair my-self—but now they're worried there are more problems we're not being up-front about. They're being totally ridiculous!"

"I understand your frustration, Liddy, but—"

"So I'm stuck out here in Salisbury Cove trying to reason with these people, when I am supposed to be at the Criterion overseeing the dress rehearsal. Can you do me a huge favor and scoot over there and check things out, make sure there are no fires I need to put out."

"Liddy, I'm working—"

"Hayley, please! You have an entire staff at your beck and call. I'm sure the restaurant won't go under if you're gone for a quick ten minutes."

Liddy apparently had no clue the monumental effort it took to run a restaurant. But if it wasn't about Liddy, then it was rarely on her radar.

Hayley sighed. "Fine. But I'm just going to go over there and make sure everything's running smoothly, and then I need to come right back to the restaurant, okay?"

"You're a lifesaver! I owe you!"

"You say that every time you ask me to do some-thing. I have a whole book of IOUs from you," Hayley said, pausing, waiting for a reply, but Liddy had already hung up.

She chuckled to herself, then walked out of her office to the kitchen where Kelton was busy whip-ping up a big batch of tonight's special risotto be-fore heading out into the dining room where her waitstaff were setting the tables and Betty, with fur-rowed brows and a drooping frown, tried figuring out the reservation situation.

"Hold down the fort, Betty. I'll be right back!"

Before Betty could protest, Hayley was out the door, greeting a large group of diners already lined up and waiting to get inside. Once she was clear of her customers, she jumped in her car and sped over to the Criterion Theatre, parking out front and waving at the elderly woman in the glass booth whom they'd hired to sell tickets.

Inside the lobby, Hayley heard loud music coming from the theater. She recognized the voice. It was Frankie Beauchemin, a local folk singer who had been tapped to perform as Jefferson O'Keefe's opening act. He had a lot of fans locally, but not Hayley. She thought he sounded like a caterwauling cat, screeching every note. She winced as he hit a high note and she fought the urge to cover her ears. The boy behind the concession stand told her she could find Jefferson backstage, so Hayley bypassed the theater to avoid having to get any closer to Frankie's shrill, deafening voice and scurried down a hall to a door that led backstage.

"Hi, Hayley, what brings you here?"

Hayley turned to discover Toby Jenkins, a local woman who had been just a few years behind her in school. Toby was what you might call a Jill-of-all-trades between raising five rambunctious kids on her own, offering psychic readings, belly dancing on the weekends at a Middle Eastern restaurant in Ellsworth, and also working as the official entertainment photographer at the *Island Times*, no doubt here to capture some exclusive behind-the-scenes photos for the paper.

"I'm just here to make sure everyone's happy," Hayley shouted over Frankie's painful warbling.

Toby gestured toward a corner while snapping away with her tiny digital camera. "Everything was peachy keen until a few minutes ago, but then *she* showed up."

Hayley looked over to see Michelle, again near tears, having an intense, serious discussion with Jefferson. He had a tortured look on his face, as if he was wishing he was anywhere else, speaking with her rather sternly as far as Hayley could tell.

"What's going on with those two?" Hayley shouted just as Frankie finished his dress rehearsal and stopped singing. Her voice carried through the entire backstage area, directing everyone's attention toward her.

Michelle instinctively knew Hayley had been referring to her and Jefferson, which just made her even more visibly emotional.

Jefferson signaled his bodyguard, a big, burly, bearded man with a shaved head, who was introduced to everybody as Bear, desperate for him to intervene. Bear ambled over, inserting his expansive jiggly belly between Michelle and Jefferson. "Sorry, ma'am, Jefferson's gotta do his sound check."

"But we're not done talking," Michelle pleaded.

Jefferson turned and walked away toward the stage as Michelle tried to chase after him, but Bear managed to block her path with his massive body like the Great Wall of China.

"I'm afraid you are, ma'am," he said firmly, holding up a giant paw that could cover a grown-man's whole face.

Michelle shrank back, sniffing back her tears as Bear stood guard, making sure she didn't try and make a run for it onto the stage where Jefferson was already testing his microphone.

Toby was thrilled to have recorded the whole ugly scene with her camera and was now euphorically swiping through all the photos.

As Michelle rushed for the door that led back out to the lobby, Hayley intercepted her. "Michelle, what's wrong? Why are you so upset?"

"It's nothing," Michelle said, brushing her off.

"It didn't look like nothing," Hayley said.

Michelle took a moment to gather her thoughts, and then said dismissively, "He's just being difficult about my menu for the party. You know how these celebrities can get. Don't worry. I'll figure it out." That's all Michelle was willing to give up. She then pushed past Hayley. "I need to go. I obviously have a lot of work to do."

Hayley hung back, perplexed. Michelle's explanation struck her as odd. Jefferson O'Keefe did not appear to Hayley as a diva who would care what kind of food was going to be served at his after-party. In fact, when Hayley had agreed to cater, Liddy had told her his only request was to make sure his favorite St. Patrick's Day drink was available, traditional Irish coffee, and also his favorite beer, Goose Island County Stout, on tap or in a bottle, it didn't matter. The whole rider controversy was mostly his manager, Cal Lions, throwing his weight around. This made no sense. Unless Michelle was lying about what had really transpired between them.

Other than this little wrinkle, the dress rehearsal was going off without a hitch, and so Hayley drove back to her restaurant, texting Liddy that everything was under control and she had nothing to worry about.

That lasted until the following morning.

The day of the performance.

Hayley was still in bed when her phone buzzed. Bruce, on his side, mumbling in his sleep, grabbed a fistful of the covers and yanked them toward him, leaving Hayley completely exposed to the unusually chilly morning air, even for March. She swung her legs out and planted them on the floor and picked up her phone.

It was Liddy.

Something in her gut told her this could not be good.

She answered the call. "Good morning, Liddy."

"There is nothing good about it! In fact, this whole day is already a complete disaster!"

"And it's only seven-fifteen in the morning. What's wrong?"

"Michelle is sick."

"What do you mean 'sick'?"

"Sick! She's sick! She's fallen ill! She's in bed and she's not getting out, so we have no one to cater the party, which is in less than fourteen hours."

"What do you want me to do?" Hayley asked, although she already knew the answer coming.

"I need you to fill in and cater the party!"

"That's asking a lot! I have nothing prepared, I already let my staff go, I haven't even run my menu by Jefferson—"

"Jefferson couldn't care less about what food you serve as long as the Goose Island and Irish coffees are flowing!"

Confirmation that Michelle was not being truthful about why she had been so upset the day before.

"Please, Hayley, you *have* to do this! There is no one else! I never should have allowed you to let Michelle take over in the first place! I knew that was going to be a huge mistake, and now look where we are!"

Liddy was the queen of "I told you so," but she did have a point. In a way, it was Hayley's fault they were in this mess, and so she could not very well leave Liddy high and dry.

"Okay, I'll do it."

"Love you, mean it, I have to run!"

Hayley set her phone down on the nightstand next to her side of the bed and sighed.

"Do what?" Bruce mumbled from underneath the covers.

"You don't even want to know."

The rest of the day was going to be backbreaking.

But Hayley just put her head down and went to work.

Her first order of business was calling her party staff, Cody, Mabel, and Cassie, and begging them to drop what they were doing and come help her. Cody was on spring vacation from MDI and had nothing else to do, retired Mabel also had all the time in the world, and Cassie, who had been scheduled to work today, was able to switch shifts with a co-worker at the last minute. They all met Hayley at Drinks Like A Fish by nine o'clock that morning. Hayley, armed with an extensive shopping list, began the Herculean task of cooking for

the party, which was now only twelve hours away.
There were many points during the day when she
strongly believed they would never be ready, especially after burning her first batch of stuffed mush-
rooms. But with Randy's help, and her three
hardworking new friends, they managed, against
all odds, to be ready by nine o'clock that night just
as Jefferson O'Keefe wrapped up his stand-up routine to thunderous applause across the street at
the Criterion Theatre.

Hayley watched through the large picture window of the bar as the doors to the theater flew
open and the happy crowd poured out into the
street, the lucky invited few making their way to
the bar for the private after-party.

Hayley smiled, secure in the knowledge that she
had averted disaster.

Nothing else could possibly go wrong tonight.

Famous last words.

Chapter Five

As the invited guests quickly filled up the bar, awaiting the imminent arrival of Jefferson O'Keefe, Hayley could not help but marvel at her crackerjack staff hard at work. Mabel and Cassie were making the rounds with trays of Hayley's bite-size appetizers, such as her perennial staples, Sweet Potato Crostini with Prosciutto Honey-Roasted Figs, Jalapeño Popper Cheese Balls with Bacon and Chives, and her personal favorite, Spinach and Ricotta Puff Pastries. Meanwhile, Randy manned the bar, serving drinks, and Cody stayed in the kitchen keeping an eye on the mini mushroom tarts baking in the oven and replenishing the serving trays just as soon as Mabel and Cassie brought them back empty. Hayley was about to relax knowing she had pulled off the nearly impossible when she suddenly heard a commotion at the door to the bar. Liddy was yelling at someone, but

Hayley couldn't hear what she was saying over the din of the crowd. She weaved her way over, plucking a cheese ball off Mabel's tray as she passed by until she could make out the man Liddy was so apparently angry with—Colin Doyle. Hayley knew him well. Born in Rhode Island, he quickly rose in the ranks of Northeast nightclub comedians with his offbeat take on life in New England, scoring a record deal for a comedy album and appearing as one of the contestants on *Last Comic Standing* during its final season. He was arguably more popular and successful than his fellow performer Jefferson O'Keefe, but Hayley had heard through the grapevine that Colin still considered him a threat. So it was a surprise to see him here in Bar Harbor trying to bully his way past Liddy into a private party for his chief rival.

"You need to leave right now! You are not on the guest list!" Liddy shouted.

"Come on, lady, most of the people here would be thrilled to have me here! I'm a celebrity!"

"D list, at best," Liddy snorted.

Colin's cheeks reddened and he gruffly tried to push past Liddy, who tried to hold him back.

Hayley was about to intervene when suddenly Jefferson's roadie and best bud, Bear, appeared, protectively stepping in front of Liddy where he towered over the much more diminutive Irish leprechaun Colin Doyle.

"You heard the lady. You're not welcome here. Out!" Bear growled.

Sizing Bear up and realizing he did not stand a chance if things ramped up and got physical, Colin finally backed off, spinning on his heel and stomping off into the night as Toby Jenkins nimbly recorded it all with her digital camera.

"Thank you, Bear. You're a lifesaver," Liddy cooed, trying to plant a kiss on his cheek, but he was just way too tall. When he finally got the message, he politely bent down so she could give him a smooch.

"Can I get you something to drink? A beer maybe?" Liddy asked.

Bear shook his head. "I'll wait for Jefferson to get here, but thanks, doll." He took the iPad with the guest list from Liddy and glanced out the window to see Colin pacing up and down the sidewalk across the street. "I'm going to stay here and keep an eye on the door to make sure that idiot doesn't try to sneak back in again."

Hayley made her way up to Liddy. "What was all that about?"

"Colin Doyle bought a front-row seat and started heckling Jefferson during his set. I was backstage and missed most of it. But apparently things got pretty tense, although I heard Jefferson handled it well and even got a few laughs at Colin's expense, which probably didn't go over very well with Colin. Anyway, he tried to slip past me, I'm sure to try and embarrass Jefferson some more when he gets here, but luckily thanks to Bear, that won't be happening on my watch."

"Why is he being such a jerk?"

"He's mad that we booked Jefferson and not him."

"I don't understand why that would bother him. We're small potatoes. The Criterion isn't exactly

Radio City Music Hall. And he's got a bigger career than Jefferson."

"Bigger career maybe, but a much smaller man. He's very petty."

"But this is Jefferson's hometown."

"It doesn't matter. He's so competitive, he can't stand the fact that Jefferson was our first choice, so he decided to come here and take him down a peg. Jefferson just booked the Comedy Cellar in New York; his career is starting to eclipse Colin's and it's driving him mad. At least that's what Jefferson told me . . . during pillow talk."

A silly giggle escaped from Liddy's lips.

"Excuse me, I work here," a voice announced near the front door. It was Michelle, trying to squeeze past Bear who was staring at the iPad.

"Sorry, but I don't see your name on the list."

"It's all right, Bear. You can let her in," Hayley said.

Bear stepped aside, allowing Michelle to slip past the human brick wall.

Hayley noticed that Michelle had spruced herself up with some makeup and was looking healthy. "Feeling better?"

"Much. Thank you for asking. I was sitting at home feeling perfectly normal so I figured I would stop by and see if you needed any help."

"I think we've pretty much got everything covered. What was wrong with you?"

Michelle shrugged. "It was just a stomach thing."

"Well, you look great," Liddy piped in. "I love that shade of eyeshadow on you. It's very becoming."

"Thank you." Michelle beamed before turning serious. "Liddy, would you mind if I had a word with Hayley privately?"

"No, of course not. You've inspired me to do a little primping myself before Jefferson gets here. I'll be in the ladies' room if you need me."

She dashed off, leaving Hayley with Michelle.

"I just wanted to apologize for the way I acted before. I don't know what was going on with me."

"You have nothing to apologize for. It's been a very stressful time trying to pull all of this together."

"I really do want to help out. Isn't there anything you can think of that I can do?"

Hayley thought about it and nodded. "Actually, there is. Jefferson should be here any second, so when he gets here I need someone to start serving our signature drink."

"The Irish coffees?"

"Yes, they're in the kitchen."

Suddenly the front door swung open and Jefferson made his grand entrance to warm applause from the guests.

"What does a guy have to do to get a drink around here?" Jefferson joked.

"Perfect timing," Hayley said.

"I'll go get started," Michelle said, scooting into the kitchen as Randy raced around from behind the bar and handed Jefferson a bottle of Goose Island.

Michelle reappeared moments later with a full tray of Irish coffees and started offering them to all the guests. Cassie followed suit, but Mabel came storming out of the kitchen empty-handed and marched over to Hayley. "I just caught Cody trying to sneak a sip of Irish coffee! He's barely seventeen!"

"I'll go talk to him. Just make sure everyone gets a coffee; Jefferson wants to make a toast," Hayley said, filling a glass of root beer from the fountain and taking it into the kitchen where she found a pouting Cody taking the mushroom tarts out of the oven, his hands in oven mitts. He had a guilty look on his face.

Cody sighed. "She told you, didn't she? It's just coffee."

"Irish coffee is not just coffee. That's where the *Irish* comes in."

"What am I supposed to drink during the toast?"

She handed him a root beer. "Problem solved. And don't try anything like that again. I am technically responsible for you, and I am not going to have you going home to your parents tipsy on whiskey."

"Fine." Cody sighed again.

Hayley started to leave but stopped and turned back around. "By the way, you're doing a great job. I can't wait for the day I turn on the Food Network to watch you with your own cooking show and I can say I knew you when."

That cheered him up.

Then she dashed back out of the kitchen to find Jefferson now standing on top of a table as all the party guests gathered around, everyone holding a glass mug of Irish coffee. She found herself standing next to a wobbly Cal, clutching his Irish coffee, staring intensely at Jefferson who had already begun his toast to Bar Harbor for being so warm and welcoming upon his return to his hometown, singling out Liddy for making it happen and all her hard work. He then went on to thank Hayley and her staff, and especially Randy for hosting, also the entertainment committee and the Criterion Theatre. He then paused, staring down at his Irish coffee.

"Did I forget anybody?"

Hayley gave Cal a sideways glance.

His whole body tensed.

"Wait, of course, sorry . . ."

Cal relaxed a bit and smiled.

"My best friend and partner in crime, Bear, who keeps me sane as we travel all over the country putting on shows! Love ya, buddy!"

Cal tensed up again and stared daggers at Jefferson.

Jefferson turned to the right to show off to the crowd the green shamrock tattoo emblazoned on his left bicep visible to everyone because he was wearing a red flannel shirt with the sleeves cut off. "I got this to commemorate my family heritage in honor of this special St. Patrick's Day. May we all be blessed with the luck of the Irish!" And with that, Jefferson raised his glass mug of Irish coffee and gulped it down as did everyone else in the bar. Randy played the Irish pub staple "The Wild Rover" by the Dubliners on the jukebox and everyone started dancing as Jefferson tapped his foot to the beat on the tabletop before stopping suddenly and

raising a hand to his throat. He stood there, a confused, frightened look on his face, then began chok-
ing. Before anyone had time to react, he tumbled
off the table onto the floor, facedown. The entire
room fell silent.

Bear rushed over and grabbed Jefferson's wrist,
desperately feeling for a pulse. Then, with an an-
guished look, he cried out, "He's dead!"

Island Food & Spirits
by
Hayley Powell

Recently, Mona, Liddy, and I were sitting around Liddy's kitchen table enjoying a couple of Irish Mudslides that Liddy had concocted for one of our many girls' night get-togethers where we catch each other up about our week.

I had been toying around with a couple of new dinner-special ideas for St. Patrick's Day at the restaurant and was asking the girls what they thought about them when Liddy mentioned that she had seen a new Irish onion soup recipe that she thought she might like to try to make the next time we got together.

Well, you would have thought Mona and I had both just been shot out of a cannon because we jumped up so fast, screaming in unison "No!"

Liddy looked at us both, rolled her eyes, and said rather haughtily, "Good Lord, a person burns one dinner and you both think I should be banned from cooking for life!"

Rendered speechless by Liddy's announcement, Mona and I just gaped at Liddy in utter disbelief as she shrugged her shoulders and continued sipping her Irish Mudslide.

I was dumbfounded. Had she honestly forgotten what had transpired a few years back on another night just like this evening when it was her turn to host the dinner, cocktails, and a night of juicy gossip?

Liddy had never been much of a cook, which we had all learned the hard way with a few cases of food poisoning, a series of unexplained upset stomachs, and quite a few burnt meals. So when Liddy suggested that perhaps she should order out when it was her turn, Mona and I were quick to sign on to that particular plan.

Cooking was just not in Liddy's wheelhouse. But on the other hand, she did get huge points for her delicious cocktail recipes, so essentially it was a "win-win" for all of us.

When Liddy's night finally rolled around, I was waiting for Mona to pick me up in her truck, when she called and said she was running a little late since she was stuck at her seafood shop waiting for a customer to pick up an order. I decided to wait for Mona on my deck since it was so lovely outside, and soon found myself dozing off in the warm setting sun. All of a sudden, I was jolted awake by the loud roar of an engine screaming down my street followed by the ear-splitting squealing of tires!

I jumped up to see what in the world was going on and saw Mona's truck screeching to a halt in my driveway. She yelled for me to hurry and jump in because she had just heard on her police scanner that there was a fire at Liddy's house! As I ran to hop in the passenger's side of Mona's pickup, she was already squealing out of my driveway in reverse while I frantically tried to fasten my seat belt, knowing it was going to be a bumpy hell-raising ride the whole way.

I kept firing off questions to Mona. How did the fire start? Was Liddy in the house at the time? Mona shook her head and said that all she heard was the dispatcher relaying Liddy's address over the police scanner and the word *Fire!* After that, she just ran out of her shop, leaving her last customer of the day staring blankly after her as she jumped in her truck and drove as fast as she could over to my house.

My heart was racing as I frantically tried calling Liddy's cell while Mona broke all speed limits as we raced along Route 3 out of town toward Liddy's house.

Just then, I heard a siren wailing behind us and I turned around. My heart sank as I spotted a police car, its blue light flashing, racing to catch up to us. I begged Mona to stop, but she refused and kept her eyes fixed on the road, determined to get to Liddy's.

I glanced back out the rear window again and the police car was now so close, I could make out the grim face of Sergio, my brother-in-law, behind the wheel. I started to panic, knowing there was no way we were going to talk our way out of a ticket especially driving at this speed! We might even be arrested and face the humiliation of seeing our names in the crime section of the very newspaper where I worked!

Then, all of a sudden, we were blessed with a miracle. The police car pulled out around us, passed us, and went racing on ahead. I exhaled a huge sigh of relief, but Mona, eyes bugged out, was mumbling, "This isn't good, Hayley, not good at all!"

I looked ahead in the distance to see smoke billowing up into the sky from what had to be Liddy's house! Finally, after what seemed like an eternity, but in reality was probably only three or four minutes, we pulled off the main road and down the gravel path a short distance to her house.

Mona and I vaulted out of the truck and ran toward the house. Outside were several fire trucks and police cars, and when I spotted an ambulance, my eyes welled up with tears. I grabbed a fistful of Mona's sweatshirt, and we pushed our way through the crowd of firemen and police officers in search of Liddy.

We both stopped in our tracks and our jaws dropped. There was Liddy, sitting in one of her living room chairs in the middle of her front lawn. She was surrounded by what looked like almost every article of clothing she owned strewn all around her while laughing and flirting with a pair of handsome paramedics as they checked her out for smoke inhalation.

Mona could not resist taking her phone out of her pocket and snapping a few pictures of Liddy. I told her to stop because Liddy would never forgive her for taking photos, because she looked frightful with her hair standing straight up in the air like she had been electrocuted and with her face covered in black soot. Her disheveled appearance did not stop her from smiling coyly and batting her eyes at the strapping paramedics attending to her. Mona obliged, shoving her phone back in her pocket, but then turned to me and said, "I just got this year's Christmas card." We both started laughing and ran to see our best friend.

Thankfully, Liddy was fine, but her kitchen was another story. According to the fire chief, it was completely destroyed.

Apparently, she had decided that she wanted to surprise us by roasting a chicken, but she'd used too small of a pan and too high of a temperature, and the grease from the chicken overflowed in the oven and caught fire while she was getting ready upstairs. By the time she opened the oven door, the entire inside of her oven was engulfed in flames. Without thinking, she did the one thing you are not supposed to do. She threw water on it, and the fire just erupted!

That's when she panicked, called 911, began grabbing all of her designer clothes that she could carry, and well, you know the rest.

Even though everyone in town, including the entire Bar Harbor Police and Fire Departments, firmly believes that Liddy is not ever meant to cook, they all can agree that she sure does make a mean cocktail. In that area, she has definitely found her niche. So we have come to a compromise since that fateful day. We do the cooking and she provides the cocktails, which makes everyone happy all around. And let's be honest, a whole lot safer.

This week I'm sharing Liddy's Irish Onion Soup recipe that she wanted to try, but thankfully she let me be the one to make it! First, however, I know you've been thinking about that Irish Mudslide ever since I first mentioned it. So, you're welcome.

Irish Mudslide for Two

Ingredients:
3 ounces Jameson Irish Whiskey
3 ounces Bailey's Irish Cream
3 ounces Kahlúa
6 ounces half-and-half (or milk)
2 cups ice
2 drops of green food coloring
Whipped cream and chocolate sauce
  for topping

Add all of your ingredients into a blender and blend until smooth. Pour into two glasses and top with whipped cream and chocolate sauce. Cheers!

Irish Stout Onion Soup

Ingredients:
3 tablespoons butter, divided
4 large, sweet onions, sliced
3 tablespoons brown sugar
3 cups beef broth, divided
3 cloves minced garlic
1 teaspoon dried thyme
¼ cup all-purpose flour
2 bottles Guinness Stout beer or your favorite stout beer
2 tablespoons apple cider vinegar
1 tablespoon stone-ground mustard
2 bay leaves
Salt and pepper to taste
Four thick slices of your favorite crusty bread buttered then toasted and then cut into cubes
1 cup white Irish cheddar cheese, grated (white cheddar cheese is good too)

In a Dutch oven, melt two tablespoons of the butter over medium-low heat.

Add your onions and brown sugar and stir until combined and onions are dark brown and caramelized. Keep stirring occasionally and add a bit of your beef broth when needed so onions won't burn. Be patient; it can take up to 30-45 minutes to obtain the yummiest flavor.

When your onions are done, add the garlic, thyme, and remaining tablespoon of butter. Stir and cook for 1 minute.

Add the flour and stir to coat your onions. Cook for 2 minutes.

Add your beer, remaining beef broth, apple cider vinegar, mustard, bay leaves, salt and pepper. Stir and bring to a boil, then lower heat and let soup simmer uncovered for 30 minutes to let soup cook and reduce.

Taste and season with more salt and pepper if needed.

Turn your oven on broil. Ladle your soup into oven-safe bowls and top soups with the toasted bread and cheese. Place bowls on a baking sheet and put into oven until cheese is melted and bubbly (5 minutes, but keep a watch because it can burn quickly).

Remove from oven and serve hot. Enjoy!

Chapter Six

There was stunned silence for a few moments
before Cal Lions, in a breathtaking display of
grief-stricken emotion, hurled his hefty frame on
top of Jefferson's prone body, screaming, "No! No!
Why? Why?" It was so over-the-top and seemingly
calculated with no discernible tears, the whole
cringe-inducing scene struck Hayley as immediately suspicious.

Bear had to use his brute strength to haul the
heavy Cal off Jefferson and shove him down in a
chair as he warned, "We need everybody to stay
away from the body until the police get here!"

Hayley had already called 911 and now sirens
were heard fast approaching. She then searched
the crowd for Liddy, who sat at a table in the corner, staring glumly at nothing, almost catatonic
from the shock. Bruce, who was at home working
on a column, must have heard the news on their

home police scanner. He kept texting her, wanting to know what was going on. Hayley typed back a quick reply promising to call him when she had a moment.

Police Chief Sergio Alvares burst through the door to Drinks Like A Fish, followed by Lieutenant Donnie and several other officers. Sergio ordered his men to herd the crowd into the back of the room, away from the body as far as possible in the small bar.

He then signaled Hayley, who hustled over to him. "What happened?"

"I don't know! One minute he was fine, standing on top of the table making a toast; the next he just toppled over and was dead."

Sergio frowned. "What's his medical history? Do you know?"

Hayley shook her head.

"He was the picture of health!" Cal Lions roared from a nearby table. "He had a physical just last week. No warning signs to speak of! How could something like this happen? I can't believe he's gone!" More wailing and sobbing followed now by a few fake tears. Cal then covered his face with his pudgy hands, but Hayley could see him watching everyone through his splayed fingers.

Sergio decided to ignore him for the moment. He examined the body for any troubling signs, then got down on his knees and put his nose up close to Jefferson's mouth, breathing in.

"What are you looking for?" Hayley asked.

He stood back up. "Sometimes cyanide leaves a bitter almond smell but sometimes it doesn't."

"You think he was *poisoned?*" Hayley gasped.

"No, not necessarily, but I can't rule anything out."

"Why cyanide?"

"Because if we are dealing with a poison, cyanide is one of the fastest-acting ones out there. You said he was fine all night until moments before he collapsed?"

Hayley nodded. "Yes."

"And he was making a toast?"

"Yes. Then he drank his Irish coffee."

"Where is it?"

Hayley scanned the area and spotted the glass mug smashed on the floor where Jefferson had dropped it when he fell, the rest of the coffee spilled onto the floor.

"Over there," she pointed.

Sergio marched over, bent down on his hands and knees, and took a whiff of the coffee. He shook his head and popped back up to his feet.

He called Lieutenant Donnie over. "Call the county forensics team and get them down here."

Donnie's eyes widened. "You think it's a homicide?"

"I think we need a thorough investigation to be sure. Also, I don't want any guests leaving until we've had a chance to question each and every one."

"Right, Chief," Donnie said, grabbing his phone.

As the other officers kept the traumatized crowd at bay, Hayley watched as one by one people were plucked from the crowd and brought into the kitchen for questioning. Everyone who was working the party went first, starting with Cody, then Mabel, then Cassie, then Randy, and next Michelle, who reached out and grabbed Hayley's hand and in a pleading voice cried, "Please, Hayley, I'm so scared. Come with me."

"Of course, Michelle," Hayley said calmly, following her into the kitchen where Chief Sergio waited. Officer Earl, who was standing by the swinging door and nearly got clocked in the forehead as they flung them open to enter, bristled at the sight of Hayley. "Sorry, but you need to wait outside until we're ready for you."

"I want her here with me," Michelle said. "Please, I will answer your questions better if I know she's by my side. I'm very, very nervous."

"Why do you have reason to be nervous?" Officer Earl asked with a raised eyebrow.

"Earl, that's enough," Sergio snapped. He turned to Michelle and gave her a warm smile. "Now, Michelle, according to Cody, Mabel, and Cassie, you were the one who served the Irish coffees to all the guests."

Michelle nodded, her hands trembling. "That's right."

"Did you personally hand Mr. O'Keefe his coffee?"

Her voice was shaky. "Y-Yes. I mean, I think so. I don't remember specifically. I was handing them out to everybody"

"They also told me you weren't supposed to be here tonight."

"That's right. I was supposed to cater the party, but I got sick, so luckily Hayley was able to take over for me at the last minute."

"Then what were you doing here tonight?"

"I-I was feeling better so I thought I would just come by and help out."

"Did you know Mr. O'Keefe personally?"

Michelle's mouth dropped open, her bottom lip quivering. She didn't respond at first.

Sergio leaned in closer. "Michelle?"

"No!" she said, almost too quickly. "No, I didn't."

Sergio eyed her suspiciously. "No?"

"No," Michelle repeated more emphatically. "Of course I knew *of* him. Everybody in town did. Local boy makes good. But we weren't friends or anything."

Hayley could tell Michelle wasn't being completely truthful, and that bothered her. What was she hiding?

Sergio consulted his notepad. "Now, Cody says that after Hayley brought him a root beer, he left the kitchen to go listen to Mr. O'Keefe's toast, but you stayed behind. Why?"

Michelle hesitated. "Because I wanted to make sure he didn't come back."

Sergio glanced at Hayley, who shrugged, oblivious. He turned back to Michelle. "Who?"

"Colin Doyle," Michelle answered.

"Who's that?" Sergio asked, clueless.

Hayley decided to step in. "Another stand-up comedian. He had heckled Jefferson during his concert at the Criterion and then tried crashing the after-party, but Bear—that's Jefferson's security guy—kicked him out."

"But he tried sneaking in through the back door just off the kitchen a few minutes later," Michelle said. "No doubt to try and cause a scene. But I caught him and warned him if he didn't leave immediately, I was going to call the police. He left without giving me any more trouble."

"Did he have the opportunity at that time to get anywhere near the Irish coffees?"

"No, we hadn't even finished making them at that point," Michelle explained.

Hayley piped in. "If he wanted to poison Jefferson, how would he even know which one to spike? There were at least forty Irish coffees in the kitchen made special for the toast."

"Valid point," Sergio agreed. Then he gave Michelle a reassuring smile. "Okay, Michelle, that's all for now. I will call you if I have any more questions."

"May I go home now?"

"Yes, you may go," Sergio said.

Michelle grabbed her bag off the counter and scooted out the back door, leaving Hayley with Sergio and Earl.

"Do you really believe someone here poisoned Jefferson?" Hayley asked, still slightly skeptical.

"The autopsy should be able to tell us for certain, but in the meantime, I'm going to cover all my yard lines."

Earl snickered, but he wasn't about to contradict his boss.

Hayley knew it was up to her. "Bases."

Sergio appeared puzzled. "What?"

"Cover your bases. Not yard lines. That's football. Bases are in baseball. That's the correct analogy."

"Hayley, I am not in the mood—"

"Okay, let's keep covering your yard lines. I'll be right back with someone for you to question," Hayley said, smiling, dashing out of the kitchen to the bar where Lieutenant Donnie and a few men were keeping watch over the jittery party guests. After conferring with Donnie, they decided to start with Jefferson's business manager, Cal Lions, whom Donnie escorted into the kitchen. Hayley glanced over to see Liddy still sitting at a corner table, staggered and distraught.

Hayley made a beeline for her, plopping down in a chair next to her and squeezing her hand. "I know this must be so hard for you, especially after—"

"It's all my fault!" Liddy sobbed.

"Liddy, don't say that!"

"It's true. If I hadn't insisted on booking Jefferson for this event, then chances are he'd still be alive," she moaned.

"We're not even sure why or how he died yet, so there's no point in taking on all this guilt."

"Someone poisoned him; I know it. I can feel it in my bones. And they chose this night to do it. They used *me* to get to him so, yes, it is my fault!"

Liddy broke down in tears and Hayley took her in her arms to comfort her. And although Hayley remained silent, she knew in her gut that Liddy was not completely wrong. If Jefferson had indeed been poisoned, the likely culprit was the Irish coffee he had swallowed right after his toast. And since everyone else in the bar also imbibed the same Irish coffee and were all just fine, it was pretty clear that Jefferson O'Keefe had been specifically targeted.

By someone who was in the room this very minute.

Chapter Seven

Hancock County Coroner Sabrina Merryweather lit up at the sight of Hayley and Randy as she opened the door to her sprawling home atop a hill overlooking the town of Bar Harbor, Frenchman's Bay, and the surrounding islands.

"What a lovely surprise! Come in, come in. I was just making some Irish coffee to celebrate St. Patrick's Day. Can I get you two some?"

"Um, that would be a hard pass," Randy said firmly.

"Thank you, Sabrina, but Irish coffee is the last thing we want to drink after what happened at Drinks Like A Fish," Hayley said.

"Oh gosh, how silly of me. Of course. Yes. Come in, come in. I have a fully stocked bar. You can have anything you want."

"It's not even noon yet," Randy said.

Sabrina gave him a baffled look, not sure what point he was trying to make. "It's my day off."

Sabrina ushered them inside her beautifully appointed living room in a coastal style with lots of muted neutral colors, sisal rugs, sea glass details, and gauzy linen drapery, creating a rather cozy interior. "Have a seat. What can I get you? I have a hard cider that will put hair on your chest."

"Not the look I'm going for today, so a glass of water will be just fine. Thank you, Sabrina," Hayley said.

"I'm feeling brave. Hit me up with the cider," Randy said.

Sabrina shuffled off into the kitchen, returning a few minutes later with a glass of water for Hayley and a cup of cider for Randy before scooting back for a mug of Irish coffee for herself and sitting down in a chair opposite the two of them, who were side by side on her couch. "So I'm guessing this isn't entirely a social call."

"No. It's always wonderful to see you, though," Hayley insisted, even though Sabrina, the reformed mean girl, used to torture her in high school. "But—"

"But you want to know about my preliminary findings in Jefferson O'Keefe's autopsy I conducted last night."

Hayley leaned forward. "We don't mean to pry—"

Sabrina nearly spit out her Irish coffee. "No, Hayley, not you. You have never been naturally curious about anything."

The sarcasm was not lost on either of them.

"Busted," Hayley said with a self-aware chuckle.

"I won't hold you in suspense. I did find traces of a foreign substance in O'Keefe's system."

"Poison?"

"Most likely, but we're still running tests to determine if that's what caused his death."

Randy bit his lip. "Cyanide?"

Sabrina shook her head. "Cyanide makes sense because it's fast acting and can kill you within minutes. Most other poisonous substances take longer— hours, sometimes days—to take the full effect. Strychnine, for instance, takes between fifteen minutes to an hour after ingestion to kick in. According to the dozens of witnesses in the bar, Mr. O'Keefe felt symptoms just moments after sipping his Irish coffee."

"But you definitely believe it was in his coffee?" Hayley asked.

Sabrina shrugged. "I'm just speculating at this point. We can't be one hundred percent certain. We're testing the water bottle he drank from that was on stage during the show for any contaminants. Unfortunately, at the after-party, the glass mug smashed to pieces on the floor when he dropped it after falling off the table, and most of the liquid soaked into the floor. We're hoping to test the remnants of the glass—the forensics guys were able to retrieve a few broken shards—so maybe we will get a few definitive answers from that." She took a sip of her Irish coffee. "Oh, this is so delicious. Are you sure I can't get you some?"

"I'm sure," Randy said, sipping his cider. "I just can't get the picture out of my head of Jefferson

O'Keefe lying dead on the floor after drinking that Irish coffee."

"Doesn't bother me," Sabrina said matter-of-factly before slurping some more. "Maybe it's because I'm around corpses all day. Nothing fazes me anymore. You have to remember, they're people, just like you and me."

Randy tossed Hayley a ruffled look before turning back to Sabrina. "Uh, not exactly. They're, like, dead."

"To-may-to, to-mah-to." Sabrina giggled. "Oh, I'm feeling this already. Don't tell anyone, but I might have used two shots of whiskey, but like I said, it's my day off."

Randy clasped his hands together and stared glumly down at the floor. "This is a disaster."

Hayley put a hand on his shoulder. "Randy, what's wrong?"

"I can't believe he died in *my* bar!"

Sabrina chugged down the rest of her Irish coffee. "Why? He had to die somewhere. I'm going to make myself another. Don't judge. It's St. Patrick's Day. It's like a national holiday, right?" Sabrina popped up to her feet and swayed a bit. "Oh, I stood up too fast."

"Are you all right?" Hayley asked, failing to correct the fact that St. Patrick's Day had been the day before.

"Never better." Sabrina giggled before stumbling off to the kitchen.

Randy turned to Hayley. "What's going to happen to my business, Hayley? A national celebrity has died at my bar!"

"I wouldn't say *national*. Regional celebrity for sure."

"That's not my point! This could ruin me. Who is going to want to drink at a bar where someone died, worse yet, was most likely murdered?"

Hayley wanted to assure her brother that he was overreacting and really had nothing to worry about, but she didn't make any promises because he could be right. Hayley herself was not all that anxious to return anytime soon to the scene where it had happened.

"I need to get to the bar. Let's go," Randy said, jumping up and making a beeline for the door.

Hayley got up to follow him. "Shouldn't we let Sabrina know we're leaving?"

"Why? She's probably passed out already or forgotten we were ever here," Randy said on his way out.

Hayley made a quick detour to the kitchen to thank Sabrina for hosting them and found her slumped over the kitchen counter splashing whiskey into a coffeepot. She said her goodbyes and then hurried after Randy.

Back at Drinks Like A Fish, Hayley accompanied Randy inside where they found Michelle on duty cleaning the mirror behind the bar with a spray bottle of Windex and a rag. Upon seeing their reflection in the mirror, she spun around to face them. "Did you talk to Sabrina?"

Randy nodded. "Yes."

"And did someone actually poison Jefferson's Irish coffee?"

"She's not sure yet," Hayley explained. "They're still doing tests."

Randy took a deep breath. "Michelle, when you helped prepare the Irish coffees, did you set one aside for Jefferson or did you just randomly hand him one from the tray?"

"I don't understand. What are you getting at?"

"There were forty Irish coffees. If someone was going to poison him, that person needed to know which one he was going to drink," Randy said.

"You think it was me, don't you?" Michelle gasped.

Randy reared back, surprised. "What? No!"

"Yes, you do," Michelle cried. "Hayley saw me upset after I talked to Jefferson at the dress rehearsal, and now you think I *killed* him!"

"Whoa, Michelle, hold on!" Randy said, trying to calm her down. "That's not what I meant to imply at all! We've worked together for years! You're like family to me!"

Michelle pointed a finger at Hayley. "And so is she, and she thinks I did it!" Before Hayley could even object, Michelle kept plowing ahead. "Well, for your information, I was so flustered when the Chief questioned me, I completely forgot about something, a key detail I just remembered this morning. I wasn't the one who served Jefferson the coffee! His friend did!"

"Bear?" Hayley asked.

"Yes, I saw him take one and personally deliver it to him. He could have slipped something in it at any time before handing it to him when his back was to the crowd! So go talk to him and stop badgering me!"

Randy held up a hand. "Michelle, we're not badgering—"

"If you think I'm capable of something so vile

and treacherous, then I should probably just quit right now!"

Randy rushed over and hugged her. "No, Michelle, please, don't quit! I'd be lost without you. You're the backbone of this whole business. I'm sorry I even mentioned it!"

Michelle stood stiffly as Randy hugged her tightly, then softened, slowly raising her arms to hug him back, satisfied he no longer suspected her of anything as horrific as homicide.

Hayley, however, was not as convinced as her brother, given Michelle's recent odd behavior, especially now in this very moment. She was being very vague and evasive, not to mention wildly defensive, and Hayley had a strong suspicion that Michelle was not being totally honest with them or the police.

She was hiding something.

And Hayley's gut was telling her it somehow involved the dearly departed Jefferson O'Keefe.

Chapter Eight

"**I** certainly hope you don't expect me to go in there!" Liddy cried, sitting in the passenger's seat of Hayley's car as she pulled into the expansive parking lot of Cost-Less. "Why not?"

"Hayley, I have a reputation to maintain. The last thing I need is for people to think I shop at a *discount* store!"

"Well, if you run into anyone you know, why would they judge you if they're in there shopping too?"

Liddy was unmoved by Hayley's logic.

"If it's all right with you, I will just wait right here in the car," Liddy sniffed.

"Fine, I will only be a minute. I'm just dropping a check off to Cassie for helping out the other night. Then we can go to T.J. Maxx and look at casual sweaters for the spring."

Liddy's nostrils flared and she scoffed. "T.J. Maxx?"

"I'm kidding. But for the record, I love that store," Hayley sighed, shaking her head in amusement. She turned on the radio to a classic rock station. "You can listen to some oldies but goodies until I get back."

She got out of her car as Bruce Springsteen belted out "Born in the U.S.A." and walked toward the sliding glass doors to the massive store. She had invited Liddy to tag along with her to Ellsworth, about thirty minutes from Bar Harbor, so she could run a few errands hoping doing so might help get her friend out of her funk. Liddy was still devastated by Jefferson's sudden passing and had holed up at home, which Hayley thought was unhealthy. So after some prodding, she had managed to convince Liddy to accompany her, failing to mention her first stop was at Cost-Less.

When Hayley entered the store, she spotted Cassie right away at register three checking out a customer with a loaded cart full of items. Although two other registers were free, Hayley waited patiently for Cassie to finish up with her customer. Unable to resist, Hayley grabbed a Mounds bar and some Tic Tacs to buy. Cassie was just handing the customer her paper receipt when she noticed Hayley in line and lit up with a bright smile. "Well, fancy meeting you here."

"Hi, Cassie," Hayley said, rummaging through her bag and pulling out a white envelope and handing it to her. "This is for you. Thanks again for helping me with the party. I'm so sorry it turned into such a terrible night."

Cassie leaned in and said in a low voice, "It was so upsetting, I still can't sleep. My Lord, that poor man. Did you hear anything more from your brother-in-law, the Chief?"

"No, they're still investigating, but the county coroner is an old high school classmate of mine, and her initial findings point to a homicide."

Cassie gasped. "*What?*"

"There were traces of poison found in Jefferson's system, which are still being tested to identify exactly what kind."

Hayley noticed Cassie had a disturbed look on her face as she waved the box of Tic Tacs over the price scanner. "Cassie, what is it?"

"It's probably nothing."

"Tell me. Anything could help."

Cassie took a deep breath and exhaled. "A few minutes before the show started, I took a tray of your snacks across the street to the Criterion as a thank-you for the staff that was working so hard backstage. And I saw that stand-up, the one who tried to crash the party . . ."

"Colin Doyle?"

"Yes, he was wandering around backstage. He said he just wanted to say hello to Jefferson, and at one point I saw him fiddling with Jefferson's water bottle. . . ."

"Did you see him put something in it?"

"No, but he was either screwing off the top to take a sip or he was putting it back on after already opening it. I couldn't tell which. Someone then came by and snatched the bottle out of his hand and told him that water had been put out for Jefferson to drink during the show. He left right after that."

"Cassie, are you sure that's what you saw?"

"Positive. I didn't think much of it until just now when you told me Jefferson was most likely poisoned."

"Thanks. You've been a big help," Hayley said, collecting her mints and candy bar and rushing out of the store and back to her car to find Liddy bopping to the beat of The Go-Go's 1980s classic "Vacation."

"We need to find Colin Doyle."

"The last person I want to see is that awful loud-mouthed jerk."

But after Hayley relayed what Cassie had just told her, Liddy was on her phone, looking up Doyle's website. Right there on the home page was a list of his upcoming events.

"He's appearing at Chuckles in Brewer tonight."

"What's Chuckles?"

"Brewer's answer to the L.A. Comedy Store. It's a dive bar slash comedy club for low-rent talent. Of course Colin Doyle is headlining there. His set starts at eight."

Hayley reached for her own phone and started typing.

"Who are you texting?"

"Bruce, to tell him there's half a roasted chicken in the fridge for dinner because I won't be home until late. We're taking a road trip to Brewer."

Liddy was completely on board, and a couple of hours later they were seated with watered-down Cosmos and a paper cup of pretzels at a small, scuffed table right in front of the main stage at Chuckles. Liddy had not been exaggerating. Calling this establishment a dive bar had been generous, given the sticky floors, walls of peeling paint, and a few musty torn-up couches that should have been discarded as trash on the street for patrons not lucky enough to score one of the half-dozen tables.

The bored owner, a big burly man in his fifties with a balding pate, stubble, his eyes at half mast, served as the master of ceremonies, introducing all the acts. After one fidgety kid in his late teens who fancied himself the next Hannibal Buress finished up his rant about his ex-girlfriend to a smattering of unenthusiastic applause from the six people besides Hayley and Liddy in the audience, the owner made a big show of announcing tonight's headliner, the one, the only, the hilarious Colin Doyle.

Liddy defiantly folded her arms, refusing to put her hands together as Colin bounded to the stage. Hayley half-heartedly clapped, not wanting to appear rude. Colin wasted no time in making fun of the owner, a risky move considering he was the one writing Doyle's paycheck. He then launched into a litany of lame jokes about living in Maine.

"You know you're living in Maine when the store advertises how many deer a freezer will hold!"

A couple of titters from the crowd.

"Maine has four seasons. Winter, Still Winter, Almost Winter, and Construction!"

A few chuckles.

Then when he transitioned into his current relationship, describing the difference between his girlfriend and a moose as "about fifty pounds and a flannel shirt," Liddy couldn't help but audibly moan.

"I see you know my girlfriend," Colin joked before recognizing her. "Oh, it's you. You're just about the last person I expected to come to my show, or are you harboring a secret crush on me?"

"If I had a crush on you, I wouldn't be secret about it. I'd get help immediately!"

Big laughs from the tiny audience for Liddy, which Colin certainly did not appreciate, but he still didn't get the hint to not tangle with the sharp-tongued Liddy Crawford.

"You could do worse, baby! I'm a real catch! I got a house and a car and some smooth moves," he cooed, doing a bit of vogueing for the patrons.

"Your mind may want to dance, but your body is a really awkward white guy," Liddy cracked.

Another big laugh, annoying Colin.

"Is this your idea of foreplay? I think she wants me, people! Wow, women falling all over themselves to flirt with me. I love my life!"

Liddy rolled her eyes. "You may love your life, but I think it just wants to be friends."

This one got applause from the audience.

Even Hayley doubled over with laughter over that one.

Colin had heard enough. "If you don't like me, why are you here to see my act?"

"You're right. This day, especially the last twenty minutes of your so-called act, has been a complete waste of makeup. Maybe I just wanted to get even with you for heckling Jefferson O'Keefe's final performance."

The audience murmured amongst themselves.

Everyone by now had heard about Jefferson's tragic death.

Fearing he had already lost the crowd, Colin spoke loudly through the microphone. "What happened to Jeffy had nothing to do with me."

"What about the water bottle?"

Everyone fell silent.

Hayley had surprised herself by blurting it out.

Colin looked genuinely perplexed. "What water bottle?"

"The one backstage at the Criterion that was left for Jefferson. A witness saw you tampering with it," Hayley calmly explained in front of the audience that had now fallen silent and was watching with rapt attention.

"Hey! Hold on! That's a loaded word! I didn't *tamper* with it. I was just going to drink it. I had no idea it was for him until someone grabbed it out of my hand."

"What were you doing backstage anyway?" Liddy barked.

"Okay, okay. Maybe I snuck backstage to let Jefferson know I was going to be in the audience, you know, play with his head a little, throw him off his game. Comedians do it to each other all the time."

"Not good ones," Liddy retorted.

Colin grimaced but plowed ahead. "Just because we competed against each other doesn't mean I hated the guy. Honestly, I respected him, even envied him a bit. But get this through your pretty little heads, I did not, repeat, did *not* kill him! Now can I get back to my show?"

Liddy stood up. "Knock yourself out. Just don't expect us to suffer through it."

She marched out of the club with Hayley on her heels. Much to Colin's chagrin, the audience applauded.

Stung, Colin screamed into the mic at Liddy, "They're applauding because you're finally leaving!"

"No, we're not," a heckler cried out. "She was better than you!"

Outside, Liddy was fuming. "I don't believe one word that Neanderthal said."

"I do," Hayley mumbled, staring at her phone.

"You do?" Liddy gasped.

Hayley showed Liddy her phone. "I just got a text from Sabrina. The water bottle tested clean. Which means the poison had to have come from the Irish coffee or something else."

After driving home from Brewer and dropping Liddy off at her house, Hayley drove directly to the Cleftstone Manor where she found Jefferson's best bud, Bear, loading the trunk of his rental car with his luggage. She had hoped to ask him some questions about what he might have seen backstage or at Drinks Like A Fish after the show. She had not expected to find him leaving town. She pulled up next to him and got out of her car.

Bear nodded solemnly. "It was nice meeting you, Hayley, even under these awful circumstances."

"Nice meeting you too, Bear."

He looked at her as if reading her mind.

"I'm not skipping town, if that's what you think. It's just too painful sticking around here. I keep reliving what happened. Jefferson was my closest friend. I'm gonna be lost without him. I left word for the police chief that I was heading back to Portland but can come back anytime if he needs me."

"Is there any way you can stay just a little while longer, Bear? I know how difficult it must be for you, but we may need your help trying to sort all this out."

"Do you really think someone deliberately poisoned Jefferson?" Bear asked, his hand on the top of the trunk, ready to close it.

Hayley nodded. "I do. There were definitely traces of poison discovered in Jefferson's system. It could have come from anywhere, even the Irish coffee you served him."

Bear's eyes widened. "I served him?" He recalled the events of the night in question. "You're right. I did. I forgot all about it. But I just randomly grabbed a coffee off the tray to give Jefferson. I swear, if it was poisoned, anyone could have drawn that unlucky number."

Hayley believed him.

She could see the pain in his eyes over losing his best friend. "Bear, I think if we all work together, we can try and figure this all out and get some justice for Jefferson."

Bear hesitated then reached in and grabbed his suitcases. "Okay, then. I trust you, Hayley. If you think me hanging around a few days more will help, then I'll do my part. Room's paid up through the weekend anyway."

Hayley clasped her hands together. "Thank you, Bear."

"But I better get a nice discount at your restaurant."

"Don't worry about that. I'll cover the whole meal!"

She would happily feed the enormous appetite of the giant Bear because deep down she knew she was going to need all the help she could get to solve this one.

Chapter Nine

When Hayley hauled her weary body up the steps of her side deck and into the house, it was already pitch-black outside and going on ten o'clock. After saying goodbye to Bear at the Cleftstone, she had driven directly to the restaurant. Although her staff had everything under control, she felt it was her duty to at least put in some face time, say hello to the customers, make sure everyone was happy with their meals.

The last table of five didn't leave until just after nine-thirty, and she had stuck around to help clean up and cash out the register before heading home.

Hayley felt she hadn't seen her husband in days. The lights were off downstairs when she dragged herself into the house, and so she trudged up to their bedroom where she found Bruce sitting up in bed working on his laptop, looking sexy in his reading glasses and nothing else above the waist. He looked up from his screen and smiled. "I've missed you."

"I know it's been a crazy couple of weeks," Hayley moaned, flopping facedown on her side of the bed. Bruce set his computer aside and gently rubbed her back. "If you try to keep up this pace, you're definitely going to come down with something, and then you'll be no good to anybody."

"I know, between planning the St. Patrick's Day party that obviously ended in disaster, keeping the restaurant running smoothly, and trying to figure out what happened to Jefferson, it's been a lot to take on."

Bruce gently turned Hayley over on her side so he could snuggle with her. They locked eyes.

"What?" Hayley asked.

"You know what I'm going to say."

"Yes, I know. Why can't I let Sergio do his job and just focus on the restaurant? Well, you've been married to me long enough to know I'm totally incapable of staying out of things like this. I have to know what happened to that poor man. I mean, he was at the top of his game, his career was just getting bigger and bigger, and then all of a sudden he's dead. All that momentum just snuffed out. Why? It's driving me crazy."

"You know what's driving me crazy?"

"What?"

"That perfume you're wearing."

"I'm not wearing perfume."

"I know. I just wanted an excuse to do this."

He wrapped his arms around her and kissed her softly on the lips. She kissed him back. He did it again, this time more passionately, and then they were pretty much off to the races as Bruce desperately tried working the buttons of Hayley's blouse. He had just about succeeded in getting them all unbuttoned when the doorbell rang downstairs.

Both of them froze.

"Who could that be at this hour?"

"I don't know and I don't care. We're not going to answer it."

He went back to trying to release that last stubborn button.

The doorbell rang again.

Hayley stopped Bruce and pushed away from him. "It might be some kind of an emergency."

"We both know it's not. It's either Mona or Liddy or your brother with some delicious gossip or lead on the case that they couldn't just text to you because they want to witness your reaction."

Hayley playfully slapped his shoulder. "I'm sure that's not true, but fine. You win. We won't answer it." She leaned in, cupping his neck with her hand and drawing him in for another kiss. "Now, where were we?"

The doorbell rang yet again.

Followed by banging on the door.

This time Bruce pulled away, resigned. "Go on. Answer it. You're never going to be able to concentrate until you know who it is."

Hayley leapt out of bed, buttoning up her blouse as she tore down the stairs to open the front door.

As Bruce had predicted, Randy stood there, an anxious look on his face. He wasn't alone. Michelle was with him.

"Who's tending the bar?"

"We closed early. It was a slow night," Randy explained.

"I hope we didn't show up here too late," Michelle whispered.

"No, I just got home. Come in," Hayley said, ushering them inside. "Can I get either of you something to drink?"

They both shook their heads.

Hayey noticed that Michelle was fidgety and nervous about something. "Michelle, is everything all right?"

"She has a confession to make. Don't you, Michelle?"

"Yes," she squeaked out, on the verge of tears.

"What is it?"

"I've been wracked with guilt because I lied to you. Randy sensed something was wrong and finally got it out of me tonight. When I told him what I had done, he suggested we come straight over here to clear the air."

This surprised Hayley. "Okay. What did you lie to me about?"

"About why I was crying and upset after talking to Jefferson the other day, before he, you know . . ."

"So he wasn't complaining about your after-party menu?" Hayley asked, studying Michelle.

"No," Michelle sniffed. "The thing is, I had met Jefferson before. Years ago, when I was barely eighteen, and I mean barely. Jefferson came back to

Bar Harbor to play that coffeehouse on Cottage Street that's no longer there. Anyway, he wasn't very famous then, but I was a huge fan. I followed him all over town like some groupie. Well, much to my shock, the night of his show, after he was finished, he came right up to me and introduced himself. I was over the moon. He actually *noticed* me! Well, then he asked me to have a drink with him, but I wasn't twenty-one so we just took a walk around town, and we really connected, and well, I'm sure you can guess the rest."

"A one-night stand," Hayley said in a soft voice.

"Not to me. I was madly in love after that. I wanted him to meet my parents! Well, that spooked him pretty good, and he got out of Dodge and never contacted me again. I was devastated. It took me months to get over him, but I did. I haven't thought much about him in years, until he showed up to play the Criterion."

"Is that why you wanted to cater the party so badly? So the two of you could cross paths again?" Hayley inquired.

"No, I was honest with you. I really am trying to get my own catering company off the ground, and I did approach Jefferson in order to get him to sign off on the menu I had prepared. But a small part of me was hoping he would remember me. I was so nervous, I didn't know what to expect. But I knew right away he had no memory of me. He looked right through me. There wasn't even a hint of recognition. When I reminded him of who I was, it took him a minute to even acknowledge we *might* have met in the past! I was so humiliated."

"It broke her heart!" Randy angrily piped in.

He had always been very protective of his best employee.

"I wanted you to know the truth, Hayley, because I am not in the habit of lying to my friends, but I was just so embarrassed and upset. I just wanted to make up something to explain my meltdown. However, I swear on my life that I did not slip anything into his Irish coffee. Revenge was the last thing on my mind that night."

"Of course I believe you, Michelle," Hayley said.

"I'd bet money on that shockingly unfunny Colin Doyle!" Randy said.

"No, he's pretty much in the clear. He may have had a motive, but he didn't have the opportunity. It had to have been someone else. The question is who?"

Just then, Bruce came ambling down the stairs, having thrown on a Patriots T-shirt, phone in hand, a somber look on his face. "I may be able to help with that."

They all turned to him.

"I just got a text from my inside source at the police department."

Hayley, Randy, and Michelle all said in unison, "Earl."

"As a journalist, I can't reveal my sources!" Bruce huffed.

"Oh, come on, Bruce, we all know it's Officer Earl. He's a legendary blabbermouth," Randy said, chortling.

"I will not confirm or deny!"

It was definitely Officer Earl.

Hayley thought it was adorable that Bruce continued to believe his big source in the police department was some big secret.

"Anyway"—Bruce sighed—"I just got word that Jefferson's manager, Cal Lions, has been arrested."

Island Food & Spirits
by
Hayley Powell

Since it's so close to St. Patrick's Day, I thought this would be the perfect time for me to make a pot of Irish stew.

I knew Bruce would love it since he is definitely a meat-and-potatoes kind of guy.

I found my recipe and skimmed over the ingredients, realizing I needed to go to the store for some potatoes and carrots, so I grabbed Leroy's leash and snapped it on his collar, deciding we would walk to the Shop 'n Save. I had been recently taste-testing probably one too many of Randy's delicious Irish coffees that he was planning to serve at his bar on St. Patrick's Day, so I definitely needed to walk off some of those extra calories I had no doubt packed on.

Leroy loved any opportunity to take a walk. When he was a puppy I had gotten in the habit of taking him to the Shop 'n Save. I would leave him inside the entryway tied to a shopping cart where he would happily soak up all the attention from the locals patting his head and scratching his chin as they entered the store.

I learned very early on, however, that I could only do this during the off-season and definitely not in the busy summertime because one July I had left him in the entryway to greet all the tourists, but when I came back out, he was gone! You can imagine how beside myself I was, frantically calling his name and searching all around the parking lot, but I just couldn't find him.

I was in full panic mode and just about to call my brother-in-law Sergio, the chief of police, when thankfully Sergio called me first and told me he had Leroy and my little boy was just fine.

Enormously relieved, I listened as Sergio explained that a well-meaning visiting tourist from Ottawa, Canada, had assumed the poor dog had been abandoned (truth be told, he was due for a bath), so he picked Leroy up and brought him directly to the police station. I learned right then and there that it was probably better to keep Leroy's greeting days to the off-season for the local residents who were more familiar with him.

Leroy has always been such a big part of our family. I can still remember the day he first came to us. He was just the cutest little ball of fur. The kids couldn't stop carrying him around, playing with him, dressing him up in the most adorable outfits, especially on all the holidays. I chuckled, thinking about one particular holiday, but believe me, I wasn't laughing back then.

It was the Saturday before St. Patrick's

Day and I had scheduled Leroy for a much-needed haircut after a long winter during which his hair grew long and shaggy and right into the poor little guy's eyes so he could barely see. I was going to drop him off at the groomer's in Town Hill, and since it would be a few hours' wait, I decided to do some shopping in Ellsworth.

The kids were dragging their heels, not wanting to go with me, preferring to stay home and eat junk food and watch Nickelodeon. My phone rang just as I was looking for Leroy's leash. It was the groomer. They needed to reschedule Leroy's appointment because the groomer had just called in sick. The kids, overhearing my conversation, were ecstatic thinking that now they didn't have to go shopping with me in Ellsworth.

Knowing they would spend most of their time whining and complaining while I tried on clothing at the department stores, I granted them a reprieve. As long as Gemma agreed to watch her little brother, I told them they could stay home. But in case of an emergency, they were to call my BFF Mona since I would be a half hour away. They excitedly nodded then bolted for the kitchen to load up on snacks.

After a few hours of shopping, I was happy with how the day turned out; I'd found a dress and two pairs of jeans on sale. As I drove back to town from Ellsworth, I thought to myself how lucky I was that my kids were getting older and more self-sufficient.

I decided to swing into my brother Randy's bar, Drinks Like A Fish, to say a quick hello before heading home.

I was driving halfway down Cottage Street, mere feet from the bar, when suddenly I caught sight of a green flash tearing down the street. I did a double take, squinting, not believing my eyes. It was a dog, a small *green* dog! And there was a tiny leprechaun's hat on its head!

I shook my head and thought to myself, *Who in their right mind would dye their poor dog green?* Upon closer inspection, I then slammed my foot on the brake and came to a screeching halt because it suddenly dawned on me that running fast behind the green dog, trying to catch it, was my daughter, my son, my brother, and my BFF Mona all screaming at the top of their lungs, "Leroy! Leroy! Come back, boy!"

Good Lord, this was *not* happening! I quickly parked and jumped out of the car. The only thing I could think to do was put two fingers in my mouth and whistle as loud as I possibly could! I saw Leroy skid to a stop, then spin around and spot me. With his tail wagging and tongue panting, he darted over in my direction, jumping up into my outstretched arms and, much to my supreme embarrassment, to the applause from the bar patrons who had spilled out onto the street to watch these crazy people chase a green dog wearing a miniscule hat down the street.

Patting Leroy, I shifted my gaze toward my kids, who were very tentatively walking toward me, not nearly as excited to see me as Leroy was. Randy and Mona, knowing I was about to explode like Mount Vesuvius, waved goodbye and hurried back into the bar, secure in the knowledge I now had the situation under control.

With one forceful gesture, I had my kids scrambling into the back seat of my car. After depositing Leroy onto the front seat, I glared at my two quivering children in the back through the rearview mirror. "I'm waiting."

They knew it was confession time. It turned out that while watching a comedy show on the Disney Channel, and seeing that one of the characters dyed a bunny pink for Easter, my kids got the bright idea to dye Leroy green for St. Patrick's Day! They put poor Leroy into the bathtub with water and green dye, which covered him completely in green, which they thought was so cute. They had to top him off with a leprechaun hat they found buried in our decorations box in the cellar.

That's when they thought it would be a fun idea to take him for a walk around

town so everyone could see their handi-
work and stop by Drinks Like A Fish to
show their uncle Randy. Everyone they
passed by on the sidewalk loved "the little
leprechaun dog," until a bleary-eyed Cappy
Linscott came stumbling out of the bar
and spotted Leroy, believing he was seeing things after one too many midday
beers! Cappy reached out to touch Leroy,
which caused him to snap at him. Cappy
reared back, bumping into Dustin, who
dropped the leash, allowing Leroy to make
a mad dash down the street as the kids
screamed for him to come back. This drew
the attention of Randy and Mona, who
was also enjoying a midday beer break,
to come running out of the bar to see
what the commotion was all about. They
all ran after Leroy, who thought they were
playing a fun game of chase. And that's
pretty much when I came in.

Let's just say the kids were assigned a
few extra chores for a couple of weeks for
dyeing the dog, but since no one was
hurt, it wasn't the end of the world. We all
did learn one big valuable lesson: food
coloring does not wash right out. Poor
Leroy was green right through Easter.
When Gemma suggested perhaps we
should dye him pink for Easter, it only
took one look from me for her not to ever
mention it again. Luckily our boy Leroy
has been his natural dirty white color ever
since.

After all that excitement I definitely deserved a refreshing Whiskey Ginger and a big comforting bowl of Irish Stew.

Whiskey Ginger

Ingredients:
2 ounces Irish whiskey
½ ounce fresh squeezed lime juice
3 ounces ginger ale
Ice

In a tall glass, add ice and then your Irish whiskey and lime juice. Top with your ginger ale, stirring slowly just to combine.

Sit back and enjoy while waiting for your hearty Irish Stew to come out of the oven.

Irish Stew

Ingredients:
2 tablespoons olive oil
3 pounds beef stew meat
¼ cup flour
1 large onion, chopped
1 tablespoon minced garlic
1 cup Irish stout beer
4 cups beef broth
4 tablespoons tomato paste
2 pounds new potatoes, halved

2 cups carrots, peeled and cut into
   one-inch pieces
1 teaspoon dried thyme
Salt and pepper to taste

Preheat your oven to 350 degrees.

In a large ovenproof pot with lid, heat your olive oil on the stove at medium-high heat.

Salt and pepper your stew meat then toss the stew meat into a bowl with the flour and stir until all meat is lighty coated. Then add to the pot, not overcrowding, and sear on all sides. Remove to a plate and repeat until all your stew meat is seared.

Add the onions to the pot and cook until tender. Add your garlic and quickly stir it into the onions so it doesn't burn, then add your stew meat back to the pot.

Add the beer, beef broth, tomato paste, potatoes, carrots, and thyme. Stir to combine and bring to a simmer.

Once the stew has come to a simmer, cover the pot and place in oven for 2½ to 3 hours or until your beef and vegetables are tender.

Remove from the oven and enjoy!

Chapter Ten

Hayley and Bruce charged into the Bar Harbor Police Department to find Officer Earl sitting behind the reception desk, his feet up, a Thor comic book on top of his ample belly, and his eyes closed as he snoozed. The door slamming behind them didn't even rouse him, so Bruce had to pound his fist a couple of times on the desk in order to wake him up. Startled, Earl snorted and swung his feet off the desk so fast, his chair nearly tipped over. He had to struggle to keep his balance and not topple onto the floor. He blinked at Hayley and Bruce, dazed, not quite sure what was going on at first, then he cleared his throat and tried acting as professional as possible.

"Bruce, Hayley, good evening. How can I help you?" Earl said with a friendly smile, folding his arms and leaning forward in his chair as it creaked from his considerable weight.

"You know why we're here, Earl. You called Bruce not ten minutes ago to let him know Cal Lions had been arrested," Hayley explained.

Bruce gave his wife a withering look as Earl's eyes popped open in horror and he cried defensively, "I am sure I have no clue what you're talking about, Hayley!" Then he glared at Bruce for giving him up as his source and seethed, "If I did anything of the sort, I could lose my job! Isn't that right, Bruce?"

"Yes, Earl. Hayley just thinks you're my source, but she has zero evidence proving it. She's just guessing."

Earl, still shaken a bit, slowly started to relax. "Anyone could have called you. The station was packed with people when Sergio and Donnie brought him in. I can't understand why anyone would think it was me. I'm not what you would call a gossip or anything like that."

Officer Earl was deluding himself.

Most people thought of him as Bar Harbor's very own town crier, but Hayley was hardly going to argue the point.

Earl was still obsessed with playing defense. "That new night dispatcher, Heidi Burch, she runs off at the mouth all the time. You can bet it's her."

Hayley was not interested in hearing Earl throw everybody in the vicinity under the bus to shield his own guilt. "Is Sergio interrogating Mr. Lions now?"

Earl shook his head. "No, the chief went home for the night."

Hayley and Bruce exchanged surprised looks.

Bruce turned back to Earl. "Did Lions confess to murdering Jefferson already?"

"Oh no, he wasn't arrested for that. Sergio got a call earlier from the FBI asking him to pick Lions up and hold him until they can get here," Earl said breathlessly, eager to share this juicy tidbit.

Bruce leaned toward Earl, intrigued. "FBI?"

Earl nodded. "Yup. Pretty cool, huh? The FBI calling *us?*" Earl glanced around to make sure there was no one around to eavesdrop. "Now you didn't hear this from me . . ."

Hayley had to suppress a laugh.

He just couldn't help himself.

Earl eagerly continued. "Apparently the FBI has been investigating Mr. Lions for massive fraud, embezzling hundreds of thousands of dollars from his clients, both past and present, Jefferson included, and now they have enough to hang him! I mean, not literally, but he will definitely be going to prison. The evidence is overwhelming according to the feds."

"Can we see him?" Bruce asked.

Earl thought it over. "I suppose so. Sergio didn't say anything about not allowing him to have any visitors." Earl hauled himself up out of his chair and grabbed some keys off the desk. "I'll take you to him. He should be done eating his dinner by now. But don't stay too long, okay? The FBI might show up any minute and I don't want to get in trouble in case they don't want him talking to anybody."

"We'll be quick," Bruce promised as Earl opened the door to the back and led them down to the two jail cells opposite each other at the end of the hall.

One was empty. In the other, Cal Lions sat on a wooden bench, slumped over, head in his hands. In front of him on the floor was a plastic tray with a half-eaten bologna sandwich and an unopened pudding cup.

"Not hungry?" Earl asked.

Cal shook his head but didn't look up.

Earl unlocked the cell, stepped inside, and picked up the tray. "So you're not going to eat your pudding?"

"No," Cal moaned.

"Can I have it?"

"Knock yourself out," Cal mumbled.

Earl picked up the half-eaten sandwich, shoved it in his mouth, and did his best to say, "You got company."

He locked the cell and hustled away. Cal slowly raised his head to see Hayley and Bruce standing outside the bars of the jail cell.

"What do you want?" Cal growled. "Here to gloat?"

"No, we thought you had been arrested for Jefferson's murder," Bruce said.

Cal scoffed. "You and the whole town, I imagine. Look, I may have diverted a few payments from concert venues to my own personal bank account without informing my clients, to cover some unexpected bills and expenses, which I was *always* going to pay back, but for the record, I did *not* kill him! Jefferson was on his way up, rising fast. He was my biggest . . ."

"Cash cow?" Hayley offered.

Cal sneered at her but didn't offer a response. He decided to ignore Hayley and only address

Bruce. "I had no reason in the world to kill my biggest client."

Bruce grimaced. "Unless he found out what you were doing and threatened to call the police?"

"No, that never happened," Cal insisted. "Jefferson had no I idea I was . . ."

"*Stealing* from him?" Hayley said pointedly.

"I'm done talking to you two," Cal snapped.

He had no desire to incriminate himself any further.

But deep down, Hayley had a strong feeling that although Cal Lions was a cheat and a liar and should be put away for a long time for his crimes, murder was not one of them.

Earl suddenly reappeared, chocolate pudding on his lips. "You better go. The FBI just called. They're crossing the Trenton Bridge now and should be here in fifteen minutes."

Resigned to his fate, Cal dropped his head back into his hands as Earl hastily ushered Hayley and Bruce out.

Outside, once they were back in Hayley's car, Bruce sat in the passenger seat, intently scrolling through some pictures on his phone.

As Hayley backed the car up to pull out of the parking space in front of the police station, she glanced over at Bruce. "What's got you so curious?"

"The *Times* just posted photos Toby took on the day Jefferson died," Bruce said.

Hayley hit the brakes and shifted the gear into park. "Can I take a look?"

Bruce shrugged. "Sure."

Hayley took the phone from him and began scrolling, studying all the photos. There were ones of Jefferson backstage before the show, during his act, mingling at the after-party, and then on top of the table at Drinks Like A Fish, making his toast, right before his death.

Something strange suddenly jumped out at her. "Bruce!"

Bruce jolted in his seat. "What?"

She held out the phone. "Look at the photo of Jefferson backstage before the performance and then look at one that was taken at the party. Do you notice anything different?"

Bruce did as instructed, eyes scanning both photos. He looked up at Hayley. "No."

She pointed at Jefferson's bicep. "Look closer. In this one, before the performance, he doesn't have a shamrock tattoo on his shoulder, but in the photo taken later at the party, it's right there in plain view."

"It could be the lighting or angle of the photo," Bruce guessed. "Maybe you just can't make it out."

"No. If it was there, we would most definitely see it," Hayley said, grabbing her phone from the cup holder, making a call, and putting it on speaker.

Liddy answered. "Hello?"

She sounded groggy and out of it.

"Did I wake you?"

"No, I'm up. I'm just drowning my sorrows with two, no wait, three vodka martinis."

"Liddy, I have something very important to ask you. When you spent the night with Jefferson—"

"Yes, he was gentle and caring and everything I hoped he would be . . ."

Bruce turned away, pretending he could not hear her.

"No, Liddy, you saw him without his shirt on. Do you remember if he had a shamrock tattoo on his bicep?"

There was a pause.

"No, he didn't."

"Are you positive?"

"Of course. I would have remembered something like that. Which is why I found it odd when I noticed he had one during his stand-up set. Why? What's going on?"

"I'll explain later. I have to go," Hayley cried, hanging up on Liddy and making another call.

This time Sabrina Merryweather answered.

"Sabrina, it's Hayley!"

"Hi, Hayley, I was just thinking about you. I'm putting a cocktail thing together next week and—"

Hayley did not wait for her to finish, interrupting her. "Sabrina, have you identified the poison in Jefferson's system yet?"

"Yes, the full toxicology report came back today. It was arsenic, or at least a version of it. How he absorbed it into his system is still anybody's guess since we found no traces on the shards from the glass mug he was drinking from or the water bottle he used during his show."

"How fast would it take to kill him?"

"It varies, maybe a few hours. Unlike cyanide, which could cause his death within minutes, this type of poison takes a lot longer to do its dirty work. He probably started feeling symptoms sooner, maybe thirty minutes after ingesting it, but he just didn't tell anyone. As they say, the show must go on."

"What about tattoo ink? Could someone have mixed the poison with tattoo ink and he absorbed it into his system that way?"

"I suppose so, yes. But, Hayley, I noticed the shamrock tattoo on O'Keefe's arm during his autopsy. Do you know when he got it?"

"The same day he dropped dead."

Chapter Eleven

Hayley was hardly surprised to hear her former boss Sal Moretti's booming voice when she walked into the front office of the *Island Times* where she'd served as office manager for almost ten years. Her replacement, Adele, was a perfectly sweet older woman in her late sixties, whose husband had passed away right around the time Hayley had been helping search for a new manager. Adele boasted secretarial skills from almost thirty years of working at a local insurance company, but she had recently retired. Now that she was on her own, Adele desperately wanted to keep her mind busy and try to shake herself out of her grief over losing the man she had married right out of high school. Adele was also patient, kind, rarely spoke ill of anybody, and always had a pleasant smile on her face. She was thoroughly suited to deal with the mercurial moods of one Editor-in-

Chief Sal Moretti. Her talents were on full display as Sal stood by the coffee station in the corner of the reception area, a ceramic mug thrust out toward his new office manager, and in typical fashion, was yelling at the top of his lungs. "Adele, if I wanted cold coffee, I would put some ice cubes in it and call it a day! Is it too much to ask to have some hot coffee on hand when I need a boost? Tell me, is that asking too much?"

"No, Sal," Adele said softly, batting her eyes, not the least bit discombobulated by his temper tantrum. She had seen him erupt way too many times. It was all just part of the job. "But you told me that typing up your notes from your interview with the town council about the new zoning law should be my top priority. I just emailed you a copy two seconds ago. So forgive me for not taking the time before now to put on a fresh pot." Adele calmly stood up and walked over to the coffee station, which Sal blocked with his body.

"Excuse me," Adele said wearily.

Frustrated, Sal stepped aside to let her pass. "Well, hurry up. I'm getting a caffeine withdrawal headache!"

"No, your headache is from too much yelling," Hayley said.

Sal spun around to see her standing near the door. "Well, look who decided to show her face around here after deserting us for greener pastures! And when I say green, I mean money. She's making a hell of a lot more with that restaurant than she ever did here!"

Adele finished pouring grounds into a filter and then placed it in the coffee maker before smiling at Hayley. "Please tell me you've come back for your old job. I would be happy to give it back to you."

"Careful, Adele!" Sal snapped.

"Sorry, I just popped in for a minute." Hayley laughed, handing Sal a paper bag she had been holding in her hand. "Here, Sal. Cheesecake brownie muffin, your favorite!"

Sal grinned with delight and excitedly snatched the bag from her. As he opened it to tear off a chunk, he glanced over at Adele, whose back was to him. "See, Adele? This is how it's done. Hayley knows how to get on my good side. You should try it sometime." She ignored him as Sal turned back to Hayley. "Last week she had the gall to bring me a zucchini walnut muffin! Can you believe that? Who wants zucchini in a muffin?"

"Your wife asked me to try and get you to eat healthier," Adele said, flipping the on button to start brewing the coffee.

"You work for me, *not* my wife!"

Hayley scrunched up her nose. "Does she though?"

"What do you mean?" Sal bellowed.

"Everyone knows Rosana is the *real* boss around here," Hayley said.

Adele snickered. "Thank you for speaking the truth, Hayley. If I dared say it, he'd fire me. Again."

Hayley raised an eyebrow. "Again?"

Adele nodded. "He fires me on average at least three times a week."

"But you never get the hint and actually *go!*" Sal roared.

"Because I know you'd be lost without me," Adele said, walking back to her desk and sitting down in her chair. "Now stop bothering me. I have to get some ads approved from the sales department."

Sal whipped around to Hayley and popped a big piece of the muffin into his mouth, talking as he chewed. "Do you see how she talks to me? This is all your fault, Hayley. You insisted I hire her."

"Looks to me like she's keeping you in line, which is the most challenging aspect of the job and should require extra hazard pay."

Sal nearly choked on his muffin but managed to swallow it. "What are you doing here anyway? You obviously want something. I'm no fool. This muffin is some kind of bribe. It doesn't take Hercule Parrot to solve that mystery!"

"Poirot," Hayley said.

"What?"

"It's Hercule Poirot. Not Parrot."

"Fine, whatever! I'm not your brother-in-law Sergio! English *is* my first language, so stop correcting me!"

"What are you going to do, fire me?"

Adele giggled from behind her desktop computer.

Sal shot her an annoyed look.

"I'm here to see Toby. Is she around?" Hayley asked.

"It's not my job to keep tabs on everyone who works here at all times—"

"She's in her office," Adele chirped.

"Thank you, Adele. Lovely to see you," Hayley

said, scooting toward the door that led to the back bullpen of offices.

She passed by Bruce's office, which was empty at the moment, and landed at the last office on the left. The door was closed so she gently knocked.

"Come in, it's open," a woman answered.

Hayley opened the door to find Toby the staff photographer perusing some of her digital photos on her desktop computer. She lit up at the sight of Hayley. "What a lovely surprise. What are you doing at your old haunt?"

"I came to see you. I was hoping you could help me."

"Of course. Pull up a chair."

Hayley sat down and quickly explained to Toby how she was investigating what happened to Jefferson O'Keefe, how she suspected the killer might have poisoned the tattoo ink used on Jefferson's arm, the time discrepancy of him not having a tattoo earlier in the day but then appearing on stage with one as well as at the after-party.

Toby leaned forward in her chair. "How can I help?"

"You were backstage most of the day and evening snapping photos for the *Times* piece on the show, right? Well, maybe you caught something that might tell us when Jefferson got the tattoo and who applied it."

Eager to help, Toby jolted upright and started banging the keys on her computer. "Let's take a look."

Hayley stood up, circled the desk, and hovered behind Toby as she scrolled down the endless rows of photos. They went through at least a hundred before Toby stopped, zeroing in on a row of six photos taken within seconds of each other. In the foreground, a couple of Criterion Theatre employees were laughing and mugging for the camera. In the shadowy background but clear enough to make out, Jefferson was sitting in a chair, a stoic look on his face, as his best buddy, Bear, bent down on one knee, was fussing with what could only be a shamrock tattoo.

"There's your answer," Toby said.

Hayley's heart sank. She couldn't imagine Bear harming his best friend. What possible motive could he have? But she hardly knew him or their history, and there could be facts about their relationship that had yet to surface. All she knew was she had to talk to him now, before he tried leaving town again.

"Thanks, Toby!" Hayley cried before dashing out of the office and back out the front door through reception, barely slowing down to say goodbye to Sal, who was complaining to Adele that his fresh cup of coffee was now too hot as he angrily blew on it.

Hayley jumped in her car and sped over to the Cleftstone Manor, stopping at the front desk to ask the clerk to call Bear's room and let him know that she was there to see him. After announcing Hayley to Bear, she directed her to his room where Hayley found him sprawled out on the bed watching a Celtics game on TV, surrounded by store-bought nachos and a six-pack of Goose Island beer.

Bear braced himself, as he couldn't help but notice the stern, pained expression on Hayley's face as he sat up. "What's wrong?"

"The coroner believes that the poison in Jefferson's system did not come from the Irish coffee or the water bottle, but instead was absorbed through the tattoo he got that day. Were you the one who applied it?"

She already knew from the photo he had, but she was curious to know if he was going to try and lie his way out of this.

"Yes," he said bluntly. "I always do."

"Always?"

"Of course. Jefferson likes to wear a temporary shamrock tattoo every St. Patrick's Day. It's sort of an annual tradition."

Of course.

A temporary tattoo.

That made total sense.

"If it's a tradition, then the killer may have known it and used that information to kill him. Who supplied the temporary tattoo?"

"I did," Bear said without hesitation.

"Where did you buy it?"

Bear shrugged. "Some discount store up in Ellsworth. Cost-Less, I think."

Hayley shuddered as alarm bells suddenly rang in her head.

Cost-Less?

Cassie, one of Hayley's part-time helpers, was a cashier at Cost-Less.

Was it just a coincidence?

"Bear, think. Do you remember who checked you out?"

Bear wracked his brain for a minute, trying to recall. "I believe it was a woman, yeah, definitely a woman. I don't remember what she looked like exactly. Maybe around your age, a little older."

"At any time, was the package out of your sight, or did you see her open it or anything?"

Bear shook his head. "No . . ." Then he gasped. "Wait. I remember she had to run a price check. She was gone for something like three or four minutes."

Enough time to open the temporary tattoo, apply the deadly poison to the adhesive side, and seal it back up again.

Cassie!

But why?

What did she have against Jefferson O'Keefe?

Chapter Twelve

Hayley scanned the line of cashiers at the checkout section of Cost-Less, but there was no sign of Cassie. She then grabbed a pack of gum and stood in line in aisle seven until a young man in his mid-twenties, hefty, rosy chubby cheeks, in a red vest with the name tag HAL was ready to scan her one item.

Hayley smiled brightly at Hal. "Hi, I'm looking for Cassie. I thought she would be working today."

Hal, with an annoyed expression, obviously wanting as little interaction with the customers as possible, shrugged after glancing around at the other cashiers on duty. "She is. She's probably just taking her break."

"Oh, where is the break room? I'd love to pop in and say hello."

"You're not allowed back there. Employees only," he said, slapping the pack of gum down on the conveyor belt after scanning it. "That'll be two fifty-six."

Hayley rummaged through her bag and handed the cashier three one-dollar bills and waited for the change, which came sliding down into the cash dispenser. Hayley scooped it up, still smiling. "Do you have any idea when her break is over?"

"I don't make up the schedule. I just work here." He sighed.

"Thank you, Hal. You've been an enormous help," Hayley said, her words dripping with sarcasm.

Hayley grabbed her gum as Hal began checking out the next customer in line. A young ponytailed tiny bag girl, probably in her late teens, finished bagging some items for a customer in aisle six, then casually wandered over to Hayley, who stood near the exit, hanging around hoping Cassie might come back soon so she could talk to her.

"She's not in the break room," the girl whispered.

Hayley glanced at the girl's name tag.

MIA.

"Hi, Mia, I'm Hayley. Can you tell me where she is?"

"She's having a smoke on the loading dock out in back of the store. She always goes there during her break to be alone. She doesn't like to mingle much with her co-workers."

That's odd, Hayley thought to herself. Cassie had struck her as friendly and open when she had first hired her to help out with the party.

"Why do you think that is, Mia?"

"She hates working here. She's just here for the

paycheck. I mean, all of us are really, but we at least try to make the most of it. But Cassie, she's insanely bitter about it. I guess it has to do with her once being some kind of a big deal."

"Big deal?"

"Yeah, rumor has it she had her own catering company, very high-end, and she used to book a lot of la-de-da VIP affairs."

"I had no idea. . . ." Hayley gasped. "She never mentioned it."

"Something bad happened, but no one knows what because nobody dared to ask her. It's a really sore subject. But the manager here heard the business went belly-up and she had to file for bankruptcy. She lost her house and everything. She was broke, and so she had to take the job here to get some cash flow going and try and make ends meet. I feel bad for her, but hey, everyone who works here has their own money problems. She's not that special."

The pieces of the puzzle were slowly coming together.

"Mia, which way to the loading dock?"

Mia opened her mouth to answer when Hal at the register, who had been eavesdropping, yelled, "She's not allowed back there! Employees only!"

Mia just rolled her eyes and turned back to Hayley. "Don't listen to him. He's just being a jerk like always. Go to the back of the store and through the gray swinging doors. If anyone tries to stop you, tell 'em you're just using the rest room and keep going all the way back to the loading dock."

"Thank you, Mia," Hayley said, crossing back through register seven, ignoring the sullen stare from Hal, then down the toy aisle all the way back until she spotted the gray doors. As she slipped through them into the back, past the restrooms, following Mia's instructions to the loading dock, the few workers around made no attempt to stop her and find out what she was doing there.

Stepping outside through the plastic deck strip curtain onto the dock, Hayley looked around at the dozens of stacked boxes packed with store inventory.

There was no sign of Cassie.

She waited a few minutes, hoping she might show up, but then, giving up, Hayley turned back around, stopping suddenly in her tracks.

Blocking her way back into the store was Cassie, a desperate, wild look on her face, brandishing a box cutter in her hand, which she held out ominously toward Hayley.

Chapter Thirteen

"Cassie, I was looking for you!" Hayley said cheerily, trying her best to remain calm and casual, but keeping an eye on the box cutter that Cassie gripped in her hand, pointed at her.

"Well, you found me, and now you know everything, don't you?" Cassie hissed.

"I'm not sure I understand—"

Cassie thrust the box cutter toward her, cutting her off. "Stop pretending! Hal came and found me and told me you were asking all kinds of questions about me, and that blabbermouth Mia couldn't wait to fill you in on all the gory details!"

"So you lost a business. I know lots of people who have; it's not the end of the world," Hayley said evenly, eyeing for some means of escape. The loading dock was high up enough that if she tried to jump, she would probably fracture an ankle.

"Why did you have to go snooping around? I

really liked you, Hayley. I was hoping we could be friends. Good friends. I don't have a lot of friends."

"I am your friend, Cassie, but—"

Cassie flinched. "But what? You're not in the habit of palling around with *murderers*?" Cassie sneered at Hayley's shocked face. "What? It's not like you haven't figured it all out by now. I could tell from the moment we met you're a sharp cookie."

"Okay, you're right. I do have it figured out," Hayley said, taking a step back toward the edge of the dock, trying to put some distance between herself and the box cutter in Cassie's hand. "You poisoned the tattoo that killed Jefferson. You must have known him from the past and were aware that he always put on a temporary shamrock tattoo every year for his St. Patrick's Day performance. You also knew that Cost-Less was the only place near town that sold the one he preferred. So you made sure you were working your shift when Bear came in to buy it. How did you know when Bear would show up at the store?"

"That was easy. Cody."

Hayley gasped. "Cody was in on it?"

Cassie scoffed. "No. I confided to him that I had a big crush on Bear, and so he was more than happy to text me when Bear told him he was heading to Cost-Less so I could be in place to wait on him. The kid thought it was so romantic. He had such a good heart, trying to help me with my pathetic love life!"

"Then when Bear came to your register with the tattoo, you pretended you needed to do a price check, giving yourself enough time to apply the poison, knowing that it would slowly seep into Jefferson's system after Bear put it on his arm."

"The plan was going like clockwork, I had everything in place, everything was perfect, until you called me and said you had pulled out of the catering gig and you no longer needed my help! I was so furious! The whole reason for me applying to work for you was so I could be there to watch Jefferson O'Keefe die!"

"Oh my God," Hayley cried. "You poisoned Michelle!"

Cassie nodded, proud of herself. "I slipped a little something in her drink at the bar. Nothing fatal, of course. I'm not some kind of serial killer. Just something to put her out of commission long enough for you to resume catering duties and I would have a legitimate reason to be at the after-party to watch all the delicious drama unfold."

"What did Jefferson do to deserve your wrath, Cassie? I'm assuming it had something to do with your business collapsing?"

Cassie's face reddened. "You have no idea how close I had gotten to reaching unimaginable heights! I was catering parties in Southern Maine and Boston for major celebrities, sports figures, politicians, a former U.S. secretary of state. Guy Fieri even got wind of me and there was talk of flying me down to New York to appear on his Food Network show! But then it all came crashing down, thanks to Jefferson O'Keefe!" She practically spit out the name, she was so disgusted by it.

"One night, in Andover, at an afternoon party I was catering for Jay Leno, who owns a home there, I served Jefferson a canapé and he got sick and missed a performance that night. He blamed my food! No proof, mind you, but he swore it was salmonella from my egg-and-bacon canapé, which I know it was *not*! But that one accusation spread like wildfire, and the next thing I knew, my phone stopped ringing! He ruined me!"

"How did he not recognize you when he saw you again?"

"Are you kidding? These self-involved celebrities never remember anyone who's not important or can't help with their careers! Besides, after my business folded, I went through a depression, gained weight, changed my hair color, got contacts. I look completely different now. Hardly anyone from my past who comes into the Cost-Less recognizes me now, which made it much easier to plan my revenge! And now it's done, he's gone, and my life will be the better for it!"

"But at what cost, Cassie?" Hayley asked, standing so close to the edge of the dock, a heavy breeze might cause her to lose her balance and fall. "Now you'll go to prison for murder. Is that really a better life?"

"I'm only going to go to prison if people find out what I did, and as far as I can tell, you're the only one who knows the whole story and can cause me any trouble. But I can take care of that . . . right now!"

Cassie raised the box cutter, about to lunge at Hayley, when suddenly, out of nowhere, a beefy hand shot out, encircled Cassie's wrist, squeezing hard. The pain forced her to drop the box cutter, which clattered to the dock.

Hayley smiled at Jefferson's best bud, Bear, who

stood behind Cassie, firmly twisting her arm behind her back and holding her in place. He grinned at Hayley. "See? I knew you'd want some back-up muscle. Safety first."

She had known something like this might happen when she confronted Cassie. She didn't have enough evidence to call in the cops yet, but the two-hundred-pound side of beef Bear was more than up to the task of keeping Hayley out of any serious danger. She was just grateful he had taken her call and agreed to play bodyguard. Otherwise things might have ended much differently for her.

Chapter Fourteen

When Hayley sauntered into Drinks Like A Fish later that evening, she was awed by how busy it was for a Wednesday night, especially during the off-season. The bar was packed, every table filled, standing-room-only in the back. Even her favorite stool at the bar, usually reserved for her, was occupied. She spotted Bear at the end of the bar, and he smiled warmly and waved at her while nursing a Goose Island. Pressing her way through the crowd, she finally reached him just as Randy came rushing out of the kitchen with a tray of food for one of the tables, winking at his sister as he glided past her.

Hayley turned to Bear. "I'm so glad I caught you before you left town. I can't thank you enough for having my back today."

"I'm just glad you called and weren't foolish enough to go up there on your own."

"Well," Hayley said, blushing, "you could say I've learned from a few past mistakes charging head-on into danger without considering all the possible outcomes."

Bear chuckled. "I'm happy I could help."

"Are you heading home tomorrow?"

"Yup. Got a call from Jefferson's lawyer earlier today. Seems he named me the executor of his will, so I've gotta go deal with all that."

"I know it's hard losing such a close friend, but it must be nice to know how much you meant to him. He put you in charge of his estate."

"We had some good times, a lot of happy memories that I will always cherish, but now . . ."

"But now what?"

"Now I'm going to do my best to look ahead once his cousins and I get through planning the funeral."

"That sounds very healthy."

Hayley noticed Bear light up like a football field on a night game at the sight of Michelle, suddenly breezing out of the kitchen. Michelle was quite taken aback by the crowded bar but immediately got to work waiting on the crush of customers waving twenty-dollar bills at her, wanting to order drinks. She paused to glance over at Bear, smiling sweetly at him and then blowing him a kiss. Bear pretended to catch it in his hand and brought it close to his heart.

Hayley watched the mushy scene, mouth agape. "Wait . . . You and Michelle?"

"Yeah," Bear practically cooed, a little embarrassed. The big guy obviously wasn't used to gushing about his feelings. "I've been hanging out here a lot while I've been in town. We got to talking, found we had a lot in common, and well . . . Yeah, me and Michelle . . . Let's say I'm gonna get back up here to Bar Harbor just as soon as I can."

She gave him a big hug. "I'm so happy for you both."

Bear grinned, gave Hayley a friendly pat on the shoulder, then slowly moved down the bar to be closer to Michelle, who was busy making drinks. Hayley loved this unexpected happy ending.

The door to the bar flew open and Mona Barnes, Hayley's other BFF and local lobsterwoman, stormed in, her eyes settling on her usual spot at the bar, which was taken by a preppy loan officer at the First National Bank, sipping a rum and Coke. Mona's nostrils flared and her cheeks reddened. "Where the hell am I supposed to sit to enjoy my Bud Light?"

Randy returned, carrying the empty tray under his arm. "Sorry, Mona. You'll just have to wait. But good news. He and his wife have a dinner reservation at McKay's so they should be leaving soon." He turned to Hayley. Can you believe this? We've been out straight all night. I can't remember the last time it was this busy!"

Mona looked around and shrugged. "Of course his business is booming. Folks have come from far and wide out of morbid curiosity."

"Morbid curiosity?" Hayley asked with a raised eyebrow.

Mona sighed, annoyed she even had to explain. "People are always drawn to places where famous people died. The Dakota in New York, John Lennon. The Chateau Marmont in L.A., John Belushi. The Ford's Theatre in D.C., Abraham Lincoln. That's its own museum! They even give tours there! And now, Drinks Like A Fish, Bar Harbor, Maine, Jefferson O'Keefe."

"That's sick," Hayley lamented, crinkling her nose.

"I'm not saying it's right, it's just a fact," Mona huffed. "Morbid, yes, but good for the bottom line."

Randy shrugged. "I agree with Hayley, but it's not my job to judge. My job is to keep my customers happy and satisfied."

And then he scooted off to tend to a table of college students who were trying to signal him for more napkins with their buffalo wings.

Hayley felt a deep pang of sadness thinking about the tragic loss of Jefferson O'Keefe. But thanks to his large library of recordings and videos, his voice would always be with us. He had left a long and lasting mark. She knew this was going to be most hard on Liddy, but she planned to be there to help get her through it.

Hayley glanced around the bar, watching Bear flirting with Michelle, Randy flitting about chatting with all the patrons, Mona staring down the preppy banker until he got so uncomfortable, he stood up and offered her the stool. Yes, life in Bar Harbor had mostly returned to normal. But in the wake of recent events, Hayley had learned to appreciate and cherish what she had because if the last week had taught her anything, it was that it all could be gone in a moment. Which was why she waved good night to everyone and marched out of the bar. She was going home to her husband who was there waiting for her. After all, that was the part of her life that she truly cherished the most.

Island Food & Spirits
by
Hayley Powell

March has been quite an atypical month in our little town of Bar Harbor. Spring is normally a little sleepy, the calm before the storm of tourists blowing onto the island during the frenetic, hectic summer season.

But with my restaurant business booming, and catering Randy's party at Drinks Like A Fish, and of course the sad sudden passing of his guest of honor, hometown boy comedian Jefferson O'Keefe, I've barely had time to catch my breath.

I'm happy to report that the *Island Times* will be doing a special story about Mr. O'Keefe, "Island Boy Dreams Big and Makes It As Famous Comedian," which I have no doubt will be a respectful and lovely tribute to our old classmate and friend.

I was taking a much-needed break this past Monday to catch up on some rest before heading into the restaurant to catch up on paperwork while at the same time trying to come up with something for dinner that evening. I was dreading having to make a trip to the Shop 'n Save to pick something up when I suddenly remembered that my indispensable chef,

Kelton, had texted me earlier to inform me that he had some leftover corned beef and cabbage from this past weekend's special in the fridge at the restaurant for me.

This was perfect since in the off-season my restaurant is closed on Mondays and Tuesdays to give the staff a well-deserved break before we return to seven days a week during the busy tourist season.

I had also been thinking how little Bruce and I had seen each other over the past few weeks, mostly my fault, and that's when I hit upon an idea. I could kill two birds with one stone (possibly not the best choice of words, considering recent events). Maybe I could go to the restaurant and get all my paperwork done while at the same time put together a romantic dinner for just the two of us with Kelton's leftovers.

I wrote a quick note telling Bruce to meet me at the restaurant at 6:00 P.M. when he got back from the trial that he was covering in Ellsworth, for a quiet dinner with his adoring wife, and then I headed out the door. When I arrived at the restaurant, I found the corned beef and cabbage that Kelton had left in our industrial-size refrigerator, put it in a Dutch oven, and then set it in the oven on low to warm while I worked. While it heated up, I got busy with my paperwork, losing all track of time. When I glanced up at the clock on the wall and saw that it was already 5:45, I figured I

had just enough time to do a little primping in the bathroom and set a romantic
table by the fireplace in the restaurant's
dining room with a bottle of wine to enjoy
with our dinner.

I had everything ready when the clock
struck six, I sat down at the table in the
large empty restaurant and waited.

And waited.

And waited.

Thirty minutes passed and there was still
no sign of Bruce. Worried, I called his cell
but got no answer. Then I called our house
landline. No answer there either. I waited
another fifteen minutes until I couldn't stand
it anymore and tried his cell and home
again.

Still nothing.

I was afraid something bad might have
happened, so I called my brother-in-law
Sergio and asked if he had heard of any
accidents on the road from Ellsworth to
the Island and he said, "No, it's been as
quiet as a church skunk."

Church mouse.

Not skunk.

Skunk wasn't even close.

But I was too worried to correct him, so
I hung up and raced home to see if Bruce
had possibly not seen my note and was
there. But when I grabbed my purse and
headed out the door, I forgot my phone
on the table where I had been waiting.

Unbeknownst to me, at that same moment, Bruce was walking through our kitchen door with a bag of Chinese food from China Hill in Ellsworth. He had decided to surprise me with all my favorite dishes (spring rolls, Kung Pao Chicken, Stinky Tofu). He meant to call and let me know after he picked up the order but realized he had left his phone at the courthouse, which was now locked up for the night, so he wouldn't be able to retrieve it until the next day.

Bruce spotted my note clear as day on the table, read it, hurried back out the door with the food, got into his car, and drove straight to the restaurant.

You can see where this is going!

A few minutes later, I pulled into our driveway, and not seeing Bruce's car, I started to hyperventilate with panic. I reached for my phone to try and call him again and realized I had left it on the table at the restaurant, so I reversed right out of the driveway, and sped back to the restaurant.

Well, as you can now imagine, Bruce showed up at the restaurant, Chinese food in hand, and hurried inside looking for me. When he couldn't find me, he used the phone at the hostess station to call our house and heard my cell ringing on the table where I had left it. So he left the bag of Chinese food on the table and went outside to the parking lot. When he didn't see my car, he started to get worried and jumped back in his car and drove home again to see if I was there.

Have you ever heard the phrase, "Two ships passing in the night?" Well, it went on like this for another forty-five minutes.

I arrived back at the restaurant and went to the table to retrieve my phone where I noticed the bag and peeked inside. Spring rolls! Yummy! It suddenly dawned on me that Bruce had been here and had the same idea, surprising me with dinner. I figured he had gone home looking for me, so I hopped back in my car and drove home again. My worry was starting to fade, but my irritation was growing mostly from low blood sugar because I was so hungry. This missing each other was starting to get ridiculous! And I could not understand why Bruce wasn't answering his phone.

Just then my cell rang and I quickly picked up. But it wasn't Bruce. It was Randy. I told him I couldn't talk because I was trying to track down Bruce, but Randy interrupted me and told me that Bruce was at the police station with him and Sergio. He told me to turn back around and go to the restaurant. The three of them were on their way to meet me.

When we were all reunited at the restaurant, Bruce filled me in on his forgotten phone. I was just so happy he was alive and well, all was quickly forgiven and we had a good laugh over it.

Sergio was already peeking in the bag Bruce had left on the table because the food smelled so good, so of course we invited them to stay for dinner. Bruce began pulling the containers of food out of the bag, Randy grabbed wineglasses for the Merlot I had set out, and I went into the kitchen and returned with a big platter of the warmed corned beef and cabbage, a veritable feast of Chinese and Irish fare, our own fusion dinner.

Once our bellies were full, Randy made his specialty Irish coffees for us to enjoy. What started out as a disaster of an evening ended up being a memorable night for us all.

Bruce and I have set aside some time next weekend for a "just us date," but I'm not getting my hopes up because you never know what's going to happen around here.

But for now, give these delicious recipes a try. I just know your own family will love them.

Happy St. Patrick's Day!

Randy's Irish Coffee

Ingredients:
Fresh brewed coffee (use your favorite,
 I like a dark roast)
1½ ounces Jameson Irish Whiskey
Splash of real maple syrup
Whipped cream (optional)

In a coffee mug add your coffee, whiskey, and maple syrup. Stir and top with whipped cream.

Kelton's Corned Beef and Cabbage

Ingredients:
3 to 4 pounds corned beef brisket with
 the spice packet
3 tablespoons whole-grain mustard
3 tablespoons brown sugar
1 teaspoon cracked black pepper
3 cups water
1 bottle of Guinness beer
5-6 garlic cloves, peeled (more, if you
 love garlic)

1 cabbage, cored and cut into wedges
1 sweet onion, peeled and cut into
 wedges
6 large carrots, peeled and cut into
 two-inch pieces
1½ pounds small baby new potatoes

Preheat your oven to 350 degrees. You will need a large Dutch oven or roasting pan.

Rinse your corned beef brisket in cold water and pat dry. Place in the Dutch oven, fatty side up.

In a bowl, combine the whole-grain mustard, brown sugar, and black pepper and rub the mixture all over the brisket.

Sprinkle the seasoning packet into the Dutch oven and pour the three cups of water and beer into the pan, careful not to pour onto the seasoned brisket. Cover your Dutch oven and bake for 1½ hours.

Remove the Dutch oven from the oven and add the rest of the ingredients, starting with the garlic, cabbage, onions, carrots, and potatoes. Spoon juice all over the vegetables. Place back in the oven and roast covered for 1 hour.

Check meat and vegetables to see if fork tender. If not, roast uncovered for 30 more minutes or until fork tender.

Remove your brisket, transfer it to a warm platter, slice it, then arrange the vegetables all around the meat. Serve and enjoy!

PERKED UP

Barbara Ross

Chapter One

"Brrr . . ." My friend Zoey Butterfield pushed open the always-unlocked back door of my mother's house in Busman's Harbor, Maine, stomping her feet on the mat outside before she entered. In the back hall, she used one foot to lever a boot off the other, revealing a bulky sock knit in florescent colors, and then repeated the action with the other foot. She smiled and held out a wet paper bag. "Good thing we decided to stay in for St. Patrick's."

Good thing, indeed. Though there really hadn't been much choice about it. Crowley's, Busman's Harbor's noisiest dive bar, was only open weekends until mid-April, and the rest of the bars and eateries wouldn't start doing business until Memorial Day. We could have driven off the peninsula, to Damariscotta or Wiscasset, or farther afield to

Brunswick or even Portland, but given the weather, it was good that we hadn't.

Instead, we had a plan that involved Irish coffees and a movie in the comfort of my mother's living room. "Something set in Ireland," Zoey had said when we'd debated possible film selections.

I opened the paper bag and put the contents out on the kitchen table. A fifth of Jameson Irish Whiskey and two quarts of whipping cream. "How much Irish coffee are we planning to drink?" I asked.

Zoey shed her bulky coat and hung it in the back hall. "As much as it takes."

I measured coffee grounds for Mom's fancy coffee maker. Since she'd started working at Linens and Pantries during the off-season, Mom had used her employee discount to line the countertops of her old-fashioned kitchen with all sorts of sleek appliances. The coffee maker was the only one I used regularly, and I hated it, encumbered as it was with far too many buttons and settings. Grumbling to myself, I loaded the coffee and filled the water reservoir.

"What?" Zoey was filling the three footed glass mugs I'd left on the counter with hot water to warm them.

"Nothing," I assured her. I left the kitchen through the swinging door and crossed the dining room into the living room to ask Mom if she'd like to join us for a drink.

And stopped dead the moment I got there. Mom wasn't alone. George McQuaig was seated in the armchair next to her. Captain George had worked for my family for three decades, piloting the tour boat we used during the summer to ferry guests to and from the island where we ran our family business. Billed as a "dining experience," the Snowden Family Clambake Company treated four hundred customers a day to an authentic Maine clambake meal—twin lobsters, soft-shelled clams called steamers, a potato, onion, ear of corn, and an egg—all cooked under seawater-soaked tarps over a roaring hardwood fire.

I hadn't heard the captain come in. Mom must have lingered in the front hall, anticipating his arrival, and let him in before he could ring the bell. There was a wood fire already burning in the hearth.

It wasn't so astonishing that George was at our house on this particular night, but that he was here on any night. He and my mother were friends, had been for decades. She usually sat in the pilot house of the *Jacquie II* with him as she commuted to her summer job running the gift shop at the Snowden Family Clambake. George had been a friend of my late father's as well, a good friend and employee of long standing. But he hadn't, as far as I knew, crossed the threshold of our house since my dad had died eleven years before.

"Hut-hum." I cleared my throat and found my voice. "Zoey and I are making Irish coffees to celebrate the day. Would either of you care for one?"

"Sounds like a lovely treat on a cold, sleety night," Mom answered.

"Wonderful!" Captain George was full of enthusiasm. "Thank you, Julia."

"We were planning to, um, watch a movie." My

eyes traveled to the television in the corner of the room. "We could use your sitting room." The only other television in the house was in the converted sunporch off Mom's bedroom. The room was drafty in the best of times and with the way the wind howled tonight . . . I shuddered, imagining the cold air hitting my neck and whooshing down my back.

"Nonsense," Mom said. "We'll watch with you here. I'm sure we can find something we'll all enjoy."

Curiouser and curiouser. The captain wasn't here to deliver any particular message to my mother. He was here to hang out, open to having a drink and seeing a movie.

On the way back through the dining room I picked the fourth footed glass mug out of the corner cabinet and took it to the kitchen.

"Mom has company," I reported to Zoey. "Captain George is here and will be joining us."

Zoey raised an eyebrow in silent question but didn't press when I didn't respond. She had a big, flat screen TV in her modern apartment over Lupine Design, her pottery shop and studio. I wondered for a moment why we hadn't chosen to gather there for our St. Patrick's celebration. But I'd done the inviting and we'd both fallen under the assumption I would host. It was my second spring living back in my mother's house—yet again—and I treated the house as my own. But I should've checked with Mom before I'd made this plan. As soon as the weather allowed, I'd be moving out to my new apartment in the fully renovated Windsholme, the mansion on Morrow Island, the island my mother had inherited and where we ran our clambakes.

I pulled a hand mixer out of a cabinet and plugged it into an outlet. Zoey poured two cups of cream into a ceramic bowl, added vanilla, and turned on the mixer.

When the coffee and whipped cream were done, we assembled the drinks.

"Where's your brown sugar?" Zoey asked.

I shook my head. "We'll use maple syrup," I said. "It's the Maine way." I poured a tablespoon into each mug then added the whiskey, stirring the mixture gently. I poured in the coffee and then Zoey spooned on the whipped cream.

I put the mugs on a wooden tray and carried them to the living room with Zoey right behind me. The drinks smelled like heaven, coffee and whiskey together. How could they be bad?

"Here we are," I called to my mother and George. "Captain, this is my friend Zoe—"

The wind blew, the windows rattled, and every light in the house went out.

"Oh!" Zoey exclaimed from behind me, taken by surprise.

Guided by the light from the fireplace, I deposited the tray on the coffee table and went to look outside. Through the pelting, wet snow, the windows on our street stared back at me, dark and empty. I was used to dark windows. Half the homes in our neighborhood belonged to seasonal residents who had fled sometime between October first and New Year's Day and wouldn't return until the spring. But the streetlights were out and so were the lights across the street at the Snuggles

Inn, a bed-and-breakfast run by our friends, the Snugg sisters.

Blackouts were relatively frequent when you lived at the end of the single transmission line that rolled into town along the two-lane road that traveled from Route 1 to the harbor. My mother was therefore prepared. I moved around the room, lighting candles, including the three in the silver candelabra that stood on a table in the front window, one of the few heirlooms my mother had from her formerly wealthy family.

Zoey and I sat at opposite ends of the long couch facing the fire, perpendicular to the matching armchairs where my mother and the captain sat. There was a bit of polite conversation. The captain asked Zoey about her successful pottery business. She asked how he'd come to captain our tour boat. Then the talk petered out. It was warm by the fire, and the first few sips of Irish coffee had me warm and relaxed from the inside, too, but it was way too early to fall into a silent stupor. The movie was out, gone along with the cable, Internet, and electricity.

"Anyone know any ghost stories?" Zoey asked. "It seems like the night for it." As if to make her point, the wind rattled the doors and windows.

"I know the perfect one for the occasion," George said. He took a gulp of his Irish coffee and sat forward in his chair, readying himself for the tale. A tall, broad-shouldered man, he filled the roomy armchair. He looked even larger seated next to my petite mother, who took up half her chair seat and whose feet barely rested on the Oriental carpet. Captain George's white hair swept behind his ears down to his collar. I'd never been able to figure out if the long hair and the white beard were part of the "Old Salt" persona he affected for his job or if they were, unironically, him.

An accomplished storyteller, Captain George provided the narration for the tourists aboard the *Jacquie II*. About eighty percent of his tales were eighty percent true. There were plenty of things to see from the boat—seals, eagles, whales, islands, and lighthouses—but when George amped his tales up with mermaids, pirates, and sunken Viking treasure, the tips the crew collected as the customers disembarked grew exponentially.

I picked up my glass mug and settled into my seat on the deep couch in happy anticipation.

The Captain's Tale

The captain began. "'Twas his own kindness and charity that doomed poor Hugh O'Hara." His voice was sonorous, as though he were talking to our customers through the *Jacquie II*'s sound system. "He was murdered in his own house on St. Patrick's night, March 17, 1867." George paused, looking at each of our faces in the firelight, to make sure he had our attention. He did. "O'Hara and his wife, Catherine, lived on the big house on the green in Busman's Center. You'll know it."

"The Kensington House, Bed and Breakfast," Mom said. She and I both knew the broad outlines of the story of Hugh O'Hara's murder, a famous local legend, but I didn't know much beyond the fact he'd been killed in his own home.

"The huge one, with the porches and the turret?" Zoey asked.

"Yes, girl," George answered. He took another sip and settled into his tale. "The story begins in the spring of 1866, when, out of the goodness of his heart, O'Hara hired a delinquent teenager, Daniel Kearney, to help with the planting. Kearney's mother and stepfather were well-respected residents of Busman's Harbor, but young Daniel had been in trouble frequently for stealing and had spent time in the state reform school. No one knows why O'Hara looked beyond this. He even advanced the boy a week's wages, bought him a new set of clothes, and let him sleep in the downstairs bedroom behind the kitchen."

The captain paused to take a long swallow of his Irish coffee. "Very good." He tipped his cup toward Zoey and me in appreciation. I took a swallow, too. It was good—warm, robustly flavorful, and comforting. Perfect for a stormy night.

Captain George settled back in his seat and continued the tale. "That night, the very first night in his new employer's home, Daniel Kearney climbed out the window of his room. The house sat high on its foundation, commanding its location. As it does today." He stopped to look at each of us. We nodded in agreement. Kensington House was an imposing sight. "Kearney shimmied down a two-by-four he had left there earlier in the day and disappeared, never to be seen on the peninsula again until that fateful night, one year later, St. Patrick's Day, March 17, 1867."

The captain raised his eyebrows and ended the paragraph with a flourish of his hand, glancing around to see if he had our attention. He did.

"Ooooh," Zoey said, egging him on.

He nodded, satisfied. "On that night, Hugh's last night on earth, he and Catherine had enjoyed an evening celebration of St. Pat's at the home of their daughter, Margaret and her husband, Martin Gleason, who lived in a big house across the way, on the other side of the town green. It was late when Hugh and Catherine walked home in a fearsome storm, just like tonight's." The captain gestured toward the front windows, splotched with icy snow.

"Wait," I said. "They were Irish, and they were Catholic, and wealthy farmers?" I knew the Europeans who settled our peninsula had been Scots Irish. They'd named our streets and local landmarks. But the Star of the Sea, Busman's Harbor's Catholic church, had been established for the Irish servants of the wealthy families that had built summer homes in Maine starting in the 1880s. I hadn't realized there had been Irish families here well before then.

As if scandalized by my ignorance, the captain's eyebrows raised and then lowered into a frown of consternation. "Don't know your local history very well, do you, girl?" he asked in what I hoped was mock indignation. "Well, you can be excused. The history of the Irish in America is most often told as a mass migration into big cities. But at the turn of the nineteenth century, one of the most successful timbering, shipbuilding, and shipping enterprises on this coast was the firm of Kavanaugh and Cottrill right up the road here in Newcastle, Maine. James Kavanaugh and Matthew Cottrill were part

of a wave of Irish immigrants who arrived after the
American Revolution, and the lads made good.
They built St. Patrick's Church in Newcastle, con-
secrated in 1808. It's the oldest standing Catholic
church in New England, still in use today."

The captain was enjoying the opportunity to ed-
ucate as well as tell a tale. It was something he ex-
celled at in his tour boat talks as well.

"Kavanaugh and Cottrill's ships regularly took
timbers, milled wood, and barrel staves to Ireland.
Rather than come back empty, with rocks for bal-
last, they took paying passengers back to Maine.
Hugh O'Hara was one of those. He came to these
shores from County Cork in 1810 in place of a pile
of rocks. He was twenty-six years-old, smart and
strong. He worked in timbering, saving money and
buying land in Busman's Center, bit by bit. By the
time he married in 1828, he had a working farm
with a cabin on it. He bought more and more land
and built the big house you see today. Hugh
O'Hara was wealthy indeed. By the 1850s his farmland stretched from the ocean to the bay, where
the Busman's Harbor Golf Club is now. He had
more acreage than any other farm on the peninsula."

"Enough with the history lesson," Zoey said.
"Let's get to the ghost."

"In good time," the captain replied, inclining
his head toward the front window where big,
sloppy flakes hiding centers of icy sleet pinged
against the glass. "Are you in a hurry to go somewhere?"

Zoey chuckled and settled back into the couch,

tucking her brightly colored socks under her bottom.

The captain picked up the tale. "Old Hugh and his wife had moved to the downstairs bedroom behind the kitchen the previous fall. Though smaller than the grand front room upstairs, it was warmer in the winter and more convenient. In the early hours of that morning, Hugh awoke to a strange noise. He roused Catherine, pushing her down between the bed and the wall and went to investigate. Hugh was eighty-three, but he was scrappy and tough. Though he had field hands, he still worked on his farm every day. It wouldn't have occurred to him to go for help.

"There was a strange smell of sulfur in the house. Hugh lit a lantern and followed a trail of burnt matches. The thief had lit them as he moved about the house, snatching valuables as he went. Hugh came upon him back in the kitchen. The intruder wore a burlap sack with eyeholes cut out of it over his head. It must have been a terrifying sight."

I pictured the scene. Old Hugh in his nightshirt and cap. Catherine in her flannel gown and kerchief, hiding behind their four-poster bed. The terrifying specter of the strange man, eyeholes gaping the burlap sack. I shivered despite the fire.

The captain continued. "Seeing the lantern, the thief ran into the O'Haras' bedroom. Catherine O'Hara saw him in the lamp glow and screamed, giving away her hiding place. The thief grabbed an ax from his belt and brought it down on her, slicing into her upper arm. Old Hugh jumped him, and a vicious fight ensued, moving back from the

bedroom into the kitchen. O'Hara fought val-
iantly, swinging his lantern while the thief sliced
madly with his ax. Suddenly, the thief pulled a pistol from his belt and fired. Old Hugh dropped to
the floor."

The captain stopped, stared pointedly at his
empty glass mug, and then at me.

"C'mon." Zoey was nearly breathless. "Finish the
story first. Then we'll make another round."

His brows drew together in a look of resignation
and Captain George went on. "In the chaos,
Catherine O'Hara had escaped and went screaming across the green to the Gleasons' house, leaving a bright red trail of blood in the snow. While
Margaret tended to Catherine, Martin went to investigate. He found his father-in-law dead on the
kitchen floor."

Zoey gasped, putting a hand to her mouth. Her
big eyes were wide. I didn't know if the tale of
Hugh O'Hara had elicited all that emotion, or if
she was thinking back to the body she'd discovered in the basement of her pottery studio the previous spring. I moved closer to her on the couch,
hoping my nearness would steady her, but she
showed no signs of wanting George to stop. Instead, she motioned him onward.

George nodded. "By that time, other men who
lived in houses or over shops around the town
green had arrived. They searched the O'Hara
house but found no one. Then Gleason spotted a
two-by-four leaning against the open window of
the dining room. The thief must have shimmied
up it to get to the window to open it. Gleason remembered Kearney had used the same method to

escape the house the year before. 'It can be no man but Kearney!' he cried.

"In the stable the men discovered a horse and bridle missing. It was easy to spot the direction of escape in the snow and mud. By the time Gleason and his companions gathered their horses, Kearney was at least an hour ahead, but he was riding a plow horse, bareback. They caught up to him on the road to Damariscotta. When he spotted them, Kearney jumped off the horse and ran into the woods. Gleason gave chase on foot and was alone when he captured him. Kearney made a full confession. He claimed he'd only meant to rob the house but had been caught in the act by Old Hugh and things had gotten out of hand from there. Gleason and his companions brought Kearney back and turned him over at the old Wiscasset jail."

Captain George sat back in his chair and exhaled noisily, presumably exhausted—and parched—from his labors.

But Zoey was not going to let him off the hook so easily. "Then who's the ghost?" she demanded. "Old Hugh O'Hara's murderer was caught. Justice was served. What's his ghost hanging around for?"

"The ghost—" The captain began, when he was interrupted by a *rat-tat-tat* staccato knocking on the glass of the front door.

Chapter Two

"Who is out on a night like this?" I hurried out of the living room. The answer was immediately apparent. When I opened the big wood and glass front door, Fee and Vee Snugg, our across-the-street neighbors, stood on the porch.

"Come in, come in!" I cried. "What in heaven's name—"

Fee was immediately inside, unwinding her purple woolen scarf and shaking the snow off her short hair, much in the manner of her beloved Scottish terrier. Her sister, Vee, entered behind her, holding out something wrapped in foil. "My Irish soda bread," she said. "Just out of the oven when the lights went out. We saw your candles in the window and thought, why should we sit alone in the dark and eat this on our own?"

The foil bundle was still warm when I took it

from her. "We're drinking Irish coffees and telling ghost stories," I told them.

"Sounds perfect." Fee was already headed toward the living room, her thick, wool socks *shushing* across the wooden floor of the front hall.

Vee sat down on a bench to remove her boots. Unlike her sister, who wore sensible, L.L. Bean boots, Vee wore, always, a pair of suede boots with thin, almost stiletto, heels, and lambswool around the tops. The boots were impractical in the extreme and the entire town was convinced she was going to kill herself in them. Somehow she never did. When she pulled them off, I saw in the candle's glow, in her only concession to the weather, she had traded her usual nylons for brown tights that matched her neat, belted brown dress. Vee was glamorous, always, and her stubborn adherence to her own exacting standards for proper dress, no matter the circumstances, both amused and delighted me.

Vee and Fee settled on the love seat in the living room across from the chairs that held the captain and my mother. The sisters were as close as could be, living together and running their bed-and-breakfast, yet they could not have been more different in their appearance. Fee, labeled "the plain one" all her life by her parents among others, leaned into the designation. She kept her steel-gray hair out of her face with a plastic barrette and peered at the world through thick lenses surrounded by colorless frames. She wore tweed trousers and a turtleneck that appeared to be a cream color in the firelight, its neck stretched out and misshapen by too many washings. On the other hand, even after their walk across the street in the blowing snow, Vee's pure white chignon was still in perfect form. Once put up every morning, even Mother Nature's best efforts couldn't move it. Vee was fully made up and must have been before the blackout. She would never appear without "her face on," even if all that was planned was an evening at home with her sister, baking and eating.

I put our empty mugs back on the tray. Zoey picked up the candle and led our way into the kitchen.

"That's the last of the glass mugs," I told Zoey.

"We'll use regular coffee mugs," she said. "I'm sure Fee and Vee won't mind."

I went into the back hall, found a battery-powered lantern, turned it on, and scanned the shelves until I located the camp percolator my mother kept for exactly this contingency—no electricity and a desperate need for coffee. As I filled the pot, another candle appeared in the kitchen, and behind it, my mother.

"So, Captain George?" I said to her, before she could speak.

"Is a friend," she answered, a bit defensively, in my opinion. "And we thought, why should each of us be alone on this night when people are celebrating?" She closed her mouth, her lips drawn tight, indicating she'd take no follow-up questions. I didn't know if she didn't want to talk in front of Zoey, or in front of me, or if there was something she wasn't admitting to herself. I studied her in the ghostly kitchen, lit by the cold florescent bulb of the lantern and the warmer glow of the candles. Her blond hair had lightened as silver threads wove through it, and there were deep laugh lines around her eyes, but she was a remarkably beautiful woman, at least to me.

Mom went to a kitchen drawer that was used so rarely, I didn't know what was in it. She fumbled around, the contents of the drawer clanking, and then pulled out an old-fashioned manual egg-beater. Carrying it carefully, flat in both hands, held out like an offering, she handed it to Zoey.

I remembered the eggbeater instantly. When my dad's mother had died a dozen years before, each of us, her children, their spouses, and her grandchildren, had been allowed to pick an item from the house where she and my grandfather had raised their six kids and then lived out their lives. My mother had picked the homely eggbeater. When I asked her why, she said it reminded her of the birthdays and holidays when my grandmother had given my mother, who was in no way, shape, or form a cook, the task of whipping the cream for the pumpkin pies or the strawberry shortcake, whatever the season and occasion called for. Mom's memories of those times with my grandmother in her tiny kitchen, when the old lobsterman's wife and the girl from a summer family that owned a private island had found common ground in conversation, were happy ones. Memories of family and belonging.

Mom took the camp percolator, loaded with coffee grounds and water, out to the living room to hang over the fire. I opened the refrigerator and was momentarily taken by surprise when the light didn't go on, despite the darkness all around me.

"What?" Zoey asked.

"I'm laughing at myself."

It took a while, but finally Zoey succeeded in whipping the cream. We loaded the bowl, maple syrup, whiskey, soda bread, butter, little plates, utensils, and mugs on two trays and carried them triumphantly out to the living room. When we arrived, the others were finishing a discussion of the weather, current and projected, a subject that was required to lead every conversation in Maine. The group fell silent as Zoey assembled the coffees and I passed the plates with the soda bread.

"Well," Vee finally said, " what are we talking about?"

The Snugg Sisters' Tale

Le Roi, our Maine Coon cat, had claimed the warm spot where I'd been sitting and I almost sat down on him, popping up at the last moment and scooting him over. He wasn't a fan of gatherings of humans, so the temperature in the house must be dropping for him to be willing to join us by the fire.

"The O'Hara murder." Captain George answered Vee's question.

Fee blew out air in irritation, her eyes behind the thick glasses moving from the captain to me. "I suppose he told you it was poor Dan Kearney that did it?"

"He confessed," Captain George protested.

"Was he convicted?" Fee challenged.

George was flustered, but only for a moment. "No. But only because he escaped."

"Escaped?" Zoey shook her thick curls. "Who's the ghost? Is it Hugh because his murder was never avenged? Or . . ." She brightened. "Maybe it is Daniel, condemned to hang around the house because he never faced justice."

"Daniel was innocent," Vee insisted.

"Wait one minute." The captain held up a warning finger. "If he was innocent, why did he run?"

"A poor boy like that?" Fee scowled. "He never would have received justice. Not when he was accused by one of the richest families in town."

"Think of it logically." Vee took up the argument. "How did a poor boy like that get a pistol? Where was he the whole year he was gone? How did he just happen to return to Busman's Center on the day of the murder?" She had the ferocity of a defense attorney pointing out the inconsistencies in the prosecution's story.

"He came back with the intent to rob his benefactor," Captain George argued. He leaned forward, bracing his elbows on the arms of his chair. His white hair flopped from behind his ear and shimmered in the firelight. "Besides, if not Daniel Kearney, then who?"

"I'm so glad you asked." Vee grabbed her coffee mug and took a long swig. She wiggled her bottom into the love seat, eager to tell.

I took a swallow of the Irish coffee as well. "Oof."

"You okay?" Zoey's eyebrows drew together with concern.

"Fine," I sputtered. Zoey had made the second round of drinks far stronger than I'd made the first. Silently, I vowed to pace myself.

Vee put down her mug and began. "I don't suppose *he* told you that Catherine O'Hara was Old Hugh's third wife?" She glared at the captain, though it was hardly necessary. He was the only *he* in the room.

"I'm not sure what difference that makes," I said. Female mortality was high in the nineteenth century. It wouldn't be extraordinary for a man as old as Hugh to have had multiple wives.

"She was twenty-three, sixty years his junior!" Fee said it triumphantly, as if the six-decade age difference was in itself proof of something.

It was true that when Captain George had spoken of Old Hugh's wife, I'd pictured someone as old as he was, or nearly so. But I had to admit the picture in my head of the old man and lady in their sleeping clothes had come more from the illustrations in our family copy of *The Night Before Christmas* than from anything the captain had said or implied.

"She was a beautiful young woman," Vee said. "She could have had her choice of suitors when the men came home from war. Instead, in 1862, when she was eighteen, she married a man in his late seventies. Why?"

"She married Old Hugh because he was wealthy. Hugh owned two hundred acres of rich farmland as well as commercial properties on both sides of the town green." Fee paused and then delivered the coup de grâce. "She married with the sole intention of becoming a rich widow. But

Hugh didn't cooperate. He lived on and on, five years past their wedding date. She could wait no longer."

"Maybe she was driven to it," Vee suggested.

"Pah," Fee mumbled under her breath.

The sisters differed not only in their looks. A true maiden lady, Fee, for Fiona, was practical and a tad judgmental. She preferred the company of her line of Scottish terriers, the current one named Mackie, to other humans. She believed he was better behaved and had better morals, though it could be argued it was the snip of the veterinarian that had brought that about, rather than the dog's inner nobility.

Vee, for Viola, had never married either. But it was common knowledge around town that she'd carried on a years-long affair with her boss at the Busman's Harbor Bank. The affair had ended two decades earlier, when the bank was swallowed by a bigger bank that was swallowed by a bigger bank and so on, until it came to its current ownership by a giant Spanish conglomerate. The boss had taken early retirement and moved to Florida with his wife, leaving Vee shattered. But her essential spirit survived intact. Vee was and would always be a romantic.

The sisters' different personalities were reflected in their views of Catherine O'Hara. They both, apparently, thought she was guilty of Hugh's murder, but they disagreed on the motive.

"Hugh O'Hara was probably a terrible, controlling man who beat her," Vee asserted, trying for the last word.

"Now just a darn minute!' Captain George was

outraged by this slander of a man who'd been dead for over 150 years. "What evidence do you have of any of this? Hugh O'Hara was a self-made man, a religious man, and an upstanding citizen. There's never been a whisper of a word otherwise."

"Regardless of the reason"—Fee shot a silencing glance at her sister—"Catherine did it. She murdered her husband."

We were quiet for a moment, absorbing this.

"How did she do it?" the captain demanded. "Explain that, will you?"

Vee took a long drink of her Irish coffee, as if steeling herself, and plunged onward. "Step one, she needed a patsy to take the blame. She went to Daniel Kearney's mother's house in Busman's Harbor. It turned out he'd sent her the address of a boardinghouse in Boston. He didn't live there— he was a homeless urchin—but the landlady allowed him to pick up his mail." Vee leaned forward, confident in her narrative. "Catherine wrote to Daniel to say all was forgiven and he should return before the spring planting. Step one of the scheme was done."

"Daniel did arrive the day of the murder, as you all no doubt heard from the captain here," Fee said. While they might have differing views on the man and the motive, on this part of the story, the sisters agreed. "He had taken a boat from Boston to Bath, paid for with money Catherine sent. Then he'd walked over twenty miles from Bath to Busman's Center, arriving wet, frozen, and exhausted. Catherine gave him dry clothes and blankets and sent him to sleep in the stable. She told him she would let Hugh know he was there." Fee paused, raising her eyebrows over her thick glasses, "But of course she didn't."

"Instead, she and Hugh walked across the road to celebrate St. Patrick's Day with his daughter and son-in-law. Later, they returned home and went to bed," Vee continued. "Catherine waited until Hugh was well asleep and then went about setting the scene, moving around the house lighting matches and hiding valuables in a sack as she went." Vee leaned toward us, drawing us in. "Then she opened the back door yelling, 'Help! Help!' so loud and long that Daniel was raised from his sleep. He picked up an ax leaning by the wall of the stable and ran to the house to rescue Catharine."

Fee spoke next. The sisters passed the story from one to the other as easily as runners passing a baton. "When he got inside, there was quite the altercation. Hugh had also been awakened by Catherine's screams and came into the kitchen clutching a lantern. One can only imagine how astonished he was to see Daniel there. He aimed the lantern at Daniel who swung the ax wildly, hitting Catherine in the upper arm. Catherine had had enough. She pulled a pistol from her robe and shot Hugh O'Hara dead."

Fee looked around with satisfaction. We were all there in the firelight with our mouths hanging open to various degrees.

Despite my earlier caution, I picked up my Irish coffee and drained it.

"Then what happened?" Zoey was breathless.

"Catherine ran across the green to her step-daughter's house, screaming that an intruder had killed Hugh, just as she'd planned it. Daniel, terrified, ran away, stealing a plow horse and bridle from the stable." Vee spoke as if each of these steps was indisputable.

"But what about the burlap sack Kearney wore over his head?" the captain asked.

"We've only Catherine's word it ever existed," Fee pointed out. "Was the sack found? Taken into evidence?"

The captain stared down at his sock-clad feet. A tiny circle of pink skin showed through near his right big toe. "No. But what evidence do you have for any of this? Was Catherine's letter to Daniel inviting him back to Busman's Center found? Is it at the historical society?"

Fee stuck out her jaw. "This was how the tale was told to our mother by someone who had reason to know. What evidence do you have for your version?"

"The boy was arrested." The captain's voice rose. "He confessed."

Vee dismissed the confession with a wave of her hand. "Alone and scared, hunted down like an animal. You can put no credence in Daniel Kearney's confession."

Captain George wasn't giving up. "Why did he run, then? And why did he escape from jail instead of facing his accusers?"

"Never mind that," Zoey interrupted. "Who is the ghost? Is Catherine the ghost, condemned to live in her former home for the sin of killing her husband?"

Vee had opened her mouth to answer Zoey's question when she was cut off by a loud rapping on the glass of the front door.

Chapter Three

Two silhouettes were barely visible through the thick glass panel. Even in the near total darkness I recognized the shapes instinctively as my former landlord, Gus, and his wife, Augustine, called Mrs. Gus. I threw open the door and greeted them.

"Hello, hello," Mrs. Gus called. "We saw the candles in the window. I hope you don't mind." She thrust forward a plate holding something covered in aluminum foil. Gus followed her through the door, cradling a bottle of Irish whiskey.

"We're staying overnight in the apartment," Mrs. Gus explained as I helped her out of her coat. "To make sure Gus can open the restaurant in the morning."

Gus opened his restaurant at 6:00 A.M., seven days a week, every month of the year except February, when the couple visited their children and

their families in Arizona and California. No matter
the weather, Gus was there to feed the lobstermen,
the town employees, the retail workers, and the
bankers. Tomorrow, he'd probably have groups of
plow drivers and utility workers as well.

The apartment where the couple were spending
the night had been my apartment, a place I'd loved,
until Gus had reclaimed it the previous spring and
renovated it for his retired son and daughter-in-
law, who had stayed there all summer.

Mrs. Gus sat on the bench to remove her boots
and spotted Vee's distinctive pair. "The sisters are
here! Lovely. That's a coffee cake," she told me as
I picked up the wrapped bundle and headed for
the kitchen. "I made it for the restaurant for tomorrow before we lost power, but then I thought,
'What the heck!'"

"Perfect," I said. "We're having Irish coffees in
honor of the day."

Gus led the way into the living room. I grabbed
the empty coffeepot and headed to the kitchen.
Zoey followed behind me with the ceramic bowl
that had held the whipped cream. I was a little
woozy from the booze and the fire, but the cold
kitchen snapped me out of it.

Zoey poured the remaining cream into the ceramic bowl and picked up the manual beater.

"Do you want me to take a turn?" I asked.

"No, thanks," she answered. "The truth is I like
it. It's a bit hypnotic."

Her forearms and shoulders were much stronger
than mine, toned by her work at the pottery wheel.
I didn't argue and instead set about filling the coffeepot.

"What do you think?" Zoey asked.

"The power probably won't be on until sometime tomorrow," I said, distracted by counting the scoops of grounds that went into the pot.

She shook her head, her curls bouncing in the lantern light. "Not that. Who killed Hugh O'Hara? Was it Daniel or Catherine? Was Hugh a pillar of the community or a violent old man?"

"One can be both," I pointed out. But I was puzzling about these questions, too. "I can see where Captain George is coming from. He's of Irish descent and Catholic. For him, Hugh O'Hara represents the first big Irish success story on our peninsula. George wouldn't want Hugh to be a terrible person."

"Maybe," Zoey allowed. "But wasn't Daniel Kearney also Irish and Catholic?"

I filled the pot. Luckily, we were on a town line, no well or pump involved, so we still had water. "I assume he was. But he does make the perfect killer. Poor. Living on the streets. Been in trouble before. Just arrived from out of town. People always want the killer to be a stranger who's come to town, not a member of the community."

"Mmm." Zoey had nearly finished whipping the cream. She had some experience of being the stranger herself, as a person From Away, who'd discovered a body in our town. "What about Fee and Vee?" she said. "They don't agree on Catherine's character, but they're both sure the killer wasn't Daniel."

"That one's easy," I answered. "The sisters may disagree on some things, but they'll always be united in their love for the underdog. Neither one

could ever see a poor, troubled boy like Daniel
Kearney as guilty of murder."

Zoey let out a long sigh. "And Catherine—faith-
ful wife, scheming sociopath, or woman driven to
murder by a cruel, controlling husband? I guess
we'll never know."

"I guess not," I said, though I wished we could.

I returned to the living room to hang the coffeepot over the fire. Mrs. Gus had settled on the
love seat with the Snugg sisters. Vee was curvy like
a painting by Rubens, while Fee was shaped like a
fire hydrant. Both of their bottoms were substantial, but Mrs. Gus was so tiny and narrow, she fit
right between them. For his part, Gus had brought
a chair from the dining room and put it down between my spot on the end of the couch and the
captain's armchair.

"Why does the town have plows out?" Gus complained as one rumbled by on the street. "Spring
storm. This'll all be gone by tomorrow afternoon.
Waste of taxpayer money."

"People still need to get to work in the morning." Captain George spoke cautiously. Gus could
wax on about the waste of taxpayer money for—
well, no one really knew for how long. It hadn't
truly been tested, but for a good long time.

"Not the teachers or the school bus drivers,"
Gus countered. "They'll call off school yet again.
In my day we went every day, no matter if the snow
was over your young head."

I returned to the kitchen before anyone responded to that.

"Brr, it's cold back here." The kitchen, far from
the hearth, was decidedly icy. Still, the snowflakes

were so big and so wet, I didn't think it could be much below freezing outside. The pipes would be fine.

Zoey had loaded the bowl of whipped cream, plates, two clean mugs, and extra utensils onto the tray.

I put a hand on her arm. "Are you okay?"

"Great." She was surprised by the question. "Why do you ask?"

"You seem very concerned about the ghost, or ghosts. Do you believe in them?"

Perhaps the body Zoey had found in her basement haunted her. Unfortunately, it wasn't the first body she'd come across. Her mother had been murdered by a boyfriend when Zoey was in high school, and she'd been the one who found her.

Zoey smiled her big-toothed smile, unoffended by my question or any unhappy associations with it. "If you're asking if I believe in specters draped in translucent sheets floating around yelling, 'Boo!' the answer is no."

"But you do believe in something?"

She shrugged. "I believe we don't know everything about the universe. Maybe, like some physicists say, all time is happening all the time. Maybe Catherine O'Hara is happily cleaning her kitchen in her conception of time while the current owners of Kensington House make breakfast for their guests in our conception of time? And maybe, just maybe, the linearity drops for a moment, and it feels a little crowded in that kitchen."

She seemed so earnest; I didn't challenge her. If she wanted to believe her mother was happily packing her a lunch for school in some alternate timeline, who was I to object?

She smiled again. "Really," she reassured me, "I'm just interested in the story."

I grabbed the lantern and the coffee cake and led the way through the swinging door into the darkened dining room and to our company beyond.

Gus's and Mrs. Gus's Tale

It took a while for the Irish coffee to get together and the coffee cake and soda bread to get distributed. Gus and Captain George speculated about how long the blackout would last and what the snow accumulation would be. Everyone reminisced about the ice storm in 1998 when the power was out for two long weeks.

I kept quiet during the conversation, as I always did when the subject came up. I'd returned to boarding school after Christmas break only two days before the '98 storm. As a result, I'd missed it all, while Mom, Dad, and Livvie lived like pioneers, melting ice over a fire, and then boiling it for household use, packing coolers with snow in an attempt to make the food that had been in the refrigerator last as long as possible, and huddling together in sleeping bags in this very room in order to keep warm at night. They had gone through it together, bonding over shared hardship, the first real family milestone in which I had no longer been part of the unit. I was glad to have avoided the cold, the lack of showers, the improvised meals, but I'd always felt my absence cost me more than I'd gained.

As I assembled the drinks, I considered making my coffee without whiskey, given the wallop of the last one, but in the face of the genial company and warm fire, my resolve crumbled. I poured the liquor into my mug, going easier than Zoey had, as I had done with all the others.

"You don't think that will happen now?" Zoey asked a trifle nervously. "A two-week blackout?"

Gus shook his head. "Nah. That was January. This is March. This sleety snow is heavy, no doubt, and it's brought something down somewhere. But for the most part it slides off the trees and wires and plops to the ground. In '98 it rained. There was warmer air above. The ground temperature was so cold, every tree, bush, house, and wire was instantly coated in inches of ice. The branches banged like gunshots as they broke off the trees. It sounded like the town was in a war zone. Everything came down. There was three inches of ice on the roads, and it took the crews days to get anywhere. This storm, the roads will be clear tomorrow."

"Oh, good." Zoey toasted him with her coffee mug.

As the company ate and drank, the conversation petered out.

"What are we talking about?" Mrs. Gus asked.

"The murder of Hugh O'Hara," the captain said.

"And ghosts," Zoey added.

Mrs. Gus ignored the addition. She looked to either side at her old friends the Snugg sisters, her lips pursed. She let the silence linger a few moments, though she was clearly about to speak. Finally, she did. "I suppose *they* told you some story about how poor Catherine O'Hara was responsible for her husband's death."

We smiled in acknowledgment. Mom laughed.

"Of course, we did," Fee responded. "Because she was."

The captain said at the same moment, "I told them it wasn't her. It was Kearney."

"Daniel Kearney?" Gus's great, white eyebrows flew up to his hairline. "Not that poor kid."

"He confessed," George protested again, though no one was listening.

"You think that slip of a girl killed her husband?" Mrs. Gus demanded, pointedly turning her head to either side to look at each Snugg sister. Her outrage appeared fresh, but I had the feeling of an old argument with dear friends worn smooth with time. Mrs. Gus then looked at the whole group, her big, blue eyes sweeping around the room. "Did they tell you young Catherine was pregnant?"

They most certainly hadn't. Neither the captain nor the Snuggs had mentioned it. I felt the ground shift again.

"Wasn't Hugh O'Hara in his eighties?" Zoey asked, eyes round.

"It's possible," Gus grumped.

"Not just possible," Mrs. Gus said. "It *was*."

"Wouldn't that be all the more reason for Catherine to kill Old Hugh?" Fee offered. "If the baby wasn't his."

"Pshaw." Mrs. Gus swept the assertion away with

a wave of her hand. "It might have been if she'd killed him before she was showing, but she was six months gone at the time of the murder. Hugh had accepted the babe as his own—because it was, we can only assume."

"Then who did it?" the captain demanded. "Who had a motive to kill Old Hugh? Tell us that."

Gauntlet flung.

Mrs. Gus lowered her voice and we all leaned in to hear above the wind outside and the *tack-tack-tack* of the sleet against the windows. "It is true that the babe was the motive. The motive for Margaret and Martin Gleason, Old Hugh's daughter and son-in-law."

"Margaret and Martin Gleason!" the captain protested. "Why would Margaret kill her own father?"

"Margaret didn't strike the fatal blow," Mrs. Gus said. "Martin did."

"The motive was the farm," Gus said. "Not wanting to split her inheritance with a new half sibling."

The assembled company mulled that over.

"Why would Margaret kill her father, and leave her pregnant stepmother alive?" Mom asked. "Killing Hugh accomplishes nothing. If anything, it takes them further from their goal. If Catherine inherited the whole farm from her husband, she could leave it only to her child if she wished, cutting the Gleasons out entirely."

"Catherine not only wasn't the murderer," Mrs. Gus insisted. "She was the intended victim."

There was a moment of stunned silence. Stunned at least on the parts of Mom, Captain George,

Zoey, and me. Vee, on the other hand, rolled her eyes, while Fee sighed, loudly and dismissively.

"Was Margaret Old Hugh's only child?" I asked when I recovered my ability to process information. Mrs. Gus had sucked me right in.

"She was his only child with his second wife," Mrs. Gus answered. "He'd had a son with his first wife, too. John, he was called. But John went off to California searching for gold in '49 and never returned."

"Even if he inherited half the farm, John would never live there or take any income from it," Gus added. "It would function as Margaret's one hundred percent."

"Then what happened that night?" Mom asked.

Mrs. Gus took a deep breath. "Margaret had never liked Catherine. She hadn't expected her father to remarry so long after her mother's death. She'd had the old man to herself for years after her brother had left town, serving as the hostess and lady of the house for both her father and her husband. She didn't take well to being usurped. That Catherine was a dozen years younger than Margaret didn't help."

Mrs. Gus paused to stir her coffee drink, the metal spoon clinking against the sides of the ceramic mug. "Poor innocent Catherine had married into a viper's nest of greed and jealousy. O'Hara had chased his only son away and filled his daughter with spite."

"I told you he was a son of a gun." Vee spoke with satisfaction, her characterization of Hugh O'Hara corroborated.

"Why do you two think she married such an old

man anyway?" Zoey asked. Her tone was even, without judgment. She had her own experience of a romantic relationship with an older man. "There must have been other suitors. I understand it was during the Civil War, but she was young. She could have waited for the men to return."

Those who did, I amended silently. Maine had contributed more men per capita to the ranks of the Union army than any other state. The losses had been massive.

"There were other suitors." Mrs. Gus responded easily and definitively, like the answer had been on the tip of her tongue. "But Catholics were very thin on the ground in Maine back then. If she wanted to remain on our peninsula, her options would have been quite limited."

"Are these *our* Gleasons?" I asked. Gleason's Hardware had stood on Main Street since the late nineteenth century and was run by the same family all these years later.

"They're related," Mrs. Gus answered. "But I'm not sure how. Margaret and Martin had no children."

If Mrs. Gus didn't know how the Gleasons were related, no one did. Her family had been on the peninsula since colonial times.

Mrs. Gus paused to sip her well-stirred coffee. "When Hugh and Catherine announced they were expecting, that was the last straw. Margaret and Martin had been married fifteen years at that point, with no sign of a child. Margaret was consumed by jealousy and anger. She determined that Catherine would have to go and got Martin to agree."

"Martin was motivated not by jealousy, but by greed," Gus added. Unlike the Snugg sisters, he and Mrs. Gus seemed to agree on the killers' motivations. "Martin had a grasping soul. It was money that had caused him to wed Margaret in the first place. Hugh had gifted the newlyweds with some of his land and had built their fine house across the green. But Martin wanted it all. No other heirs."

Zoey squinted. "But there's no house. . . ."

"It was where the fire station is now," Gus said.

"The house isn't there anymore," Mom agreed.

"The plan was in motion." Mrs. Gus took the story up again. "First, Margaret planted doubts about Catherine's baby's paternity, putting it around town that she'd frequently seen a man going in and out of the house when Hugh was away in his fields. Many believed her."

"Perhaps because it was true?" Fee suggested, happy to believe anything bad about Catherine.

"Because then, as now, people love malicious gossip, that's why." Mrs. Gus took another drink. "Where was I? Oh yes. The plan was in motion. First, damage Catherine's reputation. Second, a fall guy was needed. Margaret visited Daniel Kearney's mother in Busman's Harbor and secured his address. She wrote to him saying all was forgiven. Her father regretted accusing Daniel of stealing his wages and clothes. Hugh wanted Daniel to come back to work on the farm."

"And this letter exists?" The captain demanded. "You've seen it?"

"I don't need to," Mrs. Gus retorted. "I know what's what." She stared at each of us in turn, challenging someone to defy her. Captain George and the Snuggs stayed quiet. "When Daniel Kearney arrived back at the farm, Margaret and Martin wasted no time. After Hugh and Catherine returned from a night of overindulging in food and drink at the Gleason house, and while Daniel slept innocently in the stable, Martin stole into his in-law's house, intent on murdering Catherine. First, he left an obvious trail through the first floor, stealing objects at random and stuffing them in a bag to make it look like a burglary gone bad. Then he snuck into the bedroom behind the kitchen intent on killing."

"What Martin and Margaret hadn't counted on was Old Hugh waking up out of a sound sleep when the first blow fell on Catherine and fighting to the death," Gus said.

"But why would Catherine run to the Gleason house when she escaped?" Mom had already thought it through. "And why did she never accuse her stepson-in-law in the aftermath?"

"He wore a burlap sack on his head," Gus said. "It was dark. Catherine couldn't be sure it was him. An accusation would never have stood up in court. It would have been far too dangerous for her to identify him, if she knew or even suspected that he wouldn't be convicted."

"Margaret must have been shocked to see her stepmother run screaming across the town green straight onto her porch. But she pulled herself together and played the part of the dutiful stepdaughter," Mrs. Gus said. "Martin arrived through the back door minutes later and rushed off to 'find the killer.' He found Kearney still asleep in the stable, as planned, and told the boy to take a horse and leave quickly. Daniel's history with the family was known and, surely, he'd be accused. Then, when help arrived, Gleason led them exactly in the direction he'd told Kearney to go."

"I thought it was odd the way Gleason jumped to the conclusion Kearney was the killer based on a simple two-by-four leaning against a window," I said. "And I noticed Martin Gleason was the only one there when Kearney confessed."

"Exactly," Gus said pointing at me and then touching the tip of his nose. "Julia's got it in one."

"But then who is the ghost?" Zoey asked. "Is it Catherine O'Hara? Or her child? What became of them?"

"Catherine disappeared a few weeks after the murder," Mrs. Gus said. "Before the child was born. Hardly what you would do"—she looked at the Snugg sisters—"if your motive was to inherit. But something you might do if you were in fear for your life and believed the person who'd tried to kill you was still on the loose," Gus said. "Or living across the street. Martin and Margaret, on the other hand, wasted no time reuniting the two farms and living happily ever after."

There was a moment of silence.

"Pure speculation," the captain finally declared. "Not one shred of proof. Daniel Kearney confessed. He was arrested and put in the old Wiscasset jail. Case closed."

"Utter nonsense," Vee said. She looked at Captain George. "At least we agree about that."

"You still haven't said who the ghost is," Zoey pointed out. "Is it Margaret? Or Martin? Are they condemned to haunt the property because of their heinous crime?"

Gus opened his mouth to answer but was cut off by the sound of a heavy blade scraping icy snow off the driveway.

"Sonny's here!" Mom jumped up from her chair and made for the door. Before she could reach it, there was a blast of cold air and the voices of my sister, Livvie, and my niece, Page, talking as they made their way into the front hall.

Chapter Four

"**O**ur power is out, too. And I thought, 'Why be bored and cold at home?' Oooh." Livvie came around to the archway into the living room and halted the moment she spotted seven of us huddled around the fireplace. "It looks like a party."

"St. Patrick's Day," Mom said. "We're having Irish coffee, soda bread, and coffee cake." She gestured toward the plates on the coffee table, where one lone slice of soda bread remained. Half the cake was left, though.

My nephew, Jack, was asleep, his head resting on Livvie's shoulder, his limp legs hanging well below her hips. At four, he was getting heavy for that type of thing. He was still in his winter coat, hood pulled up to protect him from the precipitation outside. Livvie was still in her coat, too. She couldn't take it off without putting Jack down.

"That all sounds lovely," she said. "Let me go upstairs and put this guy to bed."

My niece, Page, appeared in the archway. She'd shed her coat and boots and left them in the hall. At fourteen, she was ten years older than her brother. Tall and broad-shouldered like her mother, she had fiery red hair like her dad. Over the summer she'd filled out and she now looked like exactly what she was, indisputably a teenager. I'd watched her grow closely over the last six years since I'd moved back to Busman's Harbor, but somehow I was still startled every time I saw her looking so grown-up.

"I'm going up, too." She had her phone clutched in her hand.

It wasn't that long ago that she would have begged to stay up and listen to the stories being told in the living room. The people there, Gus and Mrs. Gus, Fee and Vee, Captain George, and especially my mom were her favorite people on earth. Now she preferred huddling under her blankets, fiddling with her phone in a freezing bedroom to sitting around a cozy fire with a bunch of boring adults. Another reminder of the swift passage of time. It made me sad.

"'Night." She waved to the assembled and then followed Livvie up the stairs.

Our group sat quietly, listening to the scrape of Sonny's plow across the street in the Snuggs' driveway. For decades, Fee Snugg had tended our garden while we were away, living on Morrow Island where we ran our clambakes during the summer. In return, my father had plowed and shoveled out the Snuggs. Since he'd died, my brother-in-law,

Sonny, had taken up the duty, willingly, even cheerfully. I had my differences with Sonny, but he was a generous man. After he finished at the Snuggs', he would drive over the harbor hill and plow out the tiny parking lot beside Gus's restaurant.

Livvie returned and greeted everyone warmly, giving each person a hug. When she came to Captain George, she raised her eyebrows in Mom's direction. I could tell she was as puzzled by his presence as I'd been. Mom remained mum, not moving a single facial muscle.

Livvie pushed Le Roi unceremoniously off the couch and settled between Zoey and me. Zoey was Livvie's boss at her winter job at Lupine Design, the pottery studio and shop Zoey owned. Over the past summer their relationship had shifted from one of mutual respect for the other's skill into a friendship. Just as Zoey and I had become close, so had Livvie and Zoey. Somehow having a mutual friend to fuss over and worry about had brought me even closer to my sister.

Livvie brought everyone up to date on Page's impressive wins on the swim team, Jack's adjustment to preschool and, with smiling glances at Zoey, her own excitement about the new designs taking shape in the studio. The guests murmured appreciatively, though Livvie couldn't have helped but notice she was carrying the entire conversation. No one was chiming in with their own adventures, though that may have been because there hadn't been any to report. We were at the part of the winter when most of us moved mechanically from home to work and back again, praying for spring.

I picked up the coffeepot and gave it a shake. There was enough liquid left to offer Livvie an Irish coffee. The cream bowl was empty, so I took it to the kitchen, planning to grab a clean mug and a carton of milk from the dark, silent fridge. I was surprised when Livvie and Zoey followed right behind me.

"What is going on?" Livvie stage-whispered.

The whispering was contagious. I whisper-shouted back, "You mean George? Mom invited him. He was the first one here."

"Really?" She paused a moment, looking puzzled, and then shook her head, disinclined to pursue the subject. "No, I mean why is everyone so quiet? Were you talking about me when I walked in?"

Zoey and I both laughed, though I could see why Livvie would have wondered. "We were talking about the O'Hara murder," I told her.

Livvie's brows knit together in the lantern light, like she was going through the catalog of murders in the past few years looking for the name O'Hara.

"And the ghost at the Kensington House B and B," Zoey added helpfully.

Light dawned for Livvie. "Old Hugh O'Hara's murder."

"Everyone has a different theory about who the killer was." I gave her a quick rundown on who believed what.

"You're all arguing about a hundred and fifty-year-old murder?" Livvie's first reaction was one of disbelief. Then her mouth curled into a smile. "Sounds about right."

"More discussing than arguing," Zoey clarified, though the truth was somewhere in between.

"Unbelievable." Livvie shook her long, auburn mane. "Especially since every one of them is wrong."

"You know something about Hugh O'Hara's murder?" I would have bet anything that she knew the story only as a vague local legend, the way I did.

"I believe I do." She smiled. "But I'm not the expert. You'll have to ask—"

There was the sound of Sonny's pickup coming up the driveway, a slamming vehicle door, and then the bang of the back door as it popped open.

Sonny's Tale

"Who's here?" Sonny called from the back hall. It was too dark to see him, but the sounds were those of outer garments being shed.

"Everybody!" Livvie yelled back.

Sonny followed the three of us through the dining room and into the living room in his socks. "Hi there, everybody!"

Everybody hi'ed him back.

Sonny brought a chair in from the dining room. I made a move to grab the coffeepot to start a fresh brew, but he waved me off. He pointed to Gus's whiskey bottle sitting on the coffee table. "I'll be drinking that straight."

He placed the chair next to my mother, as close to the fire as he dared. He'd grown a thick, red winter beard. Snow and ice dripped steadily from the beard onto his Snowden Family Clambake hoodie.

There followed a conversation with Sonny, Captain George, and Gus about the nature of the evening's precipitation. Was it more snow than sleet? Sleet than rain? Rain than snow? Could it be fairly categorized as that awful breed of Maine late-winter storm we called "sneet," the worst of all possible worlds? Sonny allowed as how the snow was heavy, wet, and slippery and that all must be cautious walking home.

The discussion ended with this pronouncement. As the last person out in it, and the only one of us who had shoveled it, Sonny's word was final.

My brother-in-law, I noted, didn't seem at all surprised to see George. It might have been because Sonny wasn't there at the beginning of the gathering, so he didn't know the captain was specifically Mom's guest. On the other hand, it wouldn't have surprised me in the least if Sonny knew something Livvie and I did not, maybe from his closer friendship with Captain George, or maybe because Mom had talked to him. After a very rocky start to their relationship, when Sonny had been Livvie's teenaged boyfriend, Mom and Sonny had developed a respect for one another that had blossomed into true friendship after my father died. If she was going to confide in any of us, it might have been Sonny. Though he had loved my father, and had known him half his life, Sonny might take the news of a new relationship more easily than Livvie or I would, or at least Mom might have judged it so.

In the quiet that followed, Sonny looked around, still dripping steadily on my mother's carpet, and asked, "What are we talking about?"

Zoey tried again with "Ghosts!"

But Mrs. Gus spoke at the same time in a volume that belied her tiny frame. "The murder of Hugh O'Hara," she said.

"Ah." Sonny nodded, moving his sodden hair.

"You know the story?" I asked.

"Of course. It was one of my granny's favorites. We're related to the Kearneys on my mom's side."

The captain's interest was captured. "You're related to Daniel Kearney?"

"Not really," Sonny answered. "Kearney was Daniel's stepfather. But he was family, so to speak."

Captain George smiled and reached out to squeeze my mother's arm. "Good to know your grandchildren aren't descended from a murderer."

He meant it as a tease, but Sonny took him seriously. "Murderer? Daniel Kearney? He never did it."

"He confessed," George insisted. Once again.

Sonny gave him a flick of the shoulder and said that didn't matter.

"Well, if not Kearney," the captain persisted, "then who?"

"Martin and Margaret Gleason." Gus stated it as fact.

"Everyone knows it was Catherine," Fee insisted. In this case "everyone" appeared to include only her sister.

"Hugh O'Hara was an abusive husband," Vee added, attempting to justify Catherine's actions.

"Now wait a darn minute!" the captain shouted.

Uh-oh. In the best of circumstances, Sonny was a man who believed what he believed and fought any attempt to change his mind. During the first year I ran the Snowden Family Clambake Company, he and I had fought bitterly over any change or improvement I wanted to make. Finally, for the sake of the business, my mother, and most of all, Livvie, we'd retreated to our separate corners, Sonny running the crew that cooked the food over the wood fire, and me handling front-of-house, ordering, and finances.

Even given Sonny's usual stubbornness, a story passed down by his granny fell into a special category. Sonny had always loved her deeply, and when she moved into his house to care for his father, his brother, and him following his mother's death when Sonny was in high school, she had achieved a sort of sainthood. Her death had added to her beatification. Everything she'd ever told Sonny, including odd bits of folklore, gossip, and old wives' tales, was indisputably true in his view, and he'd defend it vehemently.

Sonny shook his head. One remaining droplet flew from his hair and hit Mom in the face.

"Whew!" She blinked hard.

"Jacqueline, I'm so sorry!" Sonny was appalled.

Mom smiled and put her hand on his shoulder. "No harm done. Tell us then, who did it?"

Sonny drained the whiskey from his mug in one gulp and made a noise of satisfaction. When he judged his dramatic pause had lasted long enough, he gave us the name. "John O'Hara."

The room erupted.

"John O'Hara!" Vee's mouth hung open.

"Hugh's son, Margaret's half brother," the captain clarified.

"Impossible,"·Gus said. "John was in California. Went out to hunt for gold in '49."

"He *was* in California," Sonny agreed. "But he'd come back. Had been back for months. Almost a year." He looked around the room, satisfaction on his face. This was new information.

"Why would John return after all that time?" Fee wrinkled her nose, pushing up her thick glasses.

"I don't know why," Gus said. "But I can guess how. When John went out to California in '49, he sailed from Boston, around the Horn. The Transcontinental Railroad wouldn't be completed until 1869, but there were vast tracts of it done in '66-67, providing far more rail service than when John went out to California. If he could get himself over the Sierra Mountains to Salt Lake City, he could ride the train east, except for a few places west of the Mississippi where he'd have to take a stagecoach or ferry. The trip was much quicker and more affordable than it had ever been. If he was going to come home that would have been the time."

"But why?" Zoey asked, forgetting her ghost question for the moment. "Why would he come home after all that time?"

Sonny smiled like a man who had a winning hand and no poker face. "He came back for his son."

Someone actually gasped. I thought it was Vee, but I couldn't be sure.

"His son?" The captain stuttered.

Sonny rubbed his big, calloused, lobsterman's hands together, anxious to get to the next reveal, but too good a storyteller not to make us wait a moment to absorb the full impact.

"You all know John O'Hara left Busman's Harbor during the gold rush. What you don't know is he left something behind. The girl he'd been keeping company with was pregnant. Her name was Bridget Murray, daughter of one of the few other Irish Catholic families in town. After John left, she had a son. When that son was five or so, she married Sean Kearney and the boy took Kearney's name, though he was never formally adopted."

"Daniel Kearney was John O'Hara's son? Hugh O'Hara's grandson?" Mrs. Gus spoke for all of us.

"He was. My granny told me there was no doubt."

"Was it widely known?" Zoey asked. "Did Hugh know, for example?"

"I don't know who knew back then," Sonny admitted. "But I do know Daniel was never acknowledged by the O'Hara family. At least not during Hugh's lifetime."

He let that tidbit sit out there for us to chew on.

"More to the point," the captain said. "Did Daniel know? Because then he had even greater motive for the robbery. He might have believed he was taking what was rightfully his. And the robbery led to the murder, so . . ."

"It certainly gives less motive to Margaret and Martin," Fee said. "With John back in town, killing Catherine wouldn't clear the way for them to inherit Hugh's entire property. They would have to split it with John, who presumably wouldn't be an absentee, silent partner, but would want to assert his rights. Maybe even move into Hugh's house."

"Though if it was the Gleasons," Gus pointed out, "if their plan had succeeded, they would not only have eliminated Catherine, but would also have framed another potential heir, Daniel Kearney. If he had been convicted, he would have been executed. Two problems solved. Or three, counting Catherine's babe. That just left John to deal with."

"John never lived in the O'Hara house, at least not after '49. Of that I am certain," Fee said.

"Which raises the question . . . If he was back in town, why wasn't he staying with his father? He would have been there the night of the murder," Mrs. Gus said.

"John wasn't staying with his father because they were estranged," Sonny said. "That's the whole reason he left in the first place. His father was grooming him to take over the farm. John may have even wanted it. He was a good farmer, strong and smart. But he and the old man were always at odds. Perhaps Hugh was too controlling. Perhaps John was too young to appreciate him. Either way, they had words and John went."

Sonny worked on his father's lobster boat during the off-season and had since he was a boy. Did Sonny identify with John, or at least remember what it had been like to work under his father back when he was twenty?

"My granny was sure John left before he knew Bridget was pregnant. He would have known eventually, probably got a letter from Bridget or someone else. But like Gus said, it wasn't practical for him to get home until after the Civil War ended, and he could travel across the continent," Sonny added.

"Why would John kill his father?" Fee Snugg asked. "If it was in'the hope of inheritance, it didn't work out. He never owned the farm or the house."

"No one knows, but my granny was convinced the reason was more complicated. Old Hugh wouldn't see John when he returned. Catherine offered to act as peacemaker between father and son. It was a long process involving many meetings between Catherine and John. He was seen coming and going from the house regularly while Hugh was out in his fields, overseeing the work on his farm. And then, one day, after more than four years of marriage, Catherine turns up pregnant."

"You think John was the father." Mrs. Gus guessed.

"My granny certainly believed he was. She was told all this by her granny, who was around at the time."

"Someone should have told that man about birth control," Mrs. Gus muttered.

"Or restraint," the captain added.

Mrs. Gus nodded. "That works, too."

"So how did it work?" I asked. "We assume Catherine and John were lovers and were in it together, right?"

"John breaks in." Sonny recited the steps as if by rote. "Takes some stuff. Leaves an obvious trail of matches. Makes it look like a burglary. His accomplice, Catherine, has told him where the bedroom is, maybe even made love to him right there in Hugh's own bed. John strikes. His old man gives him the fight of a lifetime, but in the end, hacked with an axe, bludgeoned, and shot, Old Hugh is dead."

"What about Catherine's injury?" an ever-loyal Fee demanded.

Sonny dismissed it. "A flesh wound inflicted to make the attack look real."

Mrs. Gus had said the same thing.

"Was Daniel Kearney in on the scheme then?" the captain asked.

"No. He was there by tragic coincidence. Catherine, in addition to trying to broker peace between John and his dad—at least we can only assume she was trying to do that until she became his lover—was also trying to make peace between Hugh and Daniel." Sonny explained. "John was desperate to see the son he'd never met and hoped the boy would be accepted by his grandfather Hugh as well. Catherine wrote to Daniel in Boston, asking him to return to the farm. He did return, but by tragic coincidence did so on the very night the murder was planned for. Arriving late and seeing the farmhouse dark, he ducked into the stable for a bit of sleep before what he anticipated would be the joyous family reunion. Instead, he woke to a hue and cry and shouts of murder. He didn't know what was happening and tried to escape, but Martin Gleason caught him, accused him, and hauled him to the jail."

Captain George opened his mouth to speak, but we were ahead of him. "He confessed!" we all shouted at once.

"He did," Sonny conceded, "but he didn't stay in jail long, did he? Someone busted him out."

"His father?" Livvie asked.

"That's what my granny believed," Sonny confirmed.

"Then what happened to them? John didn't inherit the farm. Daniel didn't either." Even though Livvie had heard Sonny's account before, she was as enthralled as the rest of us.

"My granny didn't say." Sonny rubbed his red beard. "They disappeared."

"Like Catherine," Zoey said.

"Like Catherine," Sonny agreed.

"You think they all went together," I guessed. "It makes sense if Catherine and John were lovers, expecting a child, and Daniel was John's son."

"But where did they go?" Livvie asked.

"Nobody knows," Sonny answered. If his granny didn't know, no one did. "They never came back, not one of them."

"They're not up in the town cemetery," Mrs. Gus said. "I can tell you that for sure. I've read every name on every stone. More than once." She was a dedicated volunteer at the cemetery.

A moody silence settled over the group as each of us pondered this. Where had Catherine, John, and Daniel gone? How to figure it out? I'd check the Internet when the power came back on, but something told me I wouldn't find them.

I was deep in thought, contemplating the puzzle pieces, when I heard heavy boots on the back porch and the door opening.

Chapter Five

"Halloo!" Jamie Dawes called from the back hall. He was a Busman's Harbor police officer, a neighbor, and my first and oldest friend. He and Livvie and I had grown up together, ranging back and forth across our adjacent backyards. He still lived behind Mom's house, now alone in his parents' big, old place. They'd decamped to Florida years earlier to live nearer to Jamie's eldest sister.

Jamie padded into the dining room in his socks and waved to one and all. Livvie levitated out of the seat beside me as if she'd been ejected. She landed on the other side of the couch, practically in Zoey's lap, leaving a Jamie-sized spot next to me. Jamie, however, grabbed a chair from the dining room and placed it squarely in front of the fireplace. Le Roi, with a speed that belied his age, jumped up on the couch and lay down in the warm spot Livvie had left. He leaned against me heavily, purring loudly.

"I just got off shift," Jamie told us. "Saw the candles in the window and Sonny's truck in the drive and thought I'd drop by for a St. Patrick's drink. I didn't realize it was a party." He'd gone home to change and was wearing jeans, a flannel shirt, and a beige pullover. His blond hair was wet, though I couldn't tell if he'd showered or if it was from coming through the backyard in a sleet storm.

"You've come to the right place." Sonny fetched a glass from the corner cabinet in the dining room, poured a generous drink from Gus's bottle and handed it to Jamie. "Cheers."

"Busy night?" Gus asked. It was the inevitable question. Gus just got there first.

Jamie looked around the room, as if calculating the number of broken bones that might result when our gathering ended and the guests headed home. "I spent a fair amount of time pushing cars out of ditches. Now, thank goodness, most seem to have got wherever they were going and stayed there."

We all demanded to know what Jamie knew, officially, about the blackout. How widespread? What caused it? And most urgently, when did the power company say it would end?

Jamie patiently went through the information he had. A substation had gone out. It would come back online sometime tonight. But the ice had downed the single line that ran from Route 1 to Busman's Harbor, as well as lots of smaller lines. Those would take some time to repair. Days, maybe.

Eventually, the guests ran out of questions for

Jamie. Sonny fetched another bottle of whiskey from the buffet in the dining room that housed Mom's small bar and offered everyone another round. I put my hand over my mug. It was late and the fire was making me drowsy.

"So," Jamie said. "What are we talking about?"

Jamie's Tale

"Of course I know the O'Hara case," Jamie said when we told him. "It's the oldest unsolved murder in town. The chief is obsessed with it. On a slow day at the station, he'll bring out the file and drill us on it."

"What do you know that we don't?" Zoey asked. "Have the police figured out who did it?"

"Yes. More than a hundred and fifty years ago. Daniel Kearney," Captain George said.

Gus exhaled noisily, an exaggerated sigh. "Here we go."

"What do you all know?" Jamie asked.

There followed a babble of voices that proved we knew everything. And nothing at all.

"I can confirm John O'Hara was back in the area well before the murder," Jamie told us after we'd finished arguing and talking over one another. "After the murder, several witnesses came forward to report it. Some suggested that John O'Hara was Daniel Kearney's father. No DNA then, of course, so no proof. No Daniel Kearney by then either. He'd disappeared." Jamie paused. "Margaret Gleason, however, denied any knowledge that her brother was in town. She claimed she hadn't seen him."

"But she would have seen him, wouldn't she, if he was coming and going from her father's house right across the green?" Mrs. Gus said. "If John was having an affair with Catherine, *which I very much doubt.*"

"He might have been discreet, sneaking in and out," Livvie suggested.

"Not very discreet," Fee pointed out, "if witnesses placed him there."

"Or Margaret was lying," Gus said. "She'd put it around that Catherine was having an affair. That was part of laying the groundwork to ruin Catherine's reputation. It was a much better story for her to accuse a handsome stranger of lurking around the house than to bring up her brother and introduce the idea of another heir."

"Right," Mrs. Gus agreed. "Margaret was better off keeping quiet. But what about John? If he was in the area and innocent, why didn't he show up to claim his property?"

"That's always troubled me as well," Jamie said. "But there's no record of John O'Hara ever interacting with the sheriff. He never was questioned in connection with his father's death. Never came forward on his own."

"Do you know where he went?" I asked.

Jamie rolled his shoulders. "No idea."

"Let's get back to Daniel Kearney," Captain George said. "You had him, he confessed, and you lost him."

"He didn't confess to us. All that's in the file is Martin Gleason's account of Daniel's confession. Besides, there was no *us* back then. The Busman's Harbor PD wouldn't be founded for another fifty

years. It was the county sheriff and the jailor." He
leaned away from the fire, putting his elbow on his
knees. "I can tell you this. Daniel Kearney didn't
break out of jail alone. He had help."

"An accomplice." Livvie rubbed her hands together. Not for warmth; the fire, resupplied with
wood by Sonny, was burning merrily.

"Accomplice*s*," Sonny insisted. "Catherine and
John."

"Perhaps," Jamie said. "Though one person could
have done it. Daniel was the only person in the jail
that night. While the jailor slept, someone strolled
in, took his keys off the hook, unlocked Daniel's
cell, and let him out."

"As easy as that?" Gus whistled. "Not very secure."

"Maybe not," Jamie responded. "But still it would
have required an accomplice. Kearney couldn't
have reached the keys from his cell."

"Could have been anyone." The captain was dismissive. "Kearney could have bribed someone."

"With what?" Vee scoffed. "A poor boy just come
up from Boston. He hadn't even started his job at
Old Hugh's farm yet, hadn't collected a wage."

"And who would he have bribed but the jailor?"
Vee asked.

"Of course, it was the jailor." Gus was incensed
by her naivete. "Public corruption, always with us."

Jamie shot him a withering look. He was proud
of his service on the Busman's Harbor PD. Gus
had the grace to stare at his lap.

"One strange thing," Jamie said. "In Kearney's
empty cell he'd carved a word into a wooden beam.
BENEDICTA. You can still see it there when you take

the tour if you know where to look. It must have taken a good long time. He only had his finger-nail."

"'Benedicta'?" Zoey repeated. "What does it mean?"

"Blessings," Mrs. Gus said.

"*Benedicta tu,*" Captain George added. "Blessed are you."

"Yes, but is he blessing his captors, or whoever helped him escape, or the townspeople or what? Was he religious? Did he know Latin?" Livvie asked.

"He was Irish and Catholic like his mother. But the nearest church was St. Patrick's in Newcastle, a six-hour walk each way. Daniel wouldn't have at-tended mass regularly as a child and probably didn't have much of a religious education."

In the firelight, from across the room, I noticed my mother, her brows drawn together, gently chewing her thin bottom lip. We had gone to the same prep school. When Mom attended, four years of Latin had been required. I had skated through with a mere two, and I barely remem-bered that. Still, something was off about the word *benedicta.* I could tell Mom felt it, too. I could prac-tically hear her declining verbs in her head.

A dry log popped in the fireplace, drawing everyone's attention.

"'Benedicta,'" Zoey said softly, gazing at the flames.

And then we all fell silent.

Chapter Six

The party broke up soon after that, after much hugging and good-byeing as people struggled into coats and boots. Livvie and Sonny helped Vee and Fee across the street while Jamie and I walked Gus and Mrs. Gus back to the apartment over their restaurant.

The road had been plowed and we walked four abreast down the middle. The black asphalt was covered with a crackly substance that was more ice than snow. Mrs. Gus let me loop my arm through hers. It was thin even with the sleeve of her wool coat wrapped around it, though could I feel the sinewy muscles she used every morning when she rose at 4:00 A.M. to make the pies for the restaurant. She was so little, I had to stoop to hold on to her, which made me even more unsteady. Even though I'd slowed down on the Irish whiskey as the rounds of drinks had continued through the

long evening, I felt fuzzy around the edges. I
hoped I wouldn't be the one to slip, bringing us
both down.

Jamie was too smart to offer Gus an arm. Instead, he rested a hand lightly on Gus's shoulder
as they walked, an early warning system. If Gus
began to slide, Jamie could grab him quickly.

The smell of woodsmoke filled the air, the only
sign of other humans, except for the scrape of a
distant plow blade. The windows of the houses we
passed were dark. The town's only traffic light, at
the corner of Main and Main where the road into
town went around the harbor hill and crossed over
itself, was out. But it didn't much matter. The light
was turned to blinking yellow from Columbus Day
to Patriot's Day in April, and there was no one on
the road in any case.

We crested the hill and started down, which was,
if anything, more difficult going. The night was
silent except for the *zuh-zuh-zuh* of our boots on
the ice and the occasional *schloop* as clumps of
heavy, sleety snow fell off branches as we passed.
We didn't talk, concentrating on each step. It had
been an evening of talking, talking, talking. I tried
to use the tiny part of my brain available to process
the stories I'd heard that night to assess what they
meant, but my unruly mind kept drifting back to
Jamie and the thought that we would be walking
home alone in the dark.

Gus's restaurant was suddenly in front of us, its
dark outlines barely visible. I heard but couldn't
see the water behind it, lapping against the building's pilings. No house lights twinkled from across
the water, usually a welcoming sight.

The apartment over the restaurant, where Mr. and Mrs. Gus were spending the night, had been my home for three years and I had loved it. I'd lived there with my ex, Chris Durand. The big studio I remembered was gone now, renovated to serve as summer living space for the old couple's retired son and his wife. I felt the loss of the apartment deeply, like a piece of my recent past had been obliterated.

Chris had been my weak-in-the-knees, can't-breathe-when-I'm-near-him, middle school crush. We'd met again as adults and fallen in love when I'd moved back into Busman's Harbor. But Chris had turned out to be man full of secrets. Some went back to when I'd first set eyes on him, when he'd been a junior in Busman's Harbor's joint middle and high school. Other secrets were newer, gathered like moss on a rolling stone in the years we'd been apart. He was a grown-up, complicated man.

It wasn't as if the scales had fallen from my eyes. I had never fallen out of love with him. But, as I'd gained a better understanding of what and who I'd be committing to, and a better understanding of my own wants and needs, I'd come to believe that it could never work. Result: heartbreak all around.

Along with Chris, my regular off-season job had disappeared as well. We'd run a winter dinner restaurant together in Gus's space. Shortly after the breakup we'd determined that continuing to work together would be too hard. And then Gus had to ask me to leave my apartment over the res-

taurant. He didn't want to, but it was for family.
The final blow.

I had muddled through the following year, un-
tethered. This winter had been much better. I was
on more solid ground emotionally. And, come to
think of it, I hadn't seen Chris once since the fall.
Busman's Harbor was a small town, so it was strange
we hadn't run into one another, but I wasn't worried. Chris had plenty of sailing friends and had
probably gone to Florida or the Caribbean to crew
for the winter.

My off-season job situation was still to be re-
solved. I'd spent time consulting with local retailers, helping with organizational issues, finances,
marketing, and anything else they needed really,
on a for-fee, or more often pro bono, basis. It was
interesting work, getting to see how so many different businesses worked, but it was far from a full-
time gig.

Even in the darkness, Gus didn't fumble getting
his key in the lock. He'd unlocked that door every
morning for over fifty years, and clearly could do it
blindfolded, if he was ever called upon to do so.
He and Mrs. Gus went inside, and I started after
them. Jamie put a hand on my arm and held me
back. Surely we should see them safely upstairs to
their apartment in the dark. "Let them go," he
whispered. I didn't follow but stood stubbornly in
the doorway until I heard their footsteps rising
and the sound of the door at the top of the stairway opening and closing.

We started back to Mom's house side by side,
walking silently, companionably, something we'd

done since we got off the yellow school bus that brought us home from Busman's Harbor Elementary.

But then there'd been a time when we couldn't be comfortable anymore. We loved each other and had since childhood, but that was the least of it. Jamie had wanted more. Since I'd returned to town, he'd tended his feelings carefully, like a banked fire, safe, but never fully out, during the years I'd lived with Chris.

I wasn't stupid. I knew how he felt long before he'd finally said the words last summer, even as I hoped he wouldn't. I imagined him as a guy in a rom-com, his buddies urging, "Tell her or you'll regret it for the rest of your life." Except I was sure he'd never spoken to anyone about his feelings for me or what he planned to say, though my sister said those feelings were as plain as the strong, straight nose on his face.

Try as I might, because I did love him, I couldn't return those feelings. My rational mind made lists. He was smart, kind, good-looking. He had a good job and, more than that, a good job in our little town where I could count the number of age-appropriate bachelors on one hand. My family loved him.

But for me, if there had ever been a time for passion, it had passed. I couldn't say when exactly. When we were teenagers, sitting around a campfire on Morrow Island on a starry summer night, when he didn't put his arm around me, and I didn't snuggle into the curve of his long body. Or when we'd watched a movie in a dark theater, blushing at the mushy parts. The urge to kiss him had never been there.

Now, we were settled, talking in shorthand, like an old married couple, the shared experience of decades together. At one time in my life, that might have been enough. If I hadn't had the other with Chris, the passion and the fire, as problematic and ultimately heartbreaking as that relationship had been.

When Jamie told me about his feelings, I'd handled him as gently as I could. I'd blocked much of the conversation from memory, but whatever had transpired, whatever each of us had said, at the end of it, somehow, we had been able to remain friends.

My family, however, hadn't given up hope, as Livvie's leap across the couch that evening demonstrated. I got it. They loved him. So did I. Just not that way.

Jamie, Zoey, and I weren't the only thirty-something single people in Busman's Harbor, but there were times when it felt that way. This fall, when Jamie had suggested a ride to the movies in Brunswick, as friends, I'd accepted, and invited Zoey along just in case. Our first outing was a success and we'd continued, traveling to Wiscasset or Damariscotta for drinks or a meal, cheering for Page at her swim meets. On one memorable occasion, we'd ice skated on the pond on the town green. Zoey instigated trips to Portland to museums or galleries. She said she needed the artistic inspiration for her pottery designs, and she was new enough to Maine that she still had a tourist's enthusiasm. In the depths of a cold, dark Maine winter, Jamie and I were more than happy to be pulled along.

Though I'd been the one inviting Zoey initially, now we were an established threesome and took it for granted we'd do things together. No awkwardness about it.

Much of the reason I was doing much better emotionally was because of the happy triumvirate Zoey, Jamie, and I had formed. I hadn't missed the shift in our relationships, the way, when the three of us were together, Jamie always seemed to know where Zoey was and whether she was comfortable and happy. I hoped that was enough to keep us all on track.

With a sound like a shot that flung me out of my reverie, a big branch broke off and fell into the road beside me. "Whoa! Whoa! Whoa!" My arms windmilled, my feet running in place. I went down.

"Julia!" Jamie grabbed for me and then fell, too. "Oof."

I landed on my back in the middle of the road, my jacket pulled up, my bare back scraping against the icy pavement. Jamie landed on top of me, facing me, the position he'd wanted to be in all along, though neither of us had pictured it in the middle of the road on a cold, dark night, swathed in layers of down and Gore-Tex.

He flexed his body and jumped off so quickly, I might have been on fire. Once he found his feet, in a wide stance, he reached down to help me up. He'd knocked the wind out of me, and I held one hand up, signaling, "I need a moment." My cheeks were flaming, so hot, I thought they'd melt the snow.

"Sorry," I said as he pulled me upright. He might have kissed me then. That's what the guy in the rom-com would have done. But he didn't.

"Don't worry," he said.

Don't worry about this, tonight? I wondered. *Or don't worry about everything that had passed between us?*

I found my feet and we went on. "Who do you think did it?" I asked him to break the silence as we walked.

"Murdered Old Hugh? I have my own idea. But I can't prove it, not after all this time. And I won't speak ill of the dead in case I'm wrong."

"Oh, c'mon," I urged him. "Who can you hurt?"

He stopped walking. Without streetlights, it was impossible to read his expression. Finally, he said, "Do your own sleuthing. You're good at it."

I slid a little on the downhill toward Mom's house. Jamie grabbed me under the elbow. "Careful. You're drunk."

"I am not!" I protested. "You can feel how slippery this road is."

He made a sound of disagreement. "Let's get you home to bed."

The front of the house was dark when we approached it. From the front hall, in the dim light still coming from the embers in the fireplace, I glimpsed the form of Captain George on the living room couch, snoring softly, covered with my mother's favorite quilt. Jamie and I followed the sound of dishes being stacked into the kitchen. Zoey was there alone.

"Everyone's gone to bed," she whispered. She'd been in the house frequently enough to know the way sound carried up the backstairs. "I tidied the dishes and silverware. I would have washed them, but . . ." She gestured toward the sink, her hand ghostly in the fluorescent light from the battery-operated lantern that sat on the kitchen table. "No hot water."

"Don't worry about it," I assured her. "You wouldn't have been able to see if they were clean anyway."

"I'll walk you home," Jamie said to Zoey.

"Don't be silly." Zoey went to the back hall to collect her coat.

"It's very slippery." Jamie looked at me for confirmation.

"It is."

"I'll be fine. It's only a few blocks." Zoey had shrugged into her big coat and pulled her knit cap over her curls. "Besides, Jamie, if you walk me home, you'll only have to walk back."

"I'll feel better knowing you're home and dry and not lying in the road somewhere with a broken leg," he insisted.

"Then I have to worry the whole time you're walking back to your house." A frownlike crease of mock-scolding formed between Zoey's eyes, but her mouth was smiling.

They were still arguing about whether Jamie was or wasn't going to accompany her as they went out the back door, even though it was apparent to each one of the three of us that he was.

Chapter Seven

I awoke in the morning, throat scratchy from thirst and a dull throbbing over my nose, just between the eyes. The smell of brewing coffee and the crackle of frying bacon filled the air. It took me a moment, standing barefoot and freezing in the hallway outside my bedroom, to realize the smells and sounds were coming up the front stairs from the living room instead of up the back. I flipped the hall light switch. Nothing. Confirmation of what I already knew.

A little later, after a long drink of water and three ibuprofen, and dressed in several layers of clothing, I wandered downstairs to the living room. My family was huddled around the fireplace. There was no sign of Captain George. The pink and green quilt that had covered him was folded neatly on the credenza.

"No school!" my niece, Page, crowed.

"Not so loud," Sonny mumbled.

"I'm going sledding on the green." She lowered her voice just a bit at the beginning of the sentence, but her enthusiasm caught up to her by the end and she was just as loud as before.

"Shush!" Livvie ordered.

As Sonny looked out the living room window, the sun caught the whiskers in his beard, red with more white than I'd ever noticed before. "If you're going sledding," he told his daughter, "you'd better go soon. This blackout's going to last longer than the snow at this rate." As if to emphasize his point, a large white blob dropped off the porch roof and fell onto the snow-covered lawn.

I let Page toast me a slice of bread over the fire as I sat wrapped in the quilt that had recently covered Captain George. She was more enthusiastic about making it than I was about eating it, but I accepted her burnt offering with as much graciousness as I could muster.

Page left to sled. Livvie went to see to things at home. Jack went with Sonny over to his father's house to check on him. I was alone in the living room with Mom. She was still in her bathrobe. Her shift at Linens and Pantries had been canceled, which meant the power outage extended at least as far as Topsham.

I didn't ask again about Captain George. Mom had made it pretty clear the night before she didn't want to talk about him.

If she'd wanted my opinion, I'd have told her I was happy to see her seeking, or at least accepting, companionship. An only child who'd spent her childhood summers on an island, my mother was a solitary sort, content with her own company. For years, decades, I'd thought my mother was alone because she came from the world of summer people and had married the son of a lobsterman. A foot in each world, she belonged to neither. But since I'd been back in Busman's Harbor, and had grown to know her as an adult, I saw solitude was her preference. My father had been enough. But he'd been gone eleven long years, and Mom had recovered from the depths of her grief.

Instead, I brought up the thing that had been bothering me from the night before. "'Benedicta,'" I said to Mom. "I saw you frown. Wrong case or wrong gender?"

"Like everything in Latin," she answered, "it depends. But I don't think it's a noun, 'blessed,' or a verb, 'to bless.' I think it's a place."

"A place? What place?"

Mom settled into her chair, put her elbows on her knees and steepled her hands. "Benedicta, Maine. It's a town, founded in the 1830s as a utopian community, a refuge for Irish Catholics."

"Really." And I'd thought I knew a lot about Maine. "I've never heard of it."

"The town never really became what they hoped, and the experiment was largely over by 1867 when Daniel Kearney escaped from jail. But there were still settlers there, working the land."

"Do you think Daniel was letting someone know where he was going?"

"He left his mother here in town, did he not?" Mom gave me a look I recognized. Of course,

Daniel would want his mother to know where he was. He'd let her know how to find him in Boston, hadn't he?

"Then, wouldn't it be obvious to other people where to find him?" I asked. "He was a wanted man. Accused of murder."

"I'm sure he counted on most people misunderstanding, as we did. Besides, Benedicta was at least a week's ride from here back then. Even if the single county sheriff had figured out what the message meant, I doubt he would have chased them."

I caught the plural. "Them?"

"They *all* disappeared," Mom reminded me. "Catherine, John, and Daniel."

"And if Daniel really was John's son . . ." I was thinking aloud. "And the baby Catherine was carrying as well."

"Indeed."

I walked to the Busman's Harbor Historical Society, which was housed in an imposing old, brick house on the town green, enjoying the sight and sounds of Page and the other kids sledding as I went.

The hours of the society were limited during the winter, and I didn't expect it to be open during a blackout in any case. But the director, Mrs. Floradale Thayer, lived above and had been known to accommodate those doing research even when the place wasn't officially open.

Summoned by my knock, Mrs. Thayer answered the front door wearing a heavy winter coat over a thick, terry bathrobe that had seen better days.

Her unbrushed gray hair was covered by a fur-lined cap, the earflaps sticking out from her head like wings. She was six feet tall, and a formidable woman, even in an ancient bathrobe and comical hat.

"Julia. What brings you here?" Her voice, hoarse and loud, was as intimidating as her appearance.

"I hope I didn't wake you."

"No, no." She waved my concern away like a bothersome gnat, then stepped back from the door, gesturing for me to come in.

The sky was gray, but the temperature was well over freezing. Cold water dripped from the little roof over the front steps onto my hair and down my back. I followed her inside.

I wasn't concerned about the lack of electricity or Wi-Fi. The historical society was a strictly analog operation. Over the years, several folks had offered to move the typed index cards in its cataloging system to a database, but Floradale Thayer didn't hold with computers. At the Busman's Harbor Historical Society, Floradale's opinion was the only one that mattered.

Once I'd explained my mission, it took her no time to locate the single file folder the society possessed. There were two sepia-colored photographs in it, both formal double portraits.

Hugh posed with Catherine, possibly on their wedding day. The photo had come to the historical society without a date on it, only with the names Hugh and Catherine O'Hara written on the back in modern ballpoint ink at a much later date.

Hugh stood ramrod straight, though at the time

of his third marriage he would have been in his late seventies. Formally dressed, he wore a full beard and a stovepipe hat. He was short and narrow. The result of genetics or childhood malnutrition? But his figure held power. I could believe that on the night of his murder, he had fought his attacker—whoever it was—ferociously.

Catherine sat in a chair in front of Hugh. Her dark hair was parted in the middle and hung in tight coils over her ears. She wore a jacket edged in lace. Her face was smooth and more than pretty. She was a beauty. Hugh's hand was on her shoulder. She didn't seem to recoil.

Neither of them smiled. Portraits were serious business back then.

The second photograph was of Margaret and Martin Gleason, taken, undoubtedly, the same day. How often did a photographer come to rural Maine in 1862? They had been posed in the same way as Hugh and Catherine. Margaret was plain, frowsy even in her wedding guest finery. She wore a lace cap over her light hair, though of course I couldn't tell the color. She was visibly older than her new stepmother.

Martin was compact, going a little thick through the middle. His facial hair was more tamed than Hugh's, a trimmed mustache and goatee. He and Margaret were well-dressed, as far as I could tell, but clearly not the couple at the center of the day's event.

I turned on my phone, which had been powered off to save the battery, and took a photo of each of the portraits. "There's nothing else?" I asked Mrs. Thayer. "Nothing about the murder?"

She pursed her lips, the picture of exasperation. "I've heard Chief Beaupre has had the file for years. I've hinted, then asked outright, then nagged, but he won't give it up. He says, 'They're official files from an open case.' Ha! As if everyone involved hasn't been dead for over a hundred years."

I thanked her and started to leave. Then I remembered one more question. "The Gleasons' house. It's not on the green in Busman's Center opposite the Kensington House anymore. Do you know what happened to it?"

Her gray eyebrows rose in surprise. "Why, you go by it every day. It was moved in 1877 to the end of your own block. It's the beautiful Gothic Revival on the corner there."

"Moved! That house is huge."

"They waited until the snow was hard-set on the road, cut the house in quarters and moved it, one piece at a time on a sled pulled by a team of a dozen horses. It was more easily done in those days."

More easily done? Without cranes to lift and trucks to drive?

Responding to the look on my face, Floradale said, "There were no wires hanging above to run into." She swept a hand around the dark, cold building. "For all the good they're doing us today."

Chapter Eight

Back at Mom's house I turned on my phone again and checked the map. Benedicta was three hours from Busman's Harbor, closer to the Canadian border than to here. It looked like an easy drive, if a long one, from our peninsula to Augusta on Route 27 and then a straight shot up Route 95.

Zoey picked up on the first ring. "Hi."

"How are you?"

"Restless. Fretting."

She would be. The power outage had idled her kilns, and wheels, and stilled the big presses that made the molded pottery. It was smack in the middle of her busiest time. Orders would be piled up from retailers who wanted goods in their stores for wedding gift season.

"Don't fret. Let's take a road trip." I told her what I proposed to do.

"Let me get this straight," she said when I was done. "You want to drive three hours each way to possibly, not even definitely, find a clue to solve a hundred-and-fifty-year-old murder."

"Have you got anything better to do?"

She hesitated. "Define 'better.' I have the usual mound of paperwork here and I have some battery left in my phone."

I tried again. "Do you have anything more *interesting* to do?"

That time she answered right away. "I'll put my boots on." Then she added, "Let's invite Jamie."

"He might have to work."

"He's not on shift until seven tonight."

How did she know that? They must have chatted about it when he walked her home.

In the end, I picked up Jamie first in front of his house and then swung around to Lupine Design to get Zoey. We were in my old but sturdy Subaru, Jamie and his long legs in the passenger seat, Zoey in the back. Her big SUV would have been more comfortable, but it was fully electric, and I wasn't sure about finding chargers where we were going.

As we drove along Route 27 toward Augusta, Zoey read from her phone. "'Benedicta, Maine, was envisioned as an agrarian refuge for Irish Catholics founded by Benedict Fenwick, the second Bishop of Boston.' Who modestly named it for himself," Zoey editorialized. "'The settlement was founded in 1833 and within a year one hundred and thirty-four families had agreed to move there. For Fenwick, the planned community addressed two problems. Most of the Irish immigrants of the era poured into American cities, which were full of temptations—drink, prostitutes, criminality. In addition, the newcomers faced virulent anti-Catholicism and nativism, including the burning of the Ursuline Convent in Charlestown, Massachusetts, by a Protestant mob.' " Zoey paused and drew a deep breath. " 'The much smaller number of Irish who did move to rural areas found themselves scattered and isolated, with no opportunity to practice their religion. Their neighbors were all Protestants and this, inevitably, led to intermarriage and the exit of Irish Catholics from their faith.' "

Zoey paused and I focused on the road, which was snow-free but wet. Farmland rolled along on either side of us until we approached the outskirts of Maine's capital city, Augusta.

"That's 1833." Jamie turned to look at Zoey in the back seat. "What would Benedicta have been like in 1867, when Catherine, John, and Daniel got there? *If* they went there."

His emphasis on the "if" annoyed me, for no justifiable reason. I supposed as a policeman he had to wait for the evidence. After all, that was what we were driving six hours to find.

In the rearview mirror I saw Zoey squint at her phone, scrolling with her thumb. "The community never really took off," she said. "At least not in the way Bishop Fenwick envisioned. The settlers got there and found not farmland but deep woods which had to be cleared."

"That would have been true of any settlers in the Appalachians," Jamie said. "It would have been the frontier back then. Beyond the beyond."

"And when the land was cleared and planted,

they had to cope with a brutally short growing season. It was a tremendously difficult life. 'But the biggest disappointment,'" she began to read again, "'was the frequent lack of a priest. Bishop Fenwick sent priests, but when they arrived, they were mostly horrified to discover that they not only had to serve mass, but build and later maintain their own church, build the road to the church, and grow their own food in order to survive. Most left as soon as they were able.

"'This was a grave disappointment to the settlers, who were there specifically because they'd been promised a church and a priest. That and the difficulties of farming led many to leave, returning to the cities, or more likely moving west with the country. But about half of them stayed, adapting to new ways of farming, and making their own contributions, like potatoes, which grew well in a cold climate.'"

"There was a town there in 1867," I said.

"Yes," Zoey confirmed. "With Irish Catholic neighbors, and a church, if not always a priest."

"And there would have been abandoned farmland, already cleared, and even the empty cabins of those who had left," Jamie added. He sounded a little more optimistic, intrigued by the possibilities.

While Zoey had read to us, we'd rolled through Augusta and entered Route 95, the huge artery that runs north and south through the East Coast of the United States. We were on the northern end of it, and we were traveling farther north still, forty miles from its terminus at the Houlton-Woodstock border crossing to New Brunswick, Canada.

We passed through Bangor and then Orono, home to the main campus of the University of Maine. It was colder farther north and farther from the coast. The snow was deeper and dryer, and still clung to the evergreen branches. We passed several plows clearing dirty, sandy slush from the side of the road so that it wouldn't melt and then freeze again when the sun went down, endangering motorists. Off to the side of the road there were miles and miles of soft pines and hardwoods, broken occasionally by fields or rivers and highway exits to small towns, though those were farther and farther apart. The sun glinted off the white snow.

" 'In 1870, Benedicta petitioned to become a plantation.' " In the rearview mirror, I saw the skin wrinkle over Zoey's pert nose. "A plantation?"

"In Maine a plantation is an in-between place," Jamie told her. "It's not wilderness, but not a town, either. It's settled. People and crops are *planted*. But there aren't enough people for a full town government. It can be a sort of pretown, a place that hopes to become a town. But some never do. There are places designated as plantations still in Maine today."

"There were four hundred people living there in 1870," she told us.

"Four hundred," I said. "And four of them were John, Daniel, Catherine, and her baby."

"Yes, it says that right here," she deadpanned.

"What!" I fell for it completely.

"Of course, it doesn't say that." Zoey put her phone back in her pocket.

"If it did, we could have saved ourselves a trip."
Jamie wiggled in his seat, trying to get comfortable.

We rode in silence, all talked out for the moment, full of speculation.

We passed the brown and white sign for Katahdin Waters National Monument and then the one for the Allagash Wilderness Waterway and Baxter State Park. We'd gone as far as I had ever been on this road.

We came around a bend and there, across a frozen lake, Mount Katahdin loomed. Beautiful, snow-covered, hulking, powerful. I tapped my brakes reflexively at the view like millions must have done before me, no doubt to the eternal irritation of the locals driving behind them. There was a scenic overlook, but it was closed for the season. I kept going.

"What's Benedicta like now?" Jamie asked Zoey.

She pulled her phone from the pocket of her coat again. "In 1987, Benedicta surrendered its plantation status and became an unorganized township administered by the State of Maine. There were around two hundred and twenty-five people living there."

"So, it never did become a town," I said.

"And lost half its population, though that's not unusual for rural Maine," Jamie said.

"Rural anywhere," I added.

The exit off Route 95 to Benedicta was marked as such and we followed the main road into town. I had expected the land to be abandoned, gone back to forest. I'd pictured us looking for ancient graves in the middle of a snowy wood. Instead, farmland rolled off in both directions, underlining stunning views of Mount Katahdin.

The church, St. Benedict's of course, established 1834, was white and tidy, in good repair. The sign announced mass on Sundays at 10:00 A.M., so it was still serving its parishioners. The graveyard next to it, though snow-covered, was obviously well-tended. It was neatly halved by a bend in the road that ran through it.

The church driveway was plowed and empty, so I pulled in and parked. Jamie stepped out of the car and stretched. "Brrr!" He opened the door to the back seat and pulled out the parka he'd left there. We put on gloves and hats.

"What do we do now?" Jamie asked.

"Look for their graves," I said. "It looks like the older ones are in the front part of the cemetery."

The dry snow squeaked under our boots. We each took one of the long rows, calling out the dates we were seeing.

"1838!"

"1870!"

"1841."

It became clear there was no chronological order, but instead multigenerational family groupings, like you'd expect anywhere.

"My feet are cold," Jamie complained.

"Suck it up," I said. "We didn't drive three hours not to finish the job."

He made a face but moved up to the row beyond, calling out names from the gravestones, none of them O'Hara.

I was shivering and my nose had begun to run.

Though the graves weren't strictly in date order, there was no question the ones I was seeing were newer, some from the twentieth century. But that was possible. Catherine or Daniel might have lived that long.

And then, just across the cemetery road from the older graves, with a view of Mount Katahdin standing like a guardian in the background:

JOHN O'HARA 1829-1899.

CATHERINE O'HARA, HIS WIFE, 1844 -1888.

Catherine had died at forty-four. It made me un-accountably sad. At least she had lived long enough to see her child to adulthood. Or I hoped she had. I called to the others who came running. I took notes and photos with my phone.

"Look." I pointed to the grave next to Catherine's.

DANIEL O'HARA 1849-1901.

"He took his father's last name when he moved here," I said.

"He was a wanted fugitive," Jamie reminded us. "He needed a different name."

And next to Daniel, a new name.

MARY O'HARA, WIFE OF DANIEL, 1854-1908.

"He married." Zoey sighed.

"Where are you going?" Jamie asked as I moved away.

I was already in the next row. "I'm looking for Catherine's baby."

But there were no more O'Haras anywhere in the graveyard.

"She could have been a girl," Zoey said. "And changed her name when she married."

"Or left town long before he or she died," Jamie put a hand on my shoulder. "Many did."

"It's good she's not here." Zoey tried to cheer me up. "It means she didn't die in childhood."

"I guess." I stamped my feet to get some feeling back in my toes. "You know what we do at a time like this?"

"Eat?" Jamie suggested with hope in his voice.

"Eat," I agreed.

We ate down the road in Sherman, in a diner attached to a convenience store and gas station. Only one linoleum-topped table was empty of customers, and we were grateful to get it. A lively takeout business kept the counter hopping. My stomach rumbled as I sat down. It had been a long time since Page had singed me that piece of bread for breakfast.

The waitress served up steaming cups of coffee and I have never been so glad to receive any liquid in my life. Zoey and I sat side by side, facing Jamie. The heat was on in the restaurant, and the lights. The door to the building opened into the convenience store next door, so there were no drafts on my back despite the constant opening and closing. I slid out of my heavy coat and hung it on the back of my chair.

The restaurant served breakfast all day, as all good diners should. This concept had been the source of a good deal of good-natured back and forth between Gus and me over the years. He maintained rigidly that people should eat food appropriate to the time of day and only that food. He had a lot of rules like that. I suspected, though, it wasn't a gustatory rule that kept Gus from serving breakfast until he closed at three, but his own sense of order. Once he cleaned the bits of egg, potato, French toast, and pancake off his grill, time had marched on. He wasn't going backward.

When the waitress returned, I ordered an omelet with ham, cooked onions, cheese, and home fries.

"English, wheat, rye, or homemade white for your toast?" She carried no pad, committing each of the orders, tableside and takeout, to memory and then shouting them to the cook, who presumably did the same.

I had planned to forego toast, but homemade was more than I could pass up.

Jamie and Zoey ordered breakfast foods as well. Blueberry pancakes and bacon for him, eggs over easy, home fries, and homemade white toast for her.

"It's them in the graveyard. I'm certain of it," I said when the waitress had moved off. "The birthdates match up."

"Do we know when they were born?" Zoey asked.

"Pretty closely." I pulled a pen from the Snowden Family Clambake tote bag I used as a purse and scribbled calculations on napkin. "Gus said John was twenty when he left for the California gold fields in 1849, so he would have been born in 1829, or close to. The captain said Daniel was eighteen when all this happened, so he was born 1849 or 1850."

"After John O'Hara left town," Zoey said.

"The jailor's notes said the same. November of 1849 I'm pretty sure," Jamie added.

"So that date we're certain of," I confirmed. "Catherine was eighteen when she married Hugh O'Hara in 1862. The birthdate on her tombstone is 1844. It fits. It couldn't be a coincidence, the names and the dates for all three of them."

We lapsed into silence, staring at the writing on the napkin.

"Hot plates!" The waitress delivered the food. The silence at our table continued, broken only by the scrape of forks on the heavy, white ceramic dishes.

When my meal was half-eaten, I slowed down, my hunger sated sufficiently that I could take my time and enjoy the wonderful flavors. "I don't like the idea of them being a family of murderers." I wanted to picture the O'Haras happy and industrious in their new home, whatever hardships the frontier brought.

Jamie finished chewing and swallowed. "Who says they were?"

"Nothing says, exactly," Zoey answered. "But they ran, for one." Jamie raised his eyebrows, so she went on. "And Daniel confessed," she added, making the captain's argument.

"Maybe," Jamie conceded. "But who benefitted from every one of the people with a claim to Hugh O'Hara's estate leaving town? And who was the only person to hear Daniel's confession? I don't think we can jump to conclusions."

"And who is the ghost?" Zoey demanded. "Obviously not Catherine, who was my most likely candidate, or John, or Daniel. They're all resting peacefully here."

I was about to ask Zoey if ghosts were required to haunt in some proximity to their graves, and if so, what was the allowed distance, when Jamie's cell phone rang. It was the first time I'd heard a phone in the noisy diner.

He squinted at the screen and stepped outside, leaving his parka behind. Evidently, he didn't think the call would take long.

My heart lightened at the idea that John O'Hara and his family might be innocent. Over the long evening before, as our guests talked around the fire, I'd given each of the characters personalities. John was strong, toughened by his time in the gold fields, and a romantic, falling in love first with Daniel's mother and then with Catherine. Catherine was brave, ready to move to the frontier with all the dangers that entailed for the sake of love. Daniel was a gawky, troubled teen, excited for adventure, who had finally found the family where he belonged.

But the images I'd constructed could be entirely wrong. John could have been a disloyal son and a profligate bedder of women who were not his wife. Catherine could have been a gold digger, marrying Old Hugh for his money and then making him a cuckhold. Daniel was a delinquent and a thief. And one or more of them could have been killers.

I was frustrated by the not knowing.

Jamie returned shortly. "We've got to go. They want me to come in early for my shift."

"Did you explain you were three hours away?" Zoey asked.

"Yup. Power's back on, by the way."

Zoey and I cheered, and I signaled for the check.

The trip back was both shorter and longer in the way of return journeys. Shorter because you knew the way and had certainty about where you were going, longer because the excitement of the adventure was over. We'd sprung forward to daylight saving time the weekend before, but the sun was dropping rapidly toward the mountains to our west.

Zoey's cell phone pinged. "Shoot."

"What's the matter?" Jamie looked over the back of his seat at her.

"Nothing. Something. An important retailer I have to get back to." She clicked around on her phone and then started typing with her thumbs.

It was quiet in the car as we rolled through Bangor. Zoey was still answering e-mails. Jamie had a look of tense concentration. I thought in some measure they were both mentally back at work in Busman's Harbor. I would have been, too, except I had no regular winter job to go to. Which got me thinking about what I would do the next day.

Almost to Augusta, Jamie sighed and looked at the window. "Six hours to find three one-hundred-plus-year-old graves. Julia, you really need to find something to do with your time."

"Julia's going to be the CEO of Lupine Design," Zoey said from the back seat.

Startled, I glanced in the rearview mirror. She didn't look up from her phone.

"In the fall, after the clambake season ends, when we can afford her," Zoey continued. "The business has gotten too big for me to handle and it's interfering with my creating new products. I'm not going through another busy season like this."

She said it matter-of-factly, as if it were a subject we'd discussed many times and the details were settled. We had never discussed it once.

After a few seconds, when the initial shock faded, I found I didn't hate the idea. There was a lot to think and talk about, working with a friend not the least of it. But I didn't hate the idea at all.

None of us said anything after that, though Jamie turned in his seat and gave me a heartfelt smile and a wink. I drove the rest of the way home, dreaming about the pottery business.

Chapter Nine

When I woke up the next morning, I knew exactly what I had to do. The room, when I threw off my covers, was blessedly warm. My phone was fully charged on my nightstand. Power. Gotta love it.

After I was showered, dressed, and fed, I pulled the Subaru out of our old three-bay garage and headed to the Registry of Probate in Wiscasset. I parked in the lot behind, walked through the metal detector at the entrance, and entered the hushed registry room with its cool blond wood and high ceilings. Around the space people toiled—genealogists and lawyers, heirs and executors, or Personal Representatives, as they were known in Maine.

I'd been there before on a previous matter. Then, the woman working behind the counter had told me proudly they had wills dating back to

1760, so I was optimistic I would find Hugh O'Hara's and the Gleasons' last testaments.

A helpful employee told me there was no will registered for Hugh O'Hara of Busman's Center in 1867 or any other year. Had it been lost, hidden in connection with his murder, or had he died intestate? It seemed unlikely that a wealthy man as old as O'Hara, with a complicated family situation, would have died without a last will and testament.

In contrast, Martin's and Margaret's wills were easily found. The registry clerk delivered them in a folder. I handled them carefully, unfolding the documents and spreading them out on the table in front of me.

Martin had died in 1877, at the age of forty-eight, only ten years after Hugh O'Hara's murder. He left all his property, which included his farm and the house on the town green, to Margaret. There was no mention of children.

Margaret lived longer, until 1908, when she would have been seventy-six, I calculated. Her will was much thicker. The property described was larger, the combined acreage of both the Gleason and O'Hara farms. The house left in the will had been her father's. She must have moved there after Martin's death, when their own home had been sold and towed down to Busman's Harbor.

I read through the whereases and whatnots, wondering who her heirs had been. Finally, I found it.

"I leave my house, farm, other properties and all my worldly goods to John O'Hara, Junior, the younger son of my half brother."

I stopped cold, staring at the page. Margaret

had left her worldly goods to her nephew, Catherine and John's son.

The document went on. The property was left, ". . . in the hope that he and his heirs will live on and farm it."

In exchange, Margaret set two conditions. The first was mildly puzzling, though it did explain some things. "That they change their name to Gleason and be known by that name throughout the county, in tribute to my late husband, Martin Gleason, as a small gesture to mitigate my sorrow for the sons I could not bear him."

And ". . . that they travel to St. Patrick's church in Newcastle as often as is practical to light a candle and pray for my husband's soul that he may someday be forgiven for his sin and enter the Kingdom of Heaven."

For his sin. Not sins. Sin.

I took photos of the documents to show to Jamie and Zoey, then folded them up and returned them to the woman behind the counter. Then I went across the hall to the Registry of Deeds to find out what had happened to the property.

Sure enough, John O'Hara Gleason had taken possession. Catherine and John's son hadn't been in the graveyard in Benedicta. He was probably in the Busman's Harbor cemetery among the myriad Gleasons buried there.

The house had been passed down again and again, as the farmland was sold for building lots and the Busman's Harbor Golf Club. The last Gleason to live there had sold it only twenty years before.

Chapter Ten

I called Zoey from my car. "You won't believe what I've found! A clue. A big one. In Hugh O'Hara's murder."

"Come right away. I need all the details."

"I'm on my way back from the Wiscasset Registry of Probate. I'll call Jamie to see if he's free to—"

"No worries! I'll call him."

Alone in my car I smiled at her eagerness. "Great. See you in twenty minutes."

With the return of electricity, Lupine Design was back in business when I entered through the loading dock door directly into the studio. The pottery wheels were turning, the press was noisily stamping out the molded pieces, and loud music with a thumping base came over the sound system. Zoey grabbed me right after I came in the door and hustled me toward the retail shop in the front. Livvie cocked a curious eyebrow at me as we passed, but she had a piece on the wheel and was up to her elbows in clay. One of us would have to fill her in later.

Jamie pulled his patrol car to the curb and braked hard. He bounded through the front door of the shop in full uniform. He was back on the day shift. "What's the big news? I can only stay a couple of minutes."

I recounted what I had found at the registries, while the two of them stood, both slightly open-mouthed, not interrupting.

"She implicated Martin in her will." Jamie said when I'd finished and finally drawn a breath. "I can't believe the answer has been there all along."

"Why would anyone have looked?" I asked. "The attorney who drew up the will would have known, but he was prevented from saying anything by his privilege. The witnesses would have known as well, but they were probably family servants. Margaret Gleason was a wealthy woman of advanced years. She would have had help, in the farm and the house. The only other people who knew about the inheritance were John O'Hara and his family. They would have seen inheriting the farm as returning to them what was rightfully theirs."

"Daniel Kearney was suspected of murder his whole life," Jamie said. "Wouldn't he have wanted the record set straight to relieve him of that burden?"

"Not if he was happily living his life as Daniel O'Hara," I answered. "He lived until 1901. He would have had the satisfaction of knowing he was cleared, and so would his family. Attempting to correct the record in any formal way only would have made everything more complicated."

"The property that was stolen from John and Catherine by the murder was returned to their son," Zoey summarized. "Is it possible they were all in on it?"

"Like a *Murder on the Orient Express* type of thing?" Jamie's mouth curled up. "Why would they? Hugh was eighty-three. If all they wanted was for him to be dead, they only had to wait. The motive had to be the inheritance."

"Hugh's will is missing," I reminded them. "He must have provided for Catherine, maybe even the child. Martin wanted them out of the way. He framed Daniel and hid Hugh's will."

But Zoey shook her head. "It must have been both of them. Martin and Margaret. She would have known her husband wasn't home when Catherine came screaming across the town green, bleeding in the snow. At a minimum, Margaret went along with it. She may have even instigated it."

"Yet Margaret doesn't ask for candles to be lit for herself or for forgiveness." Jamie said. "Why not?"

"Perhaps she felt she didn't deserve forgiveness," I answered.

Jamie turned his head, looking out the big windows of the shop, down the street toward Gleason's Hardware, though he couldn't see the store from his angle. "Do you think they know?"

"The Gleasons? It seems like the type of tale that might easily get lost generation to generation," I said.

"They must know they're connected to a notorious murder." The color drained from Zoey's face as she said it. She was connected to a notorious murder. Her mother's. She would never forget it. I wondered what she would tell any future children about it. Things were different now that they might someday discover the story on their own on the Internet.

We stood huddled in a triangle in the middle of Lupine Design's retail store, not speaking for a few moments, the shelves of graceful, shimmering, ocean-colored pottery around us.

Then Zoey brightened. "The address on the will. Where was Margaret living when she died?"

"She'd long before moved across the green to her father's house," I told them. "The Gleason house was moved to Busman's Harbor in 1878, after Martin died."

"She's the ghost! She is for sure," Zoey insisted. "If Martin never lived in that house, it must be Margaret. Wandering still, soaked in guilt and regret."

I knocked at the door to the Kensington House B and B. Zoey and Jamie stood behind me. Zoey had called to make sure it was okay for the three of us to visit. She and Jamie had both been busy with their jobs. It had taken more than two weeks to find a date that worked for everyone.

"Hello. Welcome. Come in." The woman who opened the door was not much older than we were. She had a warm smile, but then an innkeeper would. She wore a T-shirt and denim overalls liberally spattered with light blue paint.

We stepped into the hallway, leaving our boots on the rubber mat provided. The snow and ice had melted, bringing the first assault of mud season, loose dirt, soaked in fast-running water, streaming down the front walk and the driveway where Zoey had left her car.

The smell of fresh paint hit as soon as we walked through the door. The parlor was a mess, with the rug rolled up and drop clothes over the furniture that had been pulled away from the walls.

"Excuse this," Sheila Hammerman said. "Off-season project. We'll sit in the dining room."

When she'd first suggested the visit, I'd been relieved to discover that Zoey wasn't looking for a séance or to sleep at the inn overnight, only for an interview with the owners.

The dining room was large and light with tables for two and four scattered around it. Two tables had been pushed together in the center of the room and Sheila gestured for us to sit there. The paint smell had grown fainter and was overpowered by the aroma of fresh baking. A tall man with a full head of brown hair came through from the kitchen, holding a platter of scones in one hand and a coffee carafe in the other.

"My husband, Greg," Sheila said. "He's our chief cook and bottle washer."

Introductions were made all around, coffee poured, and scones passed. Cups, utensils, cream, sugar, and soft butter were already on the table. My stomach gurgled softly in anticipation.

"How long have you owned the inn?" I asked. I thought I knew but was having trouble finding a way into the conversation.

"Five years," Sheila answered. "We bought it from the Kensingtons who established the B and B."

"And they bought it from the Gleasons," Greg finished.

I had visited Gleason's Hardware in the intervening weeks. Al Gleason had been happy to see me and as accommodating as he always was with his customers. He was proud of his family's long association with the town and knew they were among the first Irish settlers. But it was a different branch of the family that had owned Old Hugh's house down through the generations and he knew little about it. Of the Gothic Revival house now standing on Main Street, clearly visible from his shop windows, he knew nothing at all. "You don't say? They moved it? Incredible."

Zoey took the bull by the horns. "You didn't seem surprised when I told you we wanted to talk about your ghost," she said to the Hammermans.

"*Everybody* wants to talk about our ghost," Sheila said.

"Not everybody." Greg laughed at the idea. "But it comes up. Frequently."

"Some guests specifically request her room," Sheila told us. "We've also had teams arrive with all kinds of microphones and gizmos to measure sound waves and whatnot."

"*Her* room?" Zoey's eyes shone. "Your ghost is a woman."

"Yes," Greg said. "There's one hundred percent consensus on that."

"Which is her room?" Jamie asked.

"Top of the stairs," Sheila said. "We'll take you up and show you after."

"Wouldn't Margaret have slept in the big front bedroom?" I asked Zoey. "She was the mistress of the house."

"She would haunt her old room," Zoey said with absolute certainty. "Remember, she grew up in this house. The room at the top of the stairs must have been hers when she was a child." Zoey looked at Sheila, who shrugged. How could she and Greg have known?

"Do you believe in ghosts?" I asked the owners.

"Not ghosts in general," Greg answered. "But in our ghost specifically. There have been too many reports to ignore."

They seemed quite at ease sharing their home with a spectral being. "You've never seen her?" I was surprised.

"Sadly, no," Sheila answered. She poured more coffee into her cup and passed the carafe around. "I like to think it's because we leave her to her own devices and take good care of her home."

"Except when subjecting her to probes by people dressed like the Ghostbusters." Greg laughed.

"She doesn't mind." Sheila objected. "Though she is sad. But that's not our doing. She's always sad."

"Sad?" Zoey, already sitting up unnaturally straight, leaned farther forward. "What do your guests who see her say? What does she look like? Does she speak to them?"

"By most, but not all reports, she's an old woman, quite stout," Sheila said.

Zoey caught my eye. *Old woman. Catherine hadn't lived to be old. Margaret had.*

"She approaches people," Sheila continued,

"floating without feet and begs them, 'Forgive me. Forgive me.' "

The three of us were silent, barely breathing. My heart was beating so hard, I wondered if the others could see it.

"Sometimes she grabs guests by the forearm as she speaks, imploring them," Greg said. "That's when they scream."

"Every time," Sheila said. "Even when they've specifically requested her room."

We went up to see the room, though by then it barely mattered. The tale was told. The book shut for each of us. The room was nice with a four-poster bed, roses on the wallpaper, and an adjoining bath made out of an old closet. Nice, but nothing special.

After we said our good-byes and thank-yous, we sat in Zoey's car in the driveway for several minutes, completely silent.

"So that's solved," Zoey said with finality. "It was Margaret who set the plan in motion. Martin was her accomplice. She tried to find forgiveness for him but couldn't do it for herself."

"I doubt Chief Beaupre will accept a confession from a ghost," Jamie said.

"Nor will Captain George, Fee and Vee, or Sonny," I said. *Especially Sonny.* "They're too committed to their own versions. At least Gus and Mrs. Gus will be happy with the news."

"It doesn't matter." Zoey backed her car out of the drive. "It's done. Mystery solved. Time to get back to work."

She was right. The earth was thawing. The Snowden Family Clambake would open in two short months. Time to line up suppliers, hire staff, clear up the winter debris on the island. Move out to Windsholme.

It was only then it occurred to me to wonder why these two people had gotten so invested they had driven all the way to Benedicta to solve the mystery and kept going for weeks afterward. I knew the answer as soon as my brain thought to ask it. *Because they were my friends.*

Zoey was right. It was time to let go of the past. And get back to work.

RECIPE

Vee's Irish Soda Bread

In Perked Up, *I gave the task of making the Irish soda bread to Vee, one of the two bakers in our story. In the real world, the recipe comes from my husband's sister's husband's mother (got it?), Marie Kent. Though it sounds like a distant relationship, Marie and I attended holiday gatherings, weddings, showers, graduation parties, and funerals together for years, outliers in my husband's huge Italian-American family. Marie was fiercely proud of her Irish heritage and never understood how she ended up in a family that drank gallons of coffee instead of tea. She is greatly missed.*

Ingredients

3⅓ cups flour
6 teaspoons baking powder
1 teaspoon salt
⅓ cup sugar
½ cup butter, softened
1 cup raisins
2 eggs, slightly beaten
¾ cup milk
Oil for greasing pan

Instructions

Preheat oven to 350 degrees.
Mix flour, baking powder, salt, and sugar.
Work in butter with your hands until the mixture has the consistency of cornmeal.

Add raisins.

Whisk eggs and milk together, stir into dry mixture to blend.

Knead for two minutes.

Pat into a lightly oiled 9-inch cake pan.

Bake approximately one hour until crust is golden and toothpick comes out clean.

Makes one loaf.

Dear Reader,

I hope you enjoyed reading about St. Patrick's night with Julia Snowden, her friends, and family in Busman's Harbor, Maine. If this is your first introduction to the Maine Clambake Mysteries, there are ten standalone novels, starting with *Clammed Up,* and as well four previous novellas.

This is the fifth appearance of a Maine Clambake novella in a holiday collection along with fellow authors and friends Leslie Meier and Lee Hollis. My stories have always been the third one in these anthologies, which challenges me to come up with a different angle on the theme. I assume, though I don't know, that killing someone with the Irish coffee will have been done by the time the reader gets to my entry. Therefore, for this novella I had the idea of a tale of murder told on a stormy night over an Irish coffee (or two, or four).

Once I determined the murder would take place in the past, the question was, when and how?

I knew almost nothing about Irish history in Maine, aside from the fact that it existed. As Zoey tells us on the trip to Benedicta, the history most often told about Irish people coming to America is one of famine-driven immigration to big cities. To fill in the gap in my knowledge, I found *They Change Their Sky: The Irish in Maine,* a collection of scholarly articles edited by Michael C. Connolly. At first, I was determined to read only those articles that pertained to the periods when my murder might be set, but the whole book was so fascinating I read it straight through. As you can tell, I found the story of Benedicta, Maine, completely compelling. If *Perked Up* has awakened an interest in the Irish in Maine or in rural areas, I urge you to read *They Change Their Sky*.

The story of Hugh O'Hara's murder has one inspiration, which I learned about from two sources. The murder of William Kenniston and his third wife, Octavia, is reported in *Ghosts of the Boothbay Region* by Greg Latimer, a book I have turned to for inspiration in earlier books and novellas in the series. Latimer, in turn, cites *History of Boothbay, Southport and Boothbay Harbor, Maine. 1623–1905* by Francis Byron Greene, a book I've used a lot in the creation of Busman's Harbor's history. I've moved the murder back from 1888 to 1867 and changed many other details. To be clear, no one except the hired boy was ever implicated. All the other suspects in the story, guilty or innocent, are entirely invented.

Besides these inspirations, there was Maine itself, where mid-March is definitely not spring.

I'm always happy to hear from readers. You can reach me at barbaraross@maineclambakemysteries.com, or find me via my website at www.barbaraross author.com, on Twitter @barbross, on Facebook www.facebook.com/barbaraannross, on Pinterest www.pinterest.com/barbara annross, and on Instagram @maineclambake. You can also follow me on Goodreads at https://www.goodreads.com/author/show/6550635.Barbara_Ross and on BookBub at https://www.bookbub.com/authors/barbara-ross.

I wish you a Happy St. Patrick's Day. If you're

reading *Irish Coffee Murder* during the season, I hope you have a warm drink at hand along with a slice of Irish soda bread. Enjoy!

Sincerely,

Barbara Ross
Key West, Florida

Visit our website at
KensingtonBooks.com
to sign up for our newsletters, read
more from your favorite authors, see
books by series, view reading group
guides, and more!

BOOK CLUB

BETWEEN THE CHAPTERS

Become a Part of Our
Between the Chapters Book Club
Community and Join the Conversation

Betweenthechapters.net